Inn by the Lake

Mary K. Tilghman

CHAMPAGNE BOOK GROUP

Inn by the Lake

This is a work of fiction. The characters, incidents and dialogues in this book are of the author's imagination and are not to be construed as real. Any resemblance to actual events or persons, living or dead, is completely coincidental.

Published by Champagne Book Group
2373 NE Evergreen Avenue, Albany OR 97321 U.S.A.

~~~

First Edition 2020

eISBN: 978-1-77155-298-1

Copyright © 2020 Mary K. Tilghman All rights reserved.

Cover Art by Robyn Hart

Champagne Book Group supports copyright which encourages creativity and diverse voices, creates a rich culture, and promotes free speech. Thank you by complying by not scanning, uploading, and distributing this book via the internet or via any other means without the permission of the publisher. Your purchase of an authorized electronic edition supports the author's rights and hard work and allows Champagne Book Group to continue to bring readers fiction at its finest.

www.champagnebooks.com

Version_1

For Ray.

Dear Reader,

A real life honeymoon inspired this story. President Grover Cleveland and his bride Frances Folsom Cleveland spent their honeymoon at the grand Deer Park Inn in Western Maryland in 1886. Although the inn no longer exists, the bottled water does! And so does a wonderful French restaurant located on the site of that storied inn.

But, alas, visitors to Deep Creek Lake will never find the Broadview Inn. It exists only in this book.

I filled my story with places I know and love: Swallow Falls State Park, Frank Lloyd Wright's Fallingwater, and, of course, Deep Creek Lake.

After twelve years as a travel writer, I love to bring these places to life as settings for my novels. I hope you enjoy the journey.

Mary

Chapter One
Your Serve

As Amanda pulled into the driveway, she took one look at the rundown inn with its faded colors and weedy garden and cursed. "Oh, hell." The website for the Broadview Inn promised a beautiful, historic house. Historic, questionable. Old, definitely. The right spot for her best friend Julie's bachelorette weekend? That remained to be seen.

Amanda's disappointment and her worries grew as she stepped from the car onto the cracked pavement. This wasn't anything like the fancy resort she originally booked. *Damn water main break.*

Her worry lifted a little as she stepped through the front door into a sunny parlor. A tall man with a stiff military bearing and a gracious smile greeted her as he placed a vase of fresh flowers on the reception desk.

"Good afternoon." His voice was deep, warm. "You must be Amanda Johnson."

"Yes, I am. Then you must be Mr. Wilson. I called yesterday to make the arrangements with you."

"Call me DeWayne. We're all ready for you." He slid an old-fashioned key from a cubby and handed it to her. It was heavy with a tiny brass tag that read *Rose Room*.

"I think you'll like your room. It's the first one on the left at the top of the stairs. It has a wonderful view of Deep Creek Lake."

Amanda reached for her overnight bag, but DeWayne rushed around the desk. "No, I'll take that. You go on up and take a look around. Make sure it's to your liking. Later on, if you want, I'm happy to give you a tour of our historic inn."

Every step creaked as she made her way upstairs. The flowers on the wallpaper had faded from what must have been red and green to pale pink and gray. The place might be old, but the heavy oak banister gleamed from a good dusting and the door to her room appeared to be freshly painted in a buttery yellow.

The condition of the room eased her worries even more. Festooned with lace and ruffles it was fussier than she liked, but it was spacious with high ceilings, well-kept, and clean. The scent of lemon oil rose from the dresser. A guide to Western Maryland rested next to a vintage lamp on the nightstand.

The pink paint on the walls matched the rose border at the ceiling and the king-sized bed was covered with a floral bedspread in a similar shade.

Amanda dropped onto the bed, flooded with relief that the inn's accommodations were in better shape than the exterior.

From her perch, she caught a glimpse of the lake below. She rushed to the window and pushed aside the frilly curtains for a better view of the waters sparkling in the late afternoon sun. There beside the lake were the tennis courts the inn's website boasted about. She needed to check them out right away.

Amanda practically ran over DeWayne as she raced down the steps on her way to get a closer look at the inn's main attractions.

Once she was standing at the water's edge, she soaked in the sunshine. A warm breeze caressed her skin, relaxing the tight muscles in her back and neck. Released from the responsibilities of work for the first time in months, she breathed in the serenity and smiled.

Water lapped gently at the shore. The property was located on the curve of a cove, fringed with neatly mowed grass and a cluster of low bushes covered with tiny white flowers. In the distance, tree-covered mountains loomed over the lake. A short pier stretched out on the other side of the tennis courts. No boat was tied up, but a pair of ducks snoozed beside a piling. The tennis courts had been built only a few yards from the lake.

Far from her cramped law office, miles away from files and clients for the first time in months, she could focus on something other than work. Three years out of law school, her life usually belonged to Jones, Jones & Taylor, LLC, but not now.

This weekend was hers, mostly anyway, and as long as she kept her phone and laptop close by, she was free to celebrate her friend's upcoming wedding.

She nearly despaired yesterday when she received the call, informing her Nemacolin Woodlands had to cancel her reservation due to a water main break. It was understandable. And disappointing.

She dreaded calling the bride, but Julie, in her usual sunny way, was unfazed. "I have a brochure for an inn out that way. I guess Frank left it here, and it looks charming. It's near where we were going to hike. As long as we're together and there's wine, it will be fine."

That was why Julie was her best friend. She never let anything ruffle her.

Things like this upset Amanda. She'd taken an uncharacteristic afternoon off to come early and make sure the weekend wouldn't be a disaster. Maybe the inn was a little battered, but the location, the view, and the tennis courts were perfect. She was satisfied.

Perhaps the weekend would turn out all right.

The sudden thwack of a tennis ball against the strings of a racquet alerted Amanda she wasn't alone. On the farthest of the six lakeside courts, a lone man tossed a ball over his head and fumbled a serve.

Oblivious to her presence, he hit the next one into the net. Then, he missed the next ball altogether. Before he tried yet again, he put his racquet under his arm to thumb a text on his phone.

He stopped long enough for Amanda to get a good look at him. He was tall and lanky with broad shoulders and muscular legs. His hair was a nut brown, curly, and perhaps in need of a visit to the barber. As he was turned away from her, she couldn't quite see his face. She had to admit she was curious.

After tucking his phone into a pocket, he served again.

Without speed nor finesse, his serve was pathetic. It was so painful to watch Amanda needed to look away. She focused on the condition of the courts, pleased to find the surface smooth and freshly painted. She'd worried for no reason about a healthy crop of weeds, torn nets, and faded lines.

The tennis courts were one reason Amanda agreed to book

the Broadview for this special weekend. She looked forward to a game with Julie the next day.

As if on cue, a text pinged on the phone stuffed in Amanda's back jeans pocket. *Well?*

Amazing. Amanda added a few emojis of smiley faces and hearts. *Are you on your way?*

She waited for a response, but none came. *Stop kissing that man and get in the damn car.* She keyed in the text, decided it was a bad idea, and erased it. *Dinner is at eight. You better be here before that.*

Finally, Julie texted her back. *Leaving Baltimore now.*

Now Amanda could relax, assured her friend had begun the three-hour drive to the southern edge of Deep Creek Lake.

She dropped onto the grass to enjoy the breeze ruffling her newly shorn locks. The air cooled her now-visible neck, much different from her usual waist-length—and heavy—style. Julie nearly cried when she saw her maid of honor's new haircut on Snapchat. She'd get over it. Amanda liked the effect of tousled curls framing her face. Not only did it look professional, it was also easier to keep.

She closed her eyes and breathed in the sweet air.

So this was Deep Creek Lake. She had been curious about it. Somewhere around here a huge development project was in the works. Files for the case were piled up on her desk—though she had only been given a fraction of them. Everything mentioned the lake, and now she was here, poised at its edge.

As she pushed away the concerns of work, a tennis ball bounced off her shoulder.

"Ouch." She rubbed the sore spot before picking up the neon yellow ball that fell in her lap and turned toward the guy on the courts.

He ran toward her with a penitent look. Dark curls dampened by perspiration and a crooked smile below clear blue eyes.

Blue eyes the color of the lake in front of her.

"I'm really sorry." Still carrying his racquet, he grinned sheepishly. "I wanted to practice my serve before my friend gets here later this weekend. Looks like I need it. Did I hurt you?"

He took the offending ball she held out.

"No, I've been whacked by hundreds of balls. Even a few racquets. I'm fine."

"Racquets must hurt. I am sorry."

"They do. Especially when your doubles partner smacks you right in the jaw." During a college tournament, her partner raced after the ball, swung back then caught her as she stretched to return the volley. Amanda learned to shout a lot louder that afternoon. She absent-mindedly touched the thin scar under her chin that reminded her of that lesson every day.

The stranger in tennis whites winced but said nothing. He twirled the racquet in his hands so feverishly Amanda was sure he didn't know what to say next.

Goodbye seemed like a fair choice. She rose and brushed loose grass off her jeans. "It was nice, um, meeting you. But I ought to get back. I wanted to see the grounds and, well, now I have."

She laughed and offered her hand. That's what she did at work; it seemed appropriate.

As he stretched out his, he fumbled his racquet, and it dropped to the ground. "Are you sure you're all right? I didn't mean to hit you, but I'm glad we met…"

"Amanda." She had to admit she liked his strong grip, maybe from years of playing tennis.

Or maybe not. His serve might be lame, but those eyes are a wonder, blue and framed with the nicest smile lines.

"I'll see you later, Roger," she said before strolling away.

"Roger? My name's Luke, not Roger."

She turned back with a wide smile. "Oh, with your serve, I was convinced you were Roger Federer. My mistake. I guess I'll talk to you later, Luke."

Part of her regretted walking away from such a handsome man, despite the possibility of playing what might have to be a questionable game of tennis. Judging from that swing, she wouldn't face much of a contest. But even a bad game of tennis might be fun with tall, dark, and luscious. She had a few hours until Julie and the two bridesmaids got here. Why not play a game or two?

Because Amanda still had things to do to get ready before then. After all, this was her party. She'd booked the rooms, bought the tickets for Fallingwater, and arranged for tonight's dinner. She still needed to check with Chef Beaumont about a picnic lunch for tomorrow's hike. Why, she hadn't even unpacked yet.

As she neared the inn, temptation in tennis whites jogged up to her, racquet in hand. "Could I at least buy you a coffee? As a way of apology?"

"No, thanks just the same. I should go in."

"Oh, a boyfriend." His bright eyes dimmed, not much but enough to warm her heart.

She decided she'd ease his misery. "No, my best friend will be here soon. We're having her bachelorette party at the inn this weekend."

His smile returned, but this time it was more polite than genuine. "Ah, well. That will keep you plenty busy. I won't keep you. Nice meeting you…"

"Amanda," she reminded him.

"Yes, Amanda."

She was about to leave when she thought better of it. It was no use. Her love for tennis was winning. She put a finger to her lips and eyed him.

"Is something wrong?" He glanced at his clothes.

No, there wasn't a thing wrong with this man. Those broad shoulders were the kind that could make Amanda weak with desire. Back when she had time for men. The strong ropy muscles in his arms hinted at many hours in the gym, if not on the tennis court.

She was tempted. Those courts were calling her, and she could really go for a spirited game right now. "No, no. Nothing at all. I was trying to decide how good an opponent you might be."

His eyes lit up and smile lines crinkled at his temples. "I may be a bit rusty, but I'm game if you are." He glanced at the stacked heels of her boots. "But those shoes aren't made for tennis."

She laid a hand on his arm and an unfamiliar tingle prickled her skin. Judging from the smile on his face, he felt it too. "Give me five."

"I'll give you ten. Then I'll come find you."

Amanda rushed through the parlor up to her room. She'd packed her tennis skirt and shoes for her game with Julie but couldn't see the harm in putting them on early. She grabbed a towel and her racquet. Excitement coursed through her as she flew down the stairs.

After a tiring week at work, she was looking forward to a little fun. She waved to Luke, bouncing a tennis ball on the nearest court as he waited for her. She arrived breathless, eager to play—when a cellphone rang.

She reached for hers, knowing at any minute Quin could call, but—

"Luke Beaumont here." He held up one finger and turned away. "Hi, Paul. Yes, sir. Yes, sir." He acknowledged the caller as if he could see. "I sent my proposal two days ago. The printed copy has to be on your desk. I worked until midnight to get it in on time. Please don't tell me—"

His frown deepened. Amanda tried not to listen. He rolled his eyes. "Business…sorry," he whispered before returning to his call. "Right away. I have the file with me. I can email it right now. Thanks, sir. I do appreciate it. Yes, I'll re-send it in a few minutes. I want to be sure I send the updated version." He punched the off button with a sheepish expression.

Amanda knew what that look meant. "You're standing me up, aren't you?"

"I'm sorry but…it's difficult to explain. Another time?"

"I doubt it. We've got the rest of the weekend booked. I'm sorry."

He smiled at her. "Too bad. But this is my job, and I can't ignore it. You understand…"

"Better than you know. I heard the phone and thought it was my office."

"You too? Sorry to hear that." Then he smiled his beautiful smile. Amanda tried not to stare. "Maybe we can find a time to play."

"We'll see." She was surprised at the disappointment that gnawed at her insides as he trotted away.

Much as she doubted Luke would be a challenge, she had looked forward to an amusing game. She liked his eyes, his crooked smile, his easy way. He wasn't demanding anything of her besides a little fun. And how she needed that.

Then there was that call from the office. Was it possible he was as career focused as she was? That could be a good thing—he wouldn't take up much of her precious time. Or that could be bad—he wouldn't have much time for her.

Best, really, that she put him out of her mind. She didn't have time for romance. This weekend, she needed to focus on Julie, her oldest and best-est friend, only months from her wedding day. Even if Amanda wasn't ready for marriage—she certainly had a lot to do before becoming a wife—she knew this get-together needed to be a celebration of friendship, love, and the future.

Once she was back in Pittsburgh, she'd have to devote all her attention to work. With a big case, a demanding boss, and six days a week in the office, romance wasn't an option.

Amanda glanced at her phone. It was nearly three o'clock. Time to go talk to the cook. Chef Henri promised a portable feast to top off their hike tomorrow. She wondered if maybe he had a few samples.

Afterward, she'd get her book and find a seat on the porch.

A phone rang again. This time, it was hers.

Chapter Two
The Family Home

Smooth, Luke. Real smooth.
Not only was he off his tennis game, his game of love was also tanking.

Plus, there was that Roger Federer guy. *Who's he?* He stopped on the porch and clicked on his phone's web app… "widely considered to be one of the greatest players of all-time." Luke groaned. *I should have known. How many people know that? Everybody but me, I guess.*

He thought about the trim woman with the short blonde curls as he opened the door. Though he desperately wanted to see her again, he decided to play it cool.

He'd find a way. After all, his room in his parents' apartment was right down the hall from the guest rooms. As the screen door slammed behind him, he had to wonder when he forgot how to hold a proper conversation with a woman. Friendly banter wasn't his style. He hadn't flirted in ages. When he did, he got tongue-tied or said something stupid.

He was comfortable, most of the time, talking to women at work. As a business development assistant for a well-respected construction firm, it was part of his job to address high-powered females making multi-million-dollar deals. Sometimes, he quaked in his shoes, especially when called before his boss, Frederika Templeton.

Tough but fair, she always seemed to be at the office and when she worked horrendous hours, so did he. It was expected. Maybe he wasn't a workaholic yet, but he was working on it.

The pretty visitor disappeared from his thoughts as he scrolled through his phone, searching for the email he sent Paul.

How could his report have been misplaced? He found the email he sent two days earlier. Back at the office, Paul assured Luke no one would read it until after Memorial Day. They underestimated Frederika.

When she announced she was taking both Thursday and Friday off, he rejoiced at the prospect of time at the lake. This was the first Friday he wasn't chained to his desk since, well, he couldn't remember when.

Before he could pocket his phone, an email popped up. This one, from Frederika, asking for the same file. He wasn't surprised. She may have told her staff she planned to be a thousand miles away at a family reunion, but Frederika wasn't like regular people, happy to be among relatives she hadn't seen in a while. Instead of sitting down to barbecue, she was going over reports.

Luke paused in the empty parlor to dash off a reply to assure her the report was on her desk, waiting for her in Wilmington. Then he promised to forward a copy right away.

He sprang up the stairs then turned away from the guest wing to the apartment his family kept in the original house.

Already, his room, the one in the corner that had always been his, was a mess. With a reluctant sigh, he tossed the balls he'd stashed in his pockets on the bed and swung his racquet before leaning it against the closet door. He used to play all the time but since he started at Windsor-Douglas three years ago, he didn't have time for it anymore. He was so rusty, a game with Amanda would have been a total embarrassment. She'd said something about playing on a college team. That meant she might be good.

His stepfather, DeWayne, kept up the courts in hopes Luke would come back and play here. He took it as a sign his fathers missed him. When he arrived last night, they smothered him in kisses and plied him with ratatouille and French bread, his favorites since he was a boy.

He was glad to be home again at last. He'd forgotten how beautiful the view was, how serene. Even more, he realized how much he missed Henri and DeWayne. Luke was lucky to be blessed with two wonderful fathers.

They'd moved here when he was a boy. DeWayne had met his father Henri in the months after Luke's mother, his *maman*, died. Both he and his grief-stricken father found a new life with

DeWayne. When the two men decided they wanted to work together far from the noise of New York City, far from sad memories, they found this inn. Henri gave up his restaurant. DeWayne said goodbye to a defense contracting gig. They built a life here.

Loving and fun, friendly and open, they were good men, and Luke hoped he was like them. He wasn't sure now, after three pressure-filled years as a marketing drone at Windsor-Douglas. All work and no fun, as the saying goes, was definitely true in the construction company's business development department.

With a sigh, he fired up his laptop. While he waited for the internet to connect, he caught a glimpse of the girl with the yellow curls pacing on the stone path that encircled the inn. She seemed lost in conversation on her phone. Before he had time to wonder how good a tennis player she was, his email files appeared.

He needed to send the missing file ASAP. Knowing Paul or Frederika might call at any time, Luke always carried his laptop, ready to work. Paul was in the office as usual for a Friday afternoon. He'd probably be there late, even on a holiday weekend.

His phone rang again.

"Luke, I am your father." The deep voice with the distinctive Parisian accent boomed into his ear.

It was an old joke, but even so, Luke chuckled before answering. "That's not funny anymore, Henri. I do admit, however, it was funny when I was eleven."

"You laughed. I heard that little snicker. DeWayne and I want to know if Frank is coming tonight. There's a big group coming in for dinner at eight."

"Yeah, the bachelorette party."

"Oh. How'd you know about that?"

"I smacked one of the ladies in the head with a tennis ball. It was a sort of meet-cute."

"More like a meet-awful if you ask me. You didn't hurt her?"

Luke appreciated the concern in his father's tone, much more than he appreciated his Star Wars voice. "No, Dad. She's fine. We even talked about playing some tennis."

"Really…"

Luke didn't have time to go into the details and gently

explained his work predicament. "I have to answer an email to Paul at work. I'll come talk to you and DeWayne the minute I hit the send button. And Dad? You don't have to wait for Frank. He isn't coming until Sunday."

Luke tossed his phone onto the desk and located the errant file. He studied it for all the most recent updates, confident this was his best work yet. He had worked on it for longer than any other proposal. The graphics and the architect's renderings were spectacular. He'd polished the prose until it made him want to build the project himself.

So what if it was only a doctors' office building? Nothing sexy like some of the company's other projects: hotels and shopping centers, even a museum. Still, he'd outdone himself to make this one shine. Evaluations were due July first. He wanted Paul and Frederika to remember how good this proposal was.

Except someone had lost it, making it now appear he missed a deadline. Something Windsor-Douglas never tolerated. He typed a quick note, reminding Paul this was the second time he was sending it and alerting him he was also sending a copy to Frederika at her request. Once he heard the swoosh of his emails heading into cyberspace, Luke closed the laptop and went to talk to Henri.

His father was, as Luke expected, sitting at the massive oak kitchen table, his usual location for planning meals. Beside him was Amanda.

There Henri was in his element. A big man with a shadow of black beard on his full cheeks, he always appeared to be ready to laugh. Unless he was, in fact, already laughing. Luke knew, of course, his father had experienced some serious sadness, including the loss of his mother soon after they emigrated to America, the sudden death of his wife Ana, who was Luke's mother, and the suffering of being outed after he finally found consolation then love with DeWayne.

Henri put his heart and soul into his family and his cooking. He loved whipping up French classics for a crowd. His passion for the kitchen made the Broadview a destination restaurant. The inn—old, creaky, and definitely not up-to-date—might be faltering, but the restaurant was a sure winner night after night, season after season.

With its menu full of French techniques, local produce and dairy, and Henri's warm hospitality, the restaurant was forced to turn away people without reservations. Often, however, he set up tables in the parlor rather than disappoint hungry guests.

Luke waited by the door to eavesdrop for a moment. He enjoyed watching his dad at work. His French accent thickened, and his laugh rose from deep inside his substantial belly. He talked about the recipes as if they'd been handed to him on stones carved on Mount Sinai.

The young woman beside him was a treat, as well. Luke could see from Amanda's twinkling eyes she was taken with Henri and his menu. She gave him her full attention, nodding as he spoke, glancing at his ever-moving hands.

"I propose petite Grand Marnier soufflés as a way to end your celebratory dinner tonight."

"Ooooh. I've never had one of those." Her answer, full of excitement and awe, brought a smile to Henri's face.

Luke was certain Amanda had charmed him because Henri rarely proposed making a soufflé. They tended to collapse before arriving at the table. Because the chef in Henri wanted the presentation to delight his guests, he found them too risky.

She folded her hands together in a gesture of pleasure. "I wasn't expecting something this elegant."

"*Mademoiselle*, for you and your bridal party, we will make everything memorable."

"Oh, no. Not me. I'm not the bride."

"*Je suis désolé.*" Henri put a hand to his cheek. "I thought…"

"No, no. I prefer the single life."

Much as Luke was happy to hear Amanda was single, it pained him to discover she preferred it. He was learning all kinds of things from where he stood.

Amanda and Henri laughed together before she explained, "I am the bride's best friend. My oldest and dearest friend Julie is getting married in September. The bridesmaids are having a bachelorette party."

"Ah, yes. You are the party girl. You explained this to me when we spoke on the phone." Henri laughed again.

The floor creaked under Luke's feet so before he could be

caught eavesdropping, he swept into the room. "I hope I'm not interrupting."

Henri jumped up to hug his son. "*Mademoiselle*, may I present my son? This is Luke. Luke, Mademoiselle Johnson."

"A pleasure, *mademoiselle*." He bowed slightly and smiled. Luke now admired the color blooming in her cheeks.

"I didn't realize you had a son. Luke and I met on the tennis court earlier today."

"Oh, no. You are the one he hit with the ball? My deepest apologies." Henri pursed his lips at Luke. "I do hope my boy did not hurt you."

"No, no, no. It was only a weak little lob."

He cringed. He didn't think his serve was that bad.

"I meant, it wasn't hard enough to hurt me. I mean it..." The pink in Amanda's cheeks deepened to a rosy hue. "All I meant was, no, I wasn't hurt."

"I am relieved." Henri smiled and stretched out a hand to a chair, inviting his son to join them. "Sit down, son. May I get you something to eat?"

Before he could race to the refrigerator, Luke stopped him. "No thank you, *mon père*. I don't want to disturb you. I'll come back when you're not busy. Do you know where DeWayne is?"

Before he headed off to see DeWayne in the business office, Luke looked once again at Amanda, hoping to catch her eye, maybe see her smile again. But she had forgotten him already, her attention focused on the menu in front of her.

It served him right. As he crossed the parlor to the cramped room behind the registration desk, Luke decided he had misread Amanda's cues.

He hadn't been able to read a woman's expression since Emily. A woman he'd never forgive. Or forget. The love of his life who decided she didn't need him anymore. More than a year ago now, she left her engagement ring on the kitchen counter, straightened her no-nonsense blue suit jacket, walked out the door, and never looked back.

Maybe he didn't lose his way with women. Maybe he never understood them at all.

He sure didn't get his first college girlfriend, Dianna. She broke up with him the day before graduation, saying she didn't need any distractions while she was going to grad school. His second girlfriend took a job on the West Coast and didn't tell him until after she flew to Seattle.

Since then, he'd been on a lot of first dates, but rarely a second. The women he met these days wouldn't bother to tell him the time if he asked, much less agree to a date.

Better that he protect his heart than try again. Not even Amanda with her long tennis legs and short blonde curls could make him forget Emily and his bad luck with high-powered women. And she even said she was happy being single. His blood ran cold at the thought. He didn't ever want another woman like Emily. From all appearances, Amanda could be the same. If she was, she was one to avoid.

Luke strolled into DeWayne's little office, expecting a happy conversation. If Henri's face was filled with delight, DeWayne's expression was one of worry. Tall and muscular from years of Army life, he stared at the paperwork littering his desk and twisted the heavy gold West Point ring on his big mocha-colored hand.

"Hey, DeWayne."

The worry disappeared as he rose to clasp Luke's hand and yank him into a hug. "It always makes me glad to see you darken my door, boy." He motioned to a chair, and Luke sat to face him.

"Everything looks great. Whoever resurfaced your courts did a terrific job. Is the pier new?" Luke knew DeWayne loved to talk about improvements to the property.

"Not this year. We re-stained the boards, but I can tell you didn't walk on it. It's a bit rickety. We couldn't afford the expense, especially after having the tennis courts fixed. Henri insisted we take care of them first."

"You've never worried about money before."

"Times have changed, I'm afraid." DeWayne glanced at the paperwork on his desk. "We have bills but not enough reservations to cover them. We noticed last summer people were opting for the newer resorts over us. We don't have a pool or a spa or a zip line or karaoke."

"They'll come. They always do."

"There's something new. Henri doesn't want to talk about it, so we haven't told you." DeWayne's voice sounded ominous.

"What?"

"We've gotten an offer to sell the property."

"Are you going to take it?" Luke couldn't imagine who would want to buy his parents' old inn.

It had stood sentry over the lake for more than a hundred years. Its plumbing was newer than the house but not by much and the electricity was probably installed by a contemporary of Thomas Edison himself. The windows were drafty. The fireplace smoked. The plaster walls were held together by a century's worth of wallpaper. The bathrooms were late twentieth century and so was the kitchen. The furniture was a collection of dusty old antiques spruced up with lemon oil and elbow grease each spring.

As much as he loved the old place, keeping it up was hard work. No matter how diligent DeWayne was, there was always another maintenance project to keep him busy. Plans for renovations and updates kept moving to the back burner.

"We don't want to. A developer wants the property. For a big new resort."

That didn't make any sense to Luke. They only owned a few acres. Not even enough for a good parking lot. "What about the house?"

"Oh they're not interested in this big old house. They want the land and, more importantly, its location. They plan to tear the house down."

"They can't do that." Luke's heart sank as if DeWayne was telling him he only had six months to live. It hurt to think about the possibility of his childhood home disappearing.

"Our neighbors have already agreed to sell, but the developer is eager to get his hands on our property. The hotel will be built behind us. The spa and the restaurant will be built at the edge of our land by the lake. We have the best location, the best view. We always knew that." DeWayne's voice sounded matter of fact now, as if he was relating dry information that didn't affect all of them.

"The Masons are selling their house?"

DeWayne nodded. "And the Evitts. And the horse farm beside them. I never remember the name of the owner there."

Luke remembered. Mr. Brown made it clear he didn't like people like DeWayne when he told Luke he couldn't take his daughter Janie on a date. A mean, narrow-minded man even if he treated his stable full of horses as if they were Triple Crown winners. "Joe Brown."

"Yeah. Joe. He never used to speak to me, not even to say hello at the farmers' market. Now he's calling me every day asking if I have agreed to sell."

"Don't do it, Pop. You and Henri always said you wouldn't leave here except in a box. They can't make you sell."

What would his parents do without the Broadview Inn? They weren't old enough to retire. They weren't the type of men to spend the day on the golf course. Neither liked to fly or even go out of sight of the inn for more than a few days. They loved winter so there was no chance of them moving to Florida.

Life wouldn't be the same without his family home. He didn't come back often enough, but this was where he grew up, where he became part of a new family after *Maman* died.

"It'll work out all right. I just thought you needed to know." DeWayne rounded his desk to put a comforting hand on Luke's shoulder. "Come on, son. It must be the cocktail hour by now. Let's go find out what's on the bar."

The five o'clock cocktail was a tradition at the Broadview. Henri specialized in old-fashioned drinks: Sazeracs, Manhattans, Rob Roys.

A drink was a good idea even if it wouldn't change a thing. The Beaumont-Wilson family was about to lose its happy home.

Chapter Three
In the Wine Cellar

"Where are they?" Amanda glanced at her phone, as if it might answer her back.

Henri handed her a citrus-scented gimlet. "Sometimes the traffic around Frederick and Hagerstown can be terrible. You're here to relax. Go sit on the porch and enjoy the sunset over the lake. I'm sure they'll be here in time for dinner."

Luke admired his father's way with women. His charm and French accent could make any Francophile swoon.

"What a wonderful idea." She held up her curvy coupe glass in a kind of salute and went outside.

Henri poured another drink and handed it to Luke. He gestured toward the door. "Maybe Amanda could use some company."

Luke mimicked her salute and followed.

Amanda had changed into a simple floral dress. The flowing skirt fell away at the knee and showed off her muscular legs. She must have caught him noticing because she smoothed the skirt so it hung more modestly.

She tipped her glass toward him. "Your father makes a delicious cocktail. I've never tasted one of these before."

"Specialty of the house. Henri loves his cocktails almost as much as his cooking."

When she laughed, her eyes twinkled. Luke couldn't help wanting to make her laugh again.

"It shows. He's passionate about it all. You should have heard him talk about the menu for tonight's dinner. And when I said picnic, he thought feast."

Amanda's admiration for his father charmed him. "Believe

me. I've heard it all. Henri has always loved cooking. He learned from his *maman*."

"I was surprised to hear you call him by his name."

"Since he and DeWayne have been together, they have preferred I call them Henri and DeWayne, although I sometimes call Henri dad or *mon pere* and DeWayne answers to pop. It's difficult to call for dad when you have two of them."

"I never thought of that. So, DeWayne's also your father?"

Luke nodded. He wasn't going to explain his family situation yet again. This being the twenty-first century, it was old news. Families came in all kinds and colors. His new family came together after his mother, his *maman,* died more than twenty years ago. To his relief, Amanda seemed to understand. Instead of asking anything else, she nursed her drink while gazing at the view.

He couldn't keep his eyes off her. Not only did she have the grace of an athlete, but she was also quick and smart. Already, she had charmed Henri. Maybe she was too good for him. It didn't matter. He had to talk to her. Her wanted to know more about her.

"Do you work in Baltimore?" Okay, the question was lame, but it might lead to something.

Amanda shook her head and explained she was a third-year associate in a Pittsburgh law firm. "If I work hard, I'll make partner in a few years. A few long years."

Luke cocked an eyebrow. "Is it a firm I would have heard of?"

"I doubt it. It's not one of those ambulance chasing firms that advertise on television. But it has an unforgettable name. Jones, Jones, and Taylor."

"Two Joneses?"

"Yeah. And they weren't related."

"Weren't? Did they leave?"

"No." She laughed. "They've been dead for twenty years. The founding members are all gone."

"So, do you go to court and argue before a jury?"

"No, I don't have the stomach to be a litigator. For other people in my firm, that's their passion. I spend most of my time in a small, messy office working on contracts and other documents. It's not very exciting."

A dullness in Amanda's eyes signaled to Luke a change of

subject was in order. Maybe tennis. "Do you play tennis in Pittsburgh?"

She laughed again, a little sad laugh. "I wish. No, I haven't played much tennis in a while. I used to play all the time. When I played on my college team, I was nationally ranked. I even kept up my training during law school. I really wanted to win a place on the Olympic team, and I got it."

She took another sip of her drink and a hint of a wrinkle appeared between her brows. Luke wondered how he could make it go away.

"I didn't get to go, though. I was named an alternate and that meant I only got to go if someone on the team wasn't able to. It turned out for the best, I guess. I got an offer to be a summer associate after my first year of law school at the firm where I really wanted to work. Since I wasn't at the Games, I could jump on it. It would have been nice to play, though." Amanda's voice was tinged with disappointment, her expression stony.

"That decides it, I guess. Much as I was hoping to play, I'm no match for an Olympian." He tasted his gimlet and wondered what to say next. What would bring the smile back to her face?

It was unusual that he wanted to charm a guest at the inn. Summer after summer, he never bothered to check out the women who stopped for a vacation by the lake. What was the point? His luck with women was laughable.

But Amanda wasn't just any guest. Something made her special, made him yearn for her. It was more than her golden curls, those great legs, the sinews in her right arm that threatened a mean backhand. She was kind to Henri, appreciative of his talents. She had a quick wit—even if it was at his expense. Obviously, she was smart. She seemed devoted to her work, like Emily. That, all by itself, was enough to make him wary of her. He sensed, though, that Amanda was different from Emily, that she was more than her job. Amanda was interested in everything around her, curious and inquisitive. The whole package challenged him from his toes to his, well, brain.

As out of practice in romance as he was in tennis, Luke was still convinced this was a woman worth getting to know. He'd go slow, protect his heart, even if he had every intention of flailing about until he hit on something that made her sit up and notice him.

While the sun sank behind the gentle Appalachians, she turned away from the darkening sky and smiled. "The man at the registration desk said he'd show me around the place."

"DeWayne? He loves showing off the inn."

She put down her glass and rose from her chair. "Where'd he go? I want to take him up on his offer."

Here was a chance Luke wasn't passing up. "I'd be happy to show you. I've been on the tour a few times."

"I bet you have. Well, lead on."

"We might as well start here on the porch, that wraps around three sides of the old house. When we bought this old place, everything—the siding, the gingerbread and trim—was painted white. DeWayne chipped off the old paint until he found the original colors. Then he got his paint brushes out and painted the trim the colors you see here."

"It's beautiful. I love historic buildings." Amanda put her hand on the porch railing, painted in three shades of green. "What a lot of work to repaint all this trim. So many colors. I love this dark shade and also the ruby red on the trim under the eaves. It's, well, wow."

Luke smiled. Not many people appreciated the work that went into keeping this place up.

In the sitting room beside the parlor, he showed her a glass topped table filled with old train tickets and timetables from the turn of the twentieth century. "Back then, the only way to get here was by train. Once upon a time, the inn had a carriage to pick up people at the station in Oakland."

Against the back wall, she ran her hand over the well-worn oak counter where Henri fixed their drinks earlier. "From all appearances, the bar is witness to some interesting stories."

"We'll never know. It's older than the house. Henri found it at a salvage yard in Cumberland. The salesman said it was rescued from an inn that burned down."

Amanda yanked her hand away from the wood surface as if it scorched her. She took a calming breath that made Luke curious. "Isn't it funny that it didn't burn during the fire?"

"Lucky for us. It was a great find, don't you think?"

After he led her through the dining room where the aromas of butter, meat, and herbs filled the air, she stopped him on the ornate staircase with a question. "Have famous guests ever stayed here?"

Luke shook his head. "This isn't the Deer Park."

She looked confused. "The Deer Park?"

"You've heard of the bottled water? It first came from a spring at the hotel called the Deer Park. The inn was famous in its day." He saw a glint of recognition and continued, "Although this place was built at the same time, the famous people stayed there. It was much bigger and grander. Three presidents stayed there."

"But none stayed here? Their mistake."

Luke led Amanda into unoccupied rooms so she could take a peek at the furnishings. "DeWayne tries to make sure all the rooms have different decor."

"This room is a lot like mine." She ran a hand across the lacy fabric of the bedspread. "This fabric is so delicate."

"There is an old story that one of those presidents visited the Broadview during his honeymoon, but the details are hazy and, anyway, we've never been able to prove it. We don't have any records from back then."

She cocked her head with interest. "Which president was it?"

"I can never remember his name. Maybe Garfield? Or Grover Cleveland? It was more than a century ago. Someone at the historical society may remember. Those people know just about everything about this county."

Amanda glanced out a window at the top of the stairs. "They should have stayed here. If only for the view. It's lovely."

He was pleased at the way Amanda gracefully leaned on the windowsill and appreciated all the years of work his fathers put into their home. When she moved to continue the tour, he showed her a door with no number. "The inn has changed a lot since it opened. This door used to lead to the original wing. The rooms had separate sitting areas and the best views. We have a few old photos and the rooms were beautiful. But that part of the inn collapsed in the 1950s."

"Oh no, what happened?"

He wasn't used to such inquisitive visitors. He was happy to talk about the house's history. "A tree fell on the roof during a storm and the previous owners had to tear down the whole wing.

This part—we call it the new wing even if it is more than fifty years old—was built to replace the original part. These rooms have modern conveniences, including bathrooms. The old rooms didn't."

They stopped in front of a second unmarked door. "This is our apartment. It's part of the original house. I can show it to you but it's pretty modern. At least it's 1980s modern. The previous owners updated it before Henri and DeWayne bought it."

Amanda shook her head, and they headed downstairs. "When was the original house built?"

"About 1880. A railroad executive originally built the house for his family but then once he got here, he realized his property was the perfect location for an inn. He added the first wing and began selling excursions. He called it the Broadview."

Luke paused at the basement door. He didn't usually take people down there. Dark and full of spiders, it held Henri's huge wine collection, as it had done for generations before him. For Amanda, Luke was willing to make an exception. She seemed more curious than most. "Would you like to see the wine cellar?"

"Oh, yes, please." Her enthusiasm surprised him, but he had to warn her.

"Are you sure? There might be spiders." He hated spiders, but she just shrugged.

"I'm game if you are." Her eyes sparkled as she smiled.

Yes, he was definitely game.

There was nothing glamorous about the dank, dreary basement. Even so, Amanda wandered through the narrow rows of dusty wine bins, rubbing dirt off the bottles' labels to read them. While Luke kept away from walls or shelves or anything else that might hide a creepy-crawly thing, she didn't seem the least bit bothered by bugs or dirt or the poor lighting as she ran her hands across the rough wood shelving.

"Some of these are quite old." Her eyes grew wide in amazement. "This one has the year I was born—1989."

"That's from Henri's own collection." He brushed dust off the label of a bordeaux. "His and *Maman*'s. The house also came with some old stuff. Henri left it here, but he doesn't include any of it on the wine list."

"I wonder if it's any good." She slipped a bottle, caked with decades of dirt, from its slot. "Look at this one—1884." She whispered the date. "Wow."

Luke leaned in for a closer look. Despite the dust and musty smell, he caught a whiff of her perfume, fresh and floral. It took all his strength to pay attention to the wine. "I didn't realize we had any that old."

Amanda stooped to slip it back onto the shelf. "It won't go back in."

Before he could stop her, she reached into the slot. "There's something stuck in here."

Luke didn't want to think about what that might be. Still, he crouched to see what she found.

She plucked her phone from her pocket. Shining its flashlight into the slot, she peered in. "I wonder what it is." She poked her hand inside again, leaning her body against him to stretch a little farther. "Got it."

Her eyes gleamed with curiosity as she extracted a tiny book, moldy now, though once it might have had a pattern stamped into its dark green leather. Though the paper was yellowed and smelled of mildew, the edges of the pages still held traces of a swirling pattern in varying shades of green.

They bent their heads together as Amanda leafed through it. Inside were page after page of childish scrawl. On many of them the words were smeared. A few pages were stuck together. Near the back of the book, the scrawl turned into proper penmanship with the script flowing more gracefully in blue-black ink.

"I think I can decipher some of the words." She held her phone light over the page to read. "'The rain has never stopped long enough to play outside. I was hoping to see the nice boy I met yesterday. Mother is bored, though Father is happy to read all day. Oh, there was one bit of excitement. The president came to visit today. Can you imagine? I met the President of the United States. And he brought his new wife! She's very pretty. It was all so thrilling. They joined some of the adults for tea in the dining room. They are on their honeymoon at the Deer Park Inn...'" Amanda stopped reading, her eyes wide and bright.

"That's all I can read. There's a splotch of ink that messes up the rest of the page." She rose to show him the book. "Do you know what this means?"

"Some little girl wrote in her diary that she was bored in the rain?"

Amanda laughed. "You did have a distinguished guest here. That's exciting. You mentioned a president and his wife who stayed at the Deer Park on their honeymoon. They came here. You have to find out who they were."

Luke shrugged. Much as the shine in her eyes fascinated him—maybe it was from the flashlight—he wasn't as impressed as she was by a child's diary.

"You need to take care of this. Put it on display, maybe." She leafed through the leather-bound book with an expression signaling she'd like to study it further. Right now, he wanted to do whatever he could to please her.

"What? It's just an old book."

She held it out to him. "This is special. You need to show it off. Preferably behind glass. It smells worse than four-day-old fish."

Luke chuckled though he accepted it with some reluctance. He had to agree about the odor, even as he assured her he would display it.

Before she turned off her flashlight, it illuminated a big, hairy arachnid hanging on a strand of web. He reacted without thought, recoiling from the nasty thing. His head was turned away when Amanda smashed it with her phone against the wine bin.

"Got it," she cried in triumph and took his arm. "Don't like bugs, huh?"

He laughed, a bit embarrassed. He hoped she couldn't see the look of horror on his face. Spiders inhabited his nightmares. "No. Hate them."

As she slipped past him to make her way through the narrow passageway to head upstairs, Amanda tripped over his foot and wobbled. Luke grabbed her arm before she could fall.

It was well-muscled and hard as iron. But her skin was soft, and from it the delicate scent of baby powder rose to his nostrils. She held onto him only a split second until she had recovered, but Luke wished it could last much longer.

No, she definitely was no Emily. His ex-fiancée would never have followed him to the basement, never would have touched a book smelling as the one they found, and certainly never

31

would have killed a bug.

When he didn't let go, she stiffened and cast her gaze down to her feet. "Sorry about that."

Her shy apology touched him. "I'm not."

She returned her gaze to his face, her eyes wide. Luke wondered how she interpreted his cheesy line. It wasn't the kind of thing he usually said but in the moment it seemed right. Especially when she didn't pull away.

"Maybe we ought to go back upstairs." That twinkle was back in her eye.

"Let's try to stay upright, hmmm?" When he squeezed her arm, she leaned into him a little, her warmth welcome in the dampness of the basement.

When they got to the sitting room, he searched for a proper spot. Someplace where the smell wouldn't offend their guests. The corner cabinet seemed like a good choice. He opened the glass door and rearranged a couple of knickknacks to place it at eye level. "How's this? We'll keep it on this shelf. If anyone wants to see it, or if you want to read it again, it will be right here."

"That's a good spot." She pointed to the key in his hand. "You have to keep it locked. That book is valuable." She wiped her hands and grimaced. "Now I have to wash off this awful smell."

Just as Amanda returned to the porch and started to take a seat next to Luke, her phone pinged. A look of regret clouded her eyes as she touched his arm. "I have to answer this. Thanks for the tour."

With that, she disappeared back into the house. Disappointed she was gone but happy about their basement adventure, Luke stretched out to enjoy the quiet moment. He was glad he came this weekend. He hadn't planned on coming until Frank, his college frat brother, suggested meeting him here.

They hadn't seen each other much since Frank took a job with a non-profit in Baltimore. Their rare get-togethers grew even less frequent once Frank found himself a girlfriend—now his fiancée. Luke was grateful to the woman who let his friend loose while she went away for the whole Memorial Day weekend. Two good reasons to come. Visiting his parents and catching up with an old friend. Maybe a third reason too. He thought of Amanda's inquisitive eyes, her curiosity, her wit, and the interest she showed the inn—and in him.

A fourth, troubling reason occurred to him. If he hadn't come, he wouldn't know about the offer to buy the inn. Something that left an expression of distress on DeWayne's face. He couldn't imagine life without the inn to come home to. Nor could he bear to see such turmoil in his stepfather's face. Henri, always protecting him, was probably just as upset.

Before his college buddy got here, Luke was going to have to sit with his fathers and get the whole story. Henri was putting on his game face, happy smiles, and warm hospitality. It was time for the truth. Luke didn't need protecting anymore. He was no longer young enough for the little boy treatment. Especially now.

Whether Henri and DeWayne were going to keep the Broadview, or find something else to do with their lives, they needed to be honest with Luke. He'd called this place home for nearly twenty years. He had a right to know what was next.

The sun began to sink toward the horizon, turning the mountains ahead of him a royal purple as the sky blazed orange and lavender. It was a sight Luke never got tired of. Since he could only rarely escape his office in time to enjoy the sunset, he made sure to stop for the daily display whenever he was at the lake.

Henri, now clad in a white chef's coat and starched apron that fell nearly to his shoes, brought a glass of rosé to Luke.

"Beautiful, isn't it?" His father shared his love of sunsets. He once told Luke the house's western view sold the pair on the place—even before they knew they wanted to run an inn. He shouted through the screen door before taking a chair. "DeWayne, come on or you'll miss it."

In a second or two, DeWayne appeared to watch with his family, his arm around Henri. The three men said nothing as the twilight deepened.

A compact black SUV rumbling up the driveway sliced through the silence, and when the driver cut the motor, a trio of giggling women, laden with luggage, emerged.

"Must be the bridal party." Henri leapt from his chair to return to the kitchen. "Back to work. Sweetie, I need your help."

DeWayne ruffled Luke's brown curls then followed Henri inside.

Not a moment passed before Amanda crashed through the screen door and down the porch steps.

"You're here at last." She hugged and kissed the driver who laughed and smoothed her long red hair. Amanda tugged on the white satin sash Julie wore that proclaimed in silver glitter, "Here Comes the Bride."

For Luke, the view kept getting better and better. From the truck emerged two other women as stunning as the driver. One, petite and dark, wrangled an armload of bags of varying sizes. The other, obviously pregnant, tossed a single red leather tote over her shoulder after twisting her long brown tresses and arranging them down the other shoulder. He could tell they were the bridesmaids from the pink glittery sashes they wore.

Deciding he should give the bridal party a bit of privacy, he reluctantly slipped inside. *Henri probably needs someone to warm the plates or stir the sauce or, well, something.*

Chapter Four
Clue in the Diary

After Julie introduced Amanda to Hannah and Marisa, DeWayne distributed guest keys and sent them upstairs to unpack. "Dinner's ready when you are."

Amanda carried Julie's suitcase into a corner room with tall, generous windows, framed by delicate lace curtains and overlooking the lake. The walls were covered in a lavender floral print and on the sleigh bed was an antique white counterpane. "What a pretty room—but very different from mine."

"You know you're not in the Holiday Inn when you stay here." Julie pulled a dark pink sash from her bag, shook it then presented it to Amanda.

She examined the glittery thing at arm's length. "I thought you said no silly 'hen party' stuff."

"I know I did. Marisa brought them. She said she bought them for her bachelorette weekend and thought maybe you wouldn't think of them."

"She's right about that." Julie's excited expression encouraged Amanda to put it on. "I haven't worn pink and glitter since…"

Julie smiled as she smoothed a twist in the back of the sash. "I've never seen you in pink and glitter. But it is kind of cute."

"You're kind of cute," Amanda retorted.

"I promise you won't have to wear it on the hike tomorrow." Julie turned again to unpack her bag. "Did you get a good look around? I'm sure you've checked out the tennis courts."

"Luke and I were going to play a game, but then he needed to send something for work."

Julie stopped unpacking and stared at Amanda. "Who's

35

Luke?"

"The owners' son." Amanda flopped into the easy chair by the window.

"Luke is here? Are you kidding me?"

"Yeah. Um, no. Do you know Luke?"

"I know who he is. I'm just surprised he's here this weekend. He went to college with Frank. They're fraternity brothers. But I haven't met him. Frank always says he's working—sounds like someone else I know."

Amanda was confused, not to mention surprised, by such a coincidence. "He said he works in Wilmington."

Julie hung up a sundress. "Yeah. That's the guy. He's the best man. I can't wait to meet him. Frank will be so surprised when he finds out. I texted him about our change of plans, but I never heard from him. I wish he were here."

Amanda jumped up to put an arm through her friend's. "No, you don't. Then the weekend would be all about your fiancé. This is our weekend. I've even put my 'Out of Office' notice on my email and promised myself I would only go through it once a day."

Julie looked skeptical. "How many times have you read it today?"

A twinge of guilt reminded her how often she missed meeting up with Julie because of work. "I had some time this morning before I left and then after I got here, I ran out of things to do. It seemed like a good time to catch up. But now it's all about you and your bachelorette weekend."

Julie hugged her. "I'm really glad you found time to do this."

"I'm sorry we couldn't go to the other hotel."

"This will be nice. The important thing is we're all together."

Amanda took a seat on the bed while her friend continued to unpack. "I have to tell you I was worried when I drove up to the inn. But I think it's going to be a good choice."

Julie batted her eyes and smiled. "Because of Luke?"

"No, not because of Luke. He did take me on a great tour of the inn while I was waiting."

Julie tucked a handful of folded lingerie into a drawer.

"You have been a busy girl."

"Oh, please. I had some time to kill and Luke seemed nice. Anyway, this inn has been here for some time. More than a hundred years. The wing where our rooms are, though, was only built in the '40s or '50s. I forget which. The cool part was what we found in the cellar."

"Is that what I smell? Icky basement funk?" Julie wrinkled her freckled nose.

"Julie..." Amanda put her hands to her face. Oh no, Julie was right. Amanda didn't get the smell off the first time she washed them. She raced into the bathroom to scrub them again.

Julie waited, sitting on the edge of the bed. "Okay. Tell me."

Breathlessly, Amanda related how she found the diary. "The owners were aware of stories about a president being here but didn't have any proof. They weren't sure when or even which president. Today while Luke was taking me on a tour, we went down into the wine cellar. The diary—"

"Oh, now you're Nancy Drew?" Julie crossed her legs and leaned her chin on her hand.

"I'm not telling you anymore." Amanda stuck her nose up in the air.

Julie giggled and slapped at Amanda's arm. "You were obsessed with those books in middle school, weren't you? They had titles like *The Secret of the Hidden Diary*. Well, didn't they?"

Amanda loved that mystery series enough to spend an entire summer between seventh and eighth grade reading every book she could get her hands on. One of her favorites, one her mother loaned her, was even called *The Clue in the Diary*. Now, the grown-up Amanda couldn't help laughing.

"You're right. They did. But this is a real book. I admit, it does smell atrocious. Luke put it on display in the sitting room by the parlor. The girl who wrote in it mentions seeing the president and first lady on their honeymoon."

Julie put the last of her cosmetics in the bath. "Awww. How romantic. You'll have to show me."

"I'd be happy to." Amanda was thrilled to share their discovery.

Hannah and Marisa barreled into the room already talking

a mile a minute. Amanda wanted Julie all to herself a bit longer but that would have to wait.

Amanda took a good look at Julie's friends as they made themselves comfortable. Julie hadn't mentioned that Marisa was pregnant. But as she eased into a chair by the window, Amanda couldn't miss the protective hand that went to her rounded belly. Hannah, by contrast, flitted around the room, examining pictures on the wall, running a hand over the heavy oak furniture, checking the view from the window.

Marisa flipped her brown hair over her shoulder. "Your room is so much better than mine."

"It is not." Hannah twirled around the room and shook her head. "This is nice, but yours is equally as nice. Even if you would have preferred staying at the Quality Inn by the ski lodge."

"That's not true. It's just that I prefer things more modern." Marisa tugged on the lacy, yellowed curtain.

Amanda opened her mouth to argue—after all, this hadn't been her original choice—but Hannah came to her defense.

"Well, I think it's quaint. The man behind the desk said the whole inn is all ours until another guest checks in tomorrow." Hannah collapsed on the bed beside Julie. "What time's dinner?"

Amanda laughed. "Chef Henri has been waiting for us."

Julie held open the door. "Then we should hurry."

~ * ~

"Everything is going according to plan." Julie took a sip of her after-dinner drink and looked much too relaxed for a woman with only a few weeks until The Big Day. "Wow, have you tasted this?" She smiled with approval at Henri. "What's in this?"

"A hotel specialty, *ma cherie*. Almond Joy coffee. It has Amaretto, chocolate vodka, and coconut rum." He winked at her. "I leave some room for the coffee."

The room was quiet as the women sipped and savored.

Marisa hesitated for a moment but then took the tiniest of tastes. "You should have this at the wedding." Then she licked her lips. "You know, a signature drink."

Hannah nodded. "That would get the crowd dancing. A little caffeine, a little alcohol and a great DJ."

"I love that idea, but I've already decided on everything." That's why Julie appeared so relaxed. She wasn't fretting about table assignments, napkin colors, or appetizers. "My fitting is a week from today. Although, Henri, if you keep feeding me food as delicious as your dinner, I'll need to let my dress out."

Henri practically skipped across the room and kissed Julie on the top of her head. "Words to make a chef dance with joy, *mademoiselle*. Now I will leave you to enjoy the rest of the evening. I left poor DeWayne and Luke alone with the dishes long enough. *Bon nuit*."

She glanced around the big, empty room. "It's strange to have the place all to ourselves."

Amanda was also puzzled. Luke said Henri had a reputation for drawing a crowd to the dining room on Friday and Saturday nights. Maybe because of the Memorial Day weekend it was quiet? That didn't make any sense though. Restaurants filled up on holidays.

On the other hand, a weekend to relax with the bridal party without the bother of other guests was a treat. They didn't have to worry about how loudly they laughed or how late they lingered in the parlor. No one else was here—at least until their one additional guest checked in the next day.

Then a thought struck her. Luke was expecting a friend tomorrow. Could it be possible Frank was coming to spend the weekend, and Julie wasn't aware of it? She had sent her fiancé a text with the change in plans.

Amanda brushed her thoughts aside to focus on Julie's conversation about school with her two teacher friends. Marisa taught first grade next to Julie's second grade classroom. Even though Hannah was their assistant principal she behaved more like a friend than a boss.

Amanda would have liked to get to know them both better if it was possible. She couldn't help it that work had kept her from Julie and Frank's engagement party. Then the wedding gown shopping trips, all three of them.

She even ordered her dress online instead of going to the bridal shop with the other bridesmaids. She had every intention of going to the bridal shower, but she ended up spending that Saturday on a conference call instead of with her friend.

Julie, good friend she always was, laughed off her absences but insisted Amanda promise to attend a bridesmaid's luncheon with her mother and grandmother. Then she made sure her best friend was free this weekend. With her demanding work schedule, Amanda was relieved to have an understanding friend.

The conversation lagged as the hour grew late. Marisa's eyelids drooped so much she couldn't pay attention.

"Sweetie, you're asleep on your feet," Julie said.

Marisa rose. "Pregnancy sucks." She trudged to the stairs then turned back with a smile. "It really doesn't. I'm quite happy about it, but it does make me tired. Good night."

When the mantel clock chimed twelve times, Hannah struggled to get off the sofa. "Ladies, my body is used to our school schedule. I have to get some sleep if we're going hiking in the morning. Good night."

"Sweet dreams." Julie hugged her friend. "Breakfast is at nine. Don't be late. We want to get to the state park before everybody else does."

Hannah agreed and headed for the stairs. "Good night, Amanda. Don't let the bride stay up much longer."

Amanda was happy they were alone again. "Hannah and Marisa are great."

"We do have fun." Then Julie frowned. "Like you and I used to have when you weren't always busy."

Amanda rubbed her forehead. "Work has been crazy. I never feel like I have time for myself, or my friends lately."

"Yes, I know." A smidgen of bitterness colored her friend's voice.

"I'll do better, I promise."

Julie put down her coffee mug. "Start right now. Amanda, you are overly busy. Maybe you need a man to distract you."

"Oh, please. Don't I wish. But until this case is over, I don't—"

"Stop. I've heard this before. You have to make time for yourself and your future. I see the way your face lights up when you talk about Luke. I know he's single. Go flirt with him."

Amanda's laughter rang through the quiet space. "Don't be ridiculous."

"I mean it. You know you want to. And I'll bet when you were busy checking out every inch of the inn, he was probably checking you out. And why not? He's handsome enough—even if

I've never met him, I've seen pictures. He's a good man who loves his parents. Frank thinks enough of him to make him his best man. What else do you need to know?"

"I don't know anything about him except his tennis serve is deplorable."

"There. Something in common. You love tennis. So, ask him to join you for a game. Or a tennis lesson to fix that serve. I'm perfectly happy to rearrange the schedule a bit for that. I'm a sucker for love. Here in this place, it would be so perfect."

If anyone could see through Amanda, Julie could. She didn't want to admit she was attracted to Luke, not now. She needed to keep focused on work. Later, maybe. Not now.

"I can see your mind going 'round and 'round." Julie patted Amanda on the shoulder and groaned. "We have to go to bed. If I don't, I won't see ten o'clock, much less nine. A teacher's day starts awfully early. I've been up, I guess, twenty hours now."

"You can sleep in if you want. The falls will still be there."

"I just might do that."

Amanda followed the bride to their rooms. When her head hit the pillow, she expected to fall asleep straightaway. Instead, she found herself fighting a losing battle. Her mind wouldn't shut down.

Memories of meeting Luke played and replayed. So did the expression on his face as he enjoyed the sunset with his parents. Not only was he handsome, he was clearly a family man.

Like her dad. After seeing Grandfather struggle with the grueling hours at the law firm, her father bypassed law school for business school.

But when Amanda applied for law school, her grandfather, not her father, discouraged her. She remembered the day he told her to teach, write for a newspaper, or dig ditches—anything but become an attorney. It still hurt to remember how he tried to dissuade her when she thought he would be proud of her decision.

She went anyway. Graduated at the top of her class. Became an associate in a prestigious firm. And worked like a dog, until late at night and nearly every Saturday.

Right now, she was glad there was no one to complain when she came home from the office long after dark. Sometimes, though, she wished her apartment wasn't so quiet or cold.

The day was coming when she'd have to figure out how to balance work and family. Some day.

She hoped it would be soon.

Chapter Five
Farmers' Market

"You're showing your age, Papa." Luke put down his grater and pointed the zucchini at his father. "Everyone agrees Alicia Vikander is a better Lara Croft than Angelina Jolie."

"Everyone your age, you mean." Henri smirked as he made his point and then added salt and pepper to the salad dressing. "Now finish grating that zucchini."

"It must be a generational thing." Luke spread the long shreds of squash onto sheets of paper towel to dry. "You older people favor Angelina. We prefer Alicia. What do you want me to do now?"

"Get the brownies from the oven and put them over there." Henri pointed to a waiting cooling rack.

The kitchen counters were covered with food in various stages of completion. It was still dark when Henri woke Luke to help him finish baking for both breakfast and the bridesmaids' picnic lunch. Already cooling, besides the brownies, were golden croissants and a couple of crisp baguettes and it wasn't even seven o'clock. The ingredients for muffins waited in a bowl for Luke's grated zucchini. Henri was pouring dressing over a mixture of cubed chicken, almonds, celery, and cranberries for the picnic. Bacon was sizzling in a pan and coffee brewed in a big urn by the dining room door.

Luke leaned on the counter next to his father and snagged a cube of chicken. His father slapped him away, and Luke laughed. "Well, you have to admit Alicia is more beautiful than Angelina and a much better actor."

"I don't know about her skills, but I will concede she is hot."

The door from the dining room swung open, and Amanda entered, a quizzical expression on her face.

"Oh, hello there. We were just talking about you." Henri smiled at Amanda and blithely went back to mixing his chicken salad.

She paused for a moment and raised an eyebrow. "Oh? I thought I heard you talking about Lara Croft as I came in."

Luke couldn't believe his ears. Here was a woman who, in a matter of a few short sentences and through a kitchen door, no less, picked up on the discussion he was having with his dad. It was their way to take apart a movie, especially if there was a remake or a sequel. If he wasn't impressed with Amanda before, he was now.

Shooting a glance at his father, Luke asked her, "Who do you think is the better Lara?"

"Everybody says Alicia Vikander is a much better actor. So, I vote for her." Amanda leaned on the last empty spot on the steel countertops and inhaled. "I had to come in and find out what that delicious smell is. It's definitely not coffee, though I'm dying for some."

"Did I tell you? I love this woman." Henri popped a cover on the salad bowl and pushed it into the overstuffed refrigerator.

Luke took the hint and handed her a steaming cup, along with the sugar bowl and a pitcher of cream.

"Thanks." She breathed in the bitter aroma and shook her head. "No, I smelled something chocolatey."

"Oh, honey. That has to be the brownies." Henri pointed to the tray cooling near the back door.

Amanda stood up tall with a smile lighting her face. "For us?"

"*Bien sûr*," Henri said. "All of this is for you."

Delight swept over her pretty face as she listened to the chef's plans for both the breakfast buffet to be served in an hour and the picnic the women would carry on their hiking trip to Swallow Falls State Park.

"Now I must send my son to the farmers' market to get the eggs and butter for breakfast."

"Do you want to tag along?" Luke tried not to appear overly eager. He was beginning to feel like a puppy glad when its owner walked through the door. *Down, boy. Not smooth.* But, oh yes, he wanted to spend time with her any way he could.

He feared she was going to say no as she frowned at her fuzzy slippers and then gave him a half-smile.

"I would, but… Can you give me five?"

"I'll give you ten." He couldn't help the wide smile that spread across his face.

Amanda put down her cup then raced from the kitchen.

"I think she likes you, my boy." Henri patted Luke on the shoulder. "I think you like her."

"If she knows her Lara Croft, she might be perfect."

Henri was still giving Luke instructions and cash for the market when Amanda returned, dressed in a long-sleeve T-shirt, black yoga pants, and flip-flops.

Luke couldn't take his eyes off her. If Alicia was more beautiful than Angelina, Amanda had them both beat. He enjoyed how her top stretched across all the right places and her pants hugged her legs. It didn't matter if she wore no make-up, skipped putting earrings in the row of holes in each lobe, or didn't bother to run a brush over her pretty curls.

"Luke?" Henri was calling him. "You're scaring our guest."

Henri's eyes twinkled in amusement as Amanda blushed. Luke realized she had a pretty good idea what he was thinking. He pulled himself together, straightened up, and cleared his throat. "I'm really sorry. I was thinking of Lara Croft and…we better get going."

He led her out the kitchen door to his Jeep, rushing to yank open the passenger side door. The damn door didn't open without a fight. He kept meaning to get it fixed but what was the point. He glanced at Amanda, embarrassed by the stubborn door that didn't budge, to find her smiling at his gesture.

Finally, he wrestled it open and waited for her to climb in. He couldn't resist letting his eye rest on her well-muscled derriere for a second before heading to the driver's seat.

Amanda leaned back. "So where is this farmers' market?"

"In Oakland. Not five minutes from here." Luke steered the car down the long driveway and turned left to take the more scenic route by the lake. He needed to say something so he told her about growing up on Deep Creek Lake. He hoped he didn't ramble on. He never could tell when he was boring a girl to death.

Yet, as he talked about the fishing trips with Henri and learning to canoe with DeWayne and swimming with his school friends, Amanda listened with interest.

Luke couldn't remember a spring day this gorgeous. Not wet, gray, and cold as it often was this time of year. White fluffy clouds scudded across the sky, and the breeze ruffled the blue waters of the lake, making it glitter. It was empty now but in a month there would be sailboats and rowboats and canoes everywhere. The trees were leafing out and wildflowers added spots of yellow, white, and purple to the green hills.

Summer took its time getting to this part of Maryland. The temperatures stayed cool long after humidity and heat plagued Baltimore, Washington, and the Delaware city where he lived, Wilmington.

He was delighted Amanda was seeing the countryside at its best. Or was it even more beautiful because she was beside him? One thing was for sure, even though she hadn't shown any real interest in him, he was glad she'd agreed to come with him.

What was it about her? It was more than curls and a smile, although he was entranced by her smile, bright enough to light up a room. She was sure of herself but not self-centered. Instead, she showed such interest in the things around her—she was even game to fight off spiders in the cellar. Amanda fit right in. He'd never seen her before yesterday and yet she seemed liked she belonged.

He'd go slow, he decided, take his time and do everything he could to get to know her. If he didn't impress her by Monday, he never would.

Just before he reached town, she turned with a question. "I can't help wondering about the Lara Croft conversation I barged in on."

"What about it?"

"Why ever were you arguing about that?"

"It's something Henri and I do. He's a movie fanatic. And he's made me one. We watched a lot of movies over the years. Sometimes we went to a real movie theatre, but we usually hung out together in the apartment and watched Turner Classic Movies and videos on TV. It was a quick escape from the kitchen."

She nodded as if she was willing to accept that simple description. At first. "Then I wonder why you call your inn the Broadview."

"What? That was its name when Henri and DeWayne bought it. They decided to keep it, I guess. Why?"

"Wouldn't it have been funny if you called it the Columbia Inn?"

"I'm sorry. I'm not following."

"The name of the inn in *White Christmas*. In Pine Tree, Vermont? Where they put on a show and save the general?"

He smiled. *And she loves movies.* "Better than Bates Motel, I guess."

She laughed out loud as he maneuvered the Jeep into a parking space on Oakland's main street. "The farmers' market is right down here."

A jumble of wooden stands, tables, and pick-up trucks were assembled in a parking lot between the old train station and the county historical society museum. A crowd was already milling about, sniffing strawberries and examining asparagus. Luke took note of a couple of chefs wearing white jackets emblazoned with their restaurant names. He waved to those he knew. They were talented enough, but none could match his father's expertise. Most of them moved on after a year or two. A few, such as Henri, decided to stay and raise families in this close-knit community.

"This is great." Amanda looked pleased as she browsed mounds of thin green spears of asparagus and baskets of ruby-red strawberries.

Luke scanned the stalls searching for the egg farmer, but found his gaze kept returning to the pretty woman beside him, perusing tables piled high with spring onions and pots of annuals.

"It's early in the season so many farmers aren't here yet. You might want to see the goat cheese maker. He always comes."

"Really? I love goat cheese. Maybe we should take some for our picnic."

"It's over here." Luke led her past a milk truck, a local bakery stand, and a stall selling bison to a table with samples of cheese in hues of white and yellow, and one veined in blue.

"Hi, Mr. McClary. My friend here loves goat cheese."

The cheesemonger offered a plate. "Please. Try some."

She speared a cube of soft cheese and popped it in her mouth. "Oh, this is delicious. I have to get some."

While she made her purchase, Luke continued his search for Mr. Yoder.

Amanda accepted the wrapped wedge from Mr. McClary and turned to Luke. "Who are you looking for?"

"Mr. Yoder. He'd better be here. If I don't find him or, worse, come home without eggs, I'll have to face Henri's wrath."

"Eggs? Really?" He smiled to himself when he saw Amanda's quizzical expression. She'd learn soon enough.

"Henri sent me specifically for Mr. Yoder's eggs. Never come home without them. That's all I'll say. Oh yes. I also need Mrs. Yoder's butter. But I don't see them today. Henri will have my…"

Amanda pointed to a man waving from behind a tiny stand. "Would that be the mysterious Mr. Yoder?"

"He's in a new place this year." Luke grabbed her hand. "Come on. You have to see his eggs."

A slight man with the trim beard held out his hand. "Luke, it's been a long time." After he shook hands, Luke introduced Amanda. "Amanda is a guest of the hotel. She wanted to visit the market."

"Happy to meet you, Miss Amanda." He smiled as he produced a wicker basket from under the table. "I saved these for your father."

The basket contained eggs as beautiful as Luke remembered. Their pastel shades of tan, blue, and green made them appear as if they had already been dyed for Easter.

"You weren't kidding." Amanda gently picked up a green egg from in the basket. "I expected white or maybe brown eggs. But these are gorgeous."

"You won't find these in any supermarket." Mr. Yoder puffed out his chest a little, proud as a rooster, as he showed off his wares. "My family has been raising chickens that produce these pretty eggs for generations."

Luke enjoyed showing the city girl the charms of his hometown. She seemed genuinely interested in meeting these farmers Luke had known all his life and looking over their homegrown wares. He couldn't help smiling as she asked Mr. Yoder about the different colors and the different breeds of hens that laid them. It was more than he'd ever thought to ask.

"I've never seen anything like them," she said.

Luke enjoyed the look of wonder on her face as he handed her the basket. "Wait until you taste them."

Amanda wrinkled her brow. "They're eggs."

"Just wait. You'll see." She had a skeptical nature, but Luke was confident he was up to the challenge. In fact, he was enjoying it. He turned to Mr. Yoder to complete the rest of his order. "Dad also needs butter."

The farmer leaned over a cooler and pulled out several enormous logs of creamy looking butter.

Luke shook his head. "We only need one today, Mr. Yoder."

The farmer frowned at the two five-pound logs of butter in his hands. "Henri usually needs ten pounds or more."

Luke laughed nervously—a sad attempt, he knew, at keeping the conversation light when the situation at home was difficult. He didn't want to tell Mr. Yoder business was off. Saying it in front of Amanda was even worse. The inn had always been a source of pride for his family before the current troubles.

"Not this time, Mr. Yoder. Amanda and her friends are our only guests this weekend. There aren't even reservations for dinner tonight. Dad's taking the night off."

"That can't be." Mr. Yoder's eyes grew wide. Then a different expression flashed across his face. As if he knew something Luke didn't. "The rumors are true then."

"Rumors?" Luke recalled his conversation with DeWayne yesterday.

A hint of a frown crossed Mr. Yoder's face. "There's talk that a big developer is buying the place to build a resort."

Luke couldn't decide whether to be honest or fudge a little—especially with a guest in tow. "That's some rumor." He kept his tone non-committal, trying to avoid the topic of the inn's future, hoping to finish his purchase quickly so he and Amanda could return to the inn. Though she was quiet she seemed to be following their conversation with interest.

"Then it is true?" Mr. Yoder wasn't going to let him go

without an answer.

Luke considered what he should say before responding. "I don't know, Mr. Yoder. DeWayne mentioned something about this yesterday. But he told me he and Henri don't want to sell. They love the inn and the community."

Mr. Yoder nodded. "Of course they do, but their neighbors are eager to sell and reap the rewards of generations of hard work. Mr. Evitt told me the other day he's hoping DeWayne and Henri will sell."

Luke forced a smile onto his face though Mr. Yoder's words shook him to his core. He didn't know if he was angry because of what Mr. Yoder said or what his parents hadn't yet told him. "We're still open for business. The inn and the restaurant both."

Mr. Yoder placed the butter in a bag and handed it to Luke. "Glad to hear it. There was talk that the inn was already closed."

The farmer's comment meant the difficulties at the inn might be worse than what DeWayne had told him. His stomach roiling and his head aching, Luke needed to get home, find out the whole truth, and figure out what they could do to improve business.

"I'm sure Henri and DeWayne aren't ready to quit just yet." Luke pulled out cash to pay for his purchases, but Mr. Yoder shook his head. "I'll put it on your tab." He smiled and touched the brim of his hat. "Nice meeting you, Miss Amanda."

Luke put his hand on the small of her back to lead her away, his thoughts full of strategies to save the inn. The inn had been part of their family for nearly twenty years. He wasn't ready to quit either. "We better get back. You must be ready for breakfast."

She nodded with a laugh. "I'm starving."

Then Mr. Yoder called his name. "I'll spread the word. Let people know the inn is still open for business. Good luck, son."

Chapter Six
Swallow Falls

Amanda picked up a pale blue egg from the basket and examined it. "These really are beautiful."

Luke was pleased their excursion impressed her, at least as far as the eggs were concerned. "I told you."

"What a shame to break these lovely shells." She put the egg back and turned her attention to the scenery passing by. It took her a moment before she rearranged herself to face Luke. "What's going on with the inn?"

He remembered her telling him she didn't have the stomach to be a litigator—from the direct question she just asked, he wasn't sure he believed her. That sounded exactly like a trial lawyer. He demurred, hesitant to explain something he didn't fully understand himself.

"Nothing much. Someone wants to buy the property and my parents don't want to sell. That's all I can say, really."

"But it's affecting the inn right now? Maybe people do think it's already closed. I mean, the place would be empty if we weren't there. Right?"

Luke gripped the wheel more tightly and focused on the road ahead of him. S*he was right. DeWayne had looked sad when he said business was bad. But how bad?*

"It's early in the season. We usually have a slow spring and then the place fills up in the summer."

"Is that all it is?"

He scowled, keeping his gaze on the road ahead of them. Their pleasant drive had become most unsettling, and he couldn't wait to get home. "These have been our neighbors for almost twenty years. I've grown up with their sons and daughters." The pain in his head worsened at the idea that people they knew so well could betray his fathers.

She gently laid her hand on his shoulder. "This is what I do for a living, Luke. I have seen how the power of money can change people. They can lose their minds and their civility in an instant." Such harsh words said in a soothing tone.

Her comment rang in Luke's thoughts as he turned off the main highway. These were good people with good hearts, people he loved and who loved the inn. They wanted things to stay as they were, as they had been for generations. He couldn't believe that people he'd known all his life could be that callous or superficial.

He shook his head. "Not around here." Even as he said it, he knew the first chance he got he would find his parents and find out what was really happening. He needed answers to Mr. Yoder's worrisome comments.

"Okay then." Her clipped words—and the silence that followed—intensified his anxiety.

A pensive Amanda settled back in her seat and crossed her arms. "It is beautiful here. I can't imagine why I've never come before."

He was relieved by the change in topic and the return to a friendlier tone. "I bet you're an Ocean City girl."

Tension eased from her face as she ran her fingers through her curls. "Through and through, hon. Growing up in a Baltimore family, it was the only place to go." She laughed with a bell-like sound, and he was lost.

Luke forced himself to act casual as the morning sun lit up her hair. To fight off the urge to touch those strands of gold, he leaned his elbow on the car window frame.

He wanted nothing more than to keep on driving with Amanda beside him. "Thought so. People break down into two camps in the summertime. Some head to the beach. Others go to Western Maryland." Living in Wilmington these past three years, Luke spent plenty of time at the ocean resorts. He liked Lewes. Good bars, good beaches. There was even a restaurant that might put up a decent challenge to Henri's cuisine—not that he'd ever tell him that. Nice as it was, it wasn't the Broadview. Nothing was.

She shifted in her seat and looked him up and down so thoroughly he felt as if he was being weighed and measured.

"You're a mountain person, I guess."

"Through and through, hon." He echoed her words with a smile. "Truth is, I go to the Delaware beaches when I can since I only live ninety minutes away. I have to admit I've never made it to Ocean City."

"Then you haven't lived. T-shirt shops, beach parties even Dewey can't compete with, and waves that are perfect for surfing."

"How have I lived without all that?" He rolled his eyes as he turned up the driveway to the inn and parked by the front porch.

"Well, you've had all this." Her words were simple enough, but they were the absolute truth.

Luke always loved his mountain home.

He opened Amanda's door and took the basket of eggs from her. "Where are you going today?"

"Swallow Falls."

"My favorite place."

Amanda climbed out and retrieved the packages of cheese and butter from the back seat. "Really? How come?"

He smiled as he led her up the porch steps. "I like to walk the path to the waterfalls—there are four of them—when I have a big decision to make. I haven't been there lately, I'm sad to say, but when I was deciding about whether to move to Wilmington—to leave Western Maryland—I walked that path for a long time. The waterfalls are loud and magnificent, they drown out the noise of the rest of the world. The hemlock forest feels like you've stepped into another time."

Amanda held the front door open for Luke. "Now I really can't wait to go."

Their conversation was cut short by the aroma of bacon wafting through the inn as they entered. Luke wondered why the scent always had such a soothing effect. Like the sound of laughter ringing out in the dining room. While Amanda joined her friends at the big dining table, he carried the eggs and butter into the kitchen where Henri was already heating his ancient cast iron skillet.

His father shooed him away without a word and focused on his work.

Despite everything weighing on his mind, Luke put his worries aside and piled a plate with fruit and muffins from antique platters arranged on the buffet table. He chose a seat at one of the smaller tables in the dining room, not wanting to bother the bridal party.

One of the women came over to him and tapped him on the arm. "Please, come join us."

Luke unfolded his napkin. "I don't want to impose."

"Impose? Nonsense! I'm Julie, your friend Frank's fiancée."

Luke jumped from his chair. "Julie. We meet at last." He kissed her cheek and blushed. He'd missed so many opportunities to see her. "I'm so sorry—"

"Come sit with us. You'll get to meet the whole bridal party."

Luke couldn't refuse Julie's warm and forgiving smile. He refolded his napkin, picked up his plate and coffee cup and took the seat next to the woman with the black hair. It was as close to Amanda as he could get.

Julie remained standing and smiled as she laid a hand on Luke's shoulder. "Everyone, this is Luke. He's the best man."

His neighbor smiled as she introduced herself. "Good morning. I'm Hannah."

"Morning."

"Are you a guest here?" She smiled at him as she nibbled on half of one of the zucchini muffins he made earlier.

"No, my parents run the Broadview."

Her smile widened. "Really? Well, they run a very nice place. And breakfast is delicious."

"Chef Henri will be happy to hear it."

While the rest of the party ate muffins and spread marmalade on Henri's croissants, they introduced themselves to Luke. Julie, Hannah, and Marisa, who was hardly touching her food, all worked at the same school. Luke sipped his coffee while they discussed their plans for the day.

As Julie was asking him for directions to the park where they planned to hike, Henri emerged from the kitchen. He carried a steaming platter full of smoky bacon and a mound of fluffy scrambled eggs. The aromas, savory and creamy, filled the room. Luke had almost forgotten how much he loved his father's breakfasts. In the past three years, he had mostly lived off cold cereal and a cup of Starbucks on his way to work. That was morning fuel. This was nectar from Olympus.

"What's in these eggs?" Hannah held her fork halfway to her mouth.

"Do you like them?" Henri waited for the usual nod before answering. "They are not fat free. There's a little cream, a little hot sauce, and Mr. Yoder's eggs. And butter, of course."

"They're delicious." Amanda leaned toward him with a knowing smile that made Luke glad he'd asked her to go to the farmers' market with him. "I'm a believer. There are eggs and then. There. Are. Eggs."

While the women lingered at the table after breakfast, Luke slipped upstairs to fire up his laptop and go through the inn's website and social media pages.

He found all of them out of date—except for the announcement of the Memorial Day picnic. Summer didn't start at this section of the lake without the inn's annual picnic. Unlike the other summer holidays, this celebration was more for neighbors than tourists. Area residents, shop owners, and other innkeepers would stop by for food and a chat before girding their loins for the summer onslaught.

Luke updated everything on the website with photos he took the previous day. The freshly painted tennis courts, the sunset last night, a shot of Henri cooking dinner. There were no photos of Amanda or her friends and the pages seemed wrong without any representation of the inn's guests enjoying themselves.

Will they mind a photo or two? A group of bridesmaids celebrating together? They are probably all about pictures.

He would have to ask them later.

He carried his laptop to the dining room to talk to Henri and DeWayne. He needed his questions answered and he had to talk to them about updates to the website to draw in business—no matter what the future held. First, he needed another muffin and coffee. Fortification before such a conversation was a must.

~ * ~

An argument over which direction the toilet paper rolled—apparently an issue among married couples Amanda wasn't yet aware of—left her out of the conversation as she drove her friends down the winding country road to Swallow Falls State Park. While her passengers laughed over toilet paper and the sin of not using a turn signal, Amanda found herself fretting over more troubling issues.

She was thinking about an earlier discussion when a hint of pain crossed Luke's face as he told her about the possible sale of the inn. It was an expression she recognized. She understood that kind of loss. She'd lost her own house when she was thirteen.

Her parents, her brother Chase, and she were away for vacation when her mother got a call from a neighbor that their house was on fire and the fire department was on its way. By the time they arrived home, all that was left was a smoldering pile of ashes behind the front stone wall. Her tearful mother grabbed her and Chase and held them close as the smell of smoke, acrid and still hot, swirled around them.

Their father stood on top of what little remained, kicking bits of debris, hoping to find something that survived. He bent and picked up a tiny shiny object, bringing it over to her mother. "Pat, your grandfather's class ring."

It was all that was left. So many memories burned up that day. Photographs and mementoes, a favorite sweater, an antique doll, Christmas decorations. Amanda never fully recovered from such a tragic loss. In a way, she understood how Luke must feel. A home isn't just a building. It's a repository of love and memories.

She turned on her blinker, a nod to her friends' debate, and turned onto the park road. Earlier, as Henri packed their picnic hamper, he told her about two of the park's waterfalls, its namesake Swallow Falls and the highest of the falls, Muddy Creek. It would be the first one they saw, he told her. She was excited to see both with her friends.

The women grew quiet as they tumbled from the car. Still a little early for most tourists, the park was empty enough to feel the silence. A stand of tall hemlocks with spreading branches of delicate needles welcomed them in.

Marisa wandered down the path to a clearing under the thick canopy, her gaze taking in the sights. Then she turned back to her friends. "What's that sound?"

They paused from unpacking to listen. Underneath the hush, a whooshing sound reverberated through the trees, low and constant.

Hannah wrestled her backpack from the trunk. "Probably traffic."

Julie shook her head. "It can't be. We're miles from the highway."

Though it did sound like cars rushing by to Amanda, she wondered if perhaps it hinted at the movement of water. Standing quietly with her friends, she realized what it was and smiled broadly. "Do you know what it is? The waterfalls. They must be close by."

She and the others hurried into their sweatshirts, scooped up their backpacks, then headed for the path.

They wound their way under the trees on a clearly marked trail. It was like walking through the middle aisle of an ancient cathedral. Dark and silent. The sun filtered through feathery branches, leaving pools of light here and there. The breeze whispered as it swirled around them. The trees soared high above, murmuring to each other and to the birds taking shelter in their branches.

"It's better than anything I saw in that brochure." Julie led the others, her gaze fixed on the trees swaying overhead. "It's spectacular."

"How much farther?" Hannah shrugged on her backpack to keep it from slipping off her thin shoulders.

"We're nearly there." Amanda pointed to a sign at the entrance to a boardwalk. "Come on, ladies. The first waterfall, Muddy Creek Falls, is down here."

They had walked less than a mile before arriving at a spot with a view of the whole waterfall. Though it was no Niagara Falls, it was majestic. The spectacle of clear water crashing blue and white over a tumble of dusky brown rock stopped Amanda and the others in their tracks.

"I've never seen a waterfall." Marisa stared up at the rushing water. "I never thought about how loud one would be."

Hannah leaned over the split-log railing to take a selfie as she shouted over the thunder of the falls. "It does make a lot of noise."

Amanda didn't say a word. As water splashed down to the river below, she wasn't sure what to say. All her time and energy had been spent on work in the past three years. She'd given almost no thought to the world around her—except for rush hour, long lines in the grocery store and her always stretched-too-thin budget. This morning she'd seen eggs in colors she'd never imagined and a family working together to make experiences like this possible. Now she was speechless watching water fall over a pile of rocks.

Her imagination was captivated by the sights and sounds before her. The dark green trees standing sentry over them. The water white and loud as it fell—she did a little figuring—about five stories to the river below. It was just as grand as Luke had promised. *His favorite place.* She could see how a place like this could provide the peace he needed to make important decisions. She imagined him here, pondering his choices, weighing his affection for his fathers, especially Henri with whom he seemed very close, how they bonded over movies.

Wait. She wasn't sure where thoughts of the innkeepers' son came from. Yet she couldn't deny it. He fascinated her even more than Mother Nature's display.

"Amanda?" Julie waved a hand in front of her friend's face. "I'm afraid Amanda has left the building."

Amanda chuckled. "I was listening to the water."

"I don't think so. You want to know what I think was on your mind?"

Amanda shook her head. "I don't need you to tell me. You think everybody is thinking about love and romance—just like you. You're so full of it you think I should be thinking about it. You know Marisa, with a baby on the way, is thinking of it. And Hannah—how long has she been married?—she must also be thinking of it."

"Love makes the world go around." Julie looped her arm through Amanda's. "Hannah has been married for, well, forever. How long, Hannah?" she called to her friend.

"Six months," Hannah answered, still struggling with her backpack.

"That's too heavy for you." Amanda rushed to help balance the weighty bag on her shoulders. "What have you got in there?"

Hannah blushed as she cracked open it enough to give Amanda a peek of champagne flutes and a bottle of wine. "Shhh. I want to keep it a surprise."

Amanda glanced at Julie to be sure she wasn't paying any attention. She wasn't. She and Marisa were posing for selfies with a waterfall backdrop.

"Let me carry it then." Amanda lifted the pack off the much smaller woman. "When do you want to open it?"

"I was planning a toast when we got to the falls. But we're already here. I wish it was champagne, but with Marisa being pregnant, I thought this would be a better choice."

Amanda laughed. "Sparkling cider is a great substitute. What a sweet thought."

Hannah smiled. "Let's find a good place and toast the bride."

They giggled like two little girls with a secret, which attracted the other two.

Julie and Marisa craned their necks to see what Amanda and Hannah were hiding. "What's going on?" Julie looked from one to the other.

Hannah's face flashed a hint of panic.

Amanda knew all she had to do was mention food to distract her friend. "We were talking about where to have our picnic."

Hannah pointed to a shaded spot next to a historical marker. "This looks good." She stopped to read the text. "This is Muddy Creek Falls, by the way. It says Henry Ford and Harvey Firestone and Thomas Edison camped here."

"Well, it must be a sign." Julie deadpanned but all she got were responses of weariness from her friends.

"You're right," Amanda finally said to put her out of her misery. "If it was good enough for Hank and Harvey and Tom…let's plan to have our picnic right here."

She loved her friend, even her horrible puns.

Marisa checked the time on the phone in her hand. "Isn't it a little early for lunch?"

"Maybe, but who cares?" Amanda pulled the picnic blanket from the hamper. "I'm here with my friends—and poor Hannah can't carry that pack another step."

Hannah laughed as she took a seat. "Besides, I'm always hungry."

As she spread the blanket, Amanda looked forward to

enjoying these last days with her only other single friend. Yet, she couldn't put Luke out of her mind, in spite of a spectacular view and the festive mood of the party.

Serving the food only made her thoughts of Luke's dilemma grow more intense. As she unwrapped baguettes, fragrant and golden, she thought of Henri's expression of pride as he detailed this feast. The aroma of chocolate from the brownies sparked memories of Luke and his father debating the merits of movie actresses. Even the chicken salad reminded her of the family's efforts to make their weekend special.

Lunch today came with a heaping side of guilt. She kept thinking about the family who owned the Broadview and how she'd already come to admire them. Luke's pain forced her to think about how she might feel if her own efforts were responsible for helping bring about the very thing he feared.

Her new case, the biggest of her career, involved buying land around the lake for a new development. With visions of hotel rooms overlooking the lake and the mountains, she hadn't considered what it might mean for a family pressured to sell. She was sure she'd never seen the name of the Broadview or Henri or DeWayne in any of the documents she read.

But what if that did happen? She had to represent her client to the best of her ability. But how could she ever hurt Henri and DeWayne—and Luke?

Chapter Seven
Friends and Enemies

It really was the perfect spot for a picnic. Sunlight, bright and golden, illuminated the ancient evergreens and warmed their spot just off the walking path. Water from the falls wafted on the spring breeze, cooling the air and dampening the grass. Marisa frowned as she searched around for a place dry enough to sit. Sympathy flooded through Amanda who could see from the look on Marisa's face how tired the pregnant woman was. But she never complained. In fact, Amanda, who expected her to speak of nothing but her pregnancy, was growing fond of her.

Once everything was ready, Amanda gave Hannah the signal. She rushed to get the bubbly ready while Amanda posed with Julie for a selfie on the viewing deck.

Amanda considered Julie a lucky woman for having such good colleagues. She couldn't name one person at her office she'd spend the weekend with—much less ask to be a bridesmaid. She had met her partner Quin's boys, heard about their accomplishments in the classroom and on the lacrosse field, saw the photos from their vacation to Alaska. But Quin was her supervisor, hardly a friend.

As for her fellow associates, Amanda still didn't know them well. They celebrated birthdays, toasted successful deals, and kept photos of their loved ones in their offices. Conversations were brief and general, touching on good restaurants or upcoming vacations. Mostly they stayed in their offices for ten hours a day or more, coming out for only a short break or a sandwich run. It was a different kind of life, the one she chose a long time ago, and yet she longed for friendships as warm as Julie's.

Amanda sidled up to her friend and put an arm around her

as they took in the view over the falls. "Marisa and Hannah are great."

Julie smiled. "They like you too. This is a beautiful place, isn't it?" Sighing, she returned her attention to the view. "I suspect you girls are cooking something up. What is it?"

"Hannah planned a very sweet gesture. I won't tell. She told me to distract you for a few minutes."

"Marisa is also in on it?"

Amanda nodded. "She's a trouper. She keeps going even though she's too tired to take another step."

Julie glanced at the pregnant woman with a maternal smile. "We may want to take it easy, if only for her sake."

"What will I do with all the rock climbing equipment? It's in my other backpack." Amanda sighed dramatically. "We'll have to wait for your first anniversary."

"When did you ever go rock climbing?" Julie rolled her eyes and both women chuckled.

They were still laughing, happy to enjoy a giddy moment, when the sound of a popping cork caught their attention.

"Showtime." Amanda linked her arm in Julie's as they made their way to the other bridesmaids.

Hannah passed around plastic flutes of her champagne substitute. "I want to propose a toast." She blushed as she fumbled to unfold a wrinkled sheet of pale pink notepaper. "To the bride. May she find happiness is hers every morning of her life. May she find joy in the tasks throughout her day. May children—many children—bring her laughter, tears, hugs, and kisses every waking moment. When the day is done, may she find peace and love in the arms of the man she has chosen."

Tears slid down Julie's cheeks. "You guys..."

"Too sappy?" Hannah wrapped her arms around her friend.

"Nothing is sappy where weddings are concerned." Marisa jumped up to hug the other two.

Hannah's words touched Amanda's heart. Especially the last sentence. She wiped away a tear, surprised the toast brought Luke to mind. She pictured him in his battered Jeep, turning to smile at her and tease her about her beach vacations. His smile, relaxed way, affection for his home and family were what really touched her.

Shaking away the image, for now at least, she pointed her phone at the love fest for a few photos. The bridesmaids would want to remember this moment.

As Amanda focused her phone for another picture, Julie called her over. "I need a picture of the whole group. All of you are going to make my day very special."

After lunch, Julie and Amanda carried Dixie cups full of Henri's lemonade to the platform overlooking the splashing water.

Julie leaned on the railing, her attention on Amanda. "I want you to be happy."

Amanda sipped her drink. "What makes you think I'm not? I'm doing what I always wanted to do." She didn't like where this conversation was headed. Besides, she would never be interested in her friend's matchmaking.

"Yes, that's true about your job. But what else makes you happy?"

The lemonade tasted bitter in Amanda's mouth. Why would Julie ask such a question? She didn't need anything else. Not now. She enjoyed her work. She enjoyed happy hour on Friday evening. Her apartment was small but comfortable. It was a good place to come home after an exhausting day to enjoy the quiet. That's all she wanted.

"I'm happy."

"You love your job, or you say you love your job. I just think you need something besides work to make you happy. I know I do. Hannah and Marisa do. I never see you anymore. This is the first time we've gotten together in months. You haven't even met Frank yet—and I've known him almost two years."

Amanda stayed silent. Her friend's words seemed to echo off the trees and boulders, a truth she already knew. She wanted to tune them out, or even argue. Yet, Julie was right. This wasn't about time constraints. It wasn't even about missing the pre-wedding events. She was guilty of always putting her job ahead of her best friend. Only Julie was too nice to say it. She knew she disappointed Julie every time she turned down an invitation to meet Frank.

She looked pointedly at the bride. "I'm not the only guilty party here. Since you two got together, you've had very little time to hang out with me."

"Yeah. I feel bad about that. It's just with the wedding plans and all…"

"Uh-huh. It's just that my workload and all…"

Julie sighed. "I see what you did there."

"I shouldn't have to do it all."

"Remember in high school? We both dreamed of getting married, having children, *and* being the world's best at our jobs. We thought we could do it all. You are well on your way to one goal. What about the others?"

Amanda shrugged. "I still want it all. Quin does it every day. So did my grandfather. But right now, I'm happy being single. I can work all hours—or I can dance until three in the morning. I couldn't do those things with a husband and the littles we might have. To tell you the truth, I haven't even had time to find the man who'd want to be my husband."

"Are you suggesting my dancing days are over?"

"Maybe. 'First comes love, then comes marriage.' What comes next?"

"The baby carriage. Yeah. We've been talking about that."

Amanda put her arm around her friend and stopped smiling. "It was inevitable. All this 'adulting.' Someday I hope to be there right alongside you with a baby or two."

"What? Amanda Johnson gets serious?"

That made Amanda laugh. "Grandfather thought I was overly serious during college."

"I remember when you told me what he said. Dig a ditch, become a reporter, or horrors, teach. You were shocked."

"He was afraid I'd focus on work and never make time for a family. The thing is people have to make sacrifices to do their job. Teachers—as you know—don't work only nine to three. They call parents at eight o'clock when they should be sitting with their husbands watching television. Newspaper reporters put themselves on the line every day. And they don't have to be in a war zone. You remember that newspaper in Annapolis? Someone came in and killed innocent people because he was mad about their coverage. I think of them every time I open a newspaper. And consider how many years ago that was. When I'm driving home at whatever hour, those ditch diggers are working under big glaring lights, and will be until sunrise."

Julie crossed her arms. "Are you finished with your TED talk?"

"Almost. And yet they combine family and work. I don't know how your friends do it. Or how you will do it." She mock bowed. "And thank you for coming to my TED talk."

"You're welcome. You know, though, we will do it. Your grandfather only wanted the best for you. He did it and admitted it was hard. I'm sure he knew you could handle both."

Amanda laughed. "First I need a man."

"That's easy. I'll spell it for you. L-U-K-E. At breakfast, he kept looking at you. More importantly, I can see you're interested in him."

"I'm happy the way things are." Even as she objected, a blush heated Amanda's cheeks. "It doesn't hurt to look. Besides, he's busy with his own work and his family."

"Things would be much better if you give him a chance to get to know you." Julie took on her motherly tone. "What would be the harm in letting go this weekend?"

"But this is a bachelorette weekend. I'm not supposed to be hunting for a date."

Julie rolled her eyes. "It's not a Bible retreat. It's a three-day party. Celebrating love. Go find some of your own."

Amanda downed the rest of her lemonade. "Can I get you another drink? I need some more. You know, before I go hunting for true love."

~ * ~

Amanda picked up the phone she'd purposely left on the dresser in order to ignore the email notifications all day. But, before climbing into bed for the night, she couldn't resist the urge to look for anything important among the hundred and twenty-one messages still unread.

She scrolled through them. Missing lunch. Birthday cake. Lights on in the garage. Street closing. Meeting Tuesday…

She clicked on the last one, the one from Quin. Amanda glanced at the timestamp, eleven-thirty—only a half hour ago.

I need to get you up to speed. The zoning board's hearing has been scheduled, and I need you to go over all the documents before I meet with local counsel. We have a holdout, but Ted Lowrey's working on it. You're in Western Maryland? Could you swing by an old inn called the Broadview? Mr. Lowrey says it's an old, once-beautiful hotel. It's on the best of all the parcels, and he's determined to get it. Can you take a look at it? Thanks.

Amanda sat before she fell, her hand shaking as she scanned the email, hoping she misread it. Her stomach grew queasy as the message confirmed her suspicions. Her head ached as she realized that, even worse, Quin expected her to spy for the enemy. No, that wasn't right, the attorney part of her corrected the thought. Quin wanted her to do a bit of research for their client.

Amanda tossed the phone onto the dresser and held her pounding head in her hands, wishing she had left her email for another day. Tuesday was so far away. Why did she have to read this now? How could she face Luke in the morning when she knew this? What would she say?

Best, she decided, to say nothing at all. After all, she was an attorney working on a case, nothing more. She owed Quin her best work. But what about Luke? She remembered the pain on his face when the egg farmer mentioned the sale of the inn. The ache in her head—and the guilt—squeezed like a vise until she grew faint.

There was no denying how this simple email affected her. Her hands trembled, and her limbs went weak. Her heart thudded in her chest and her breathing was as ragged as a runner crossing the finish line of a marathon.

The trouble was, she was beginning to see she was about to start a marathon. The whole picture was coming into focus. Up to now, she and a fellow junior associate had only seen documents for land sales in this area. They knew it was part of a much bigger project but only now, she saw just how big and just how personal it would be to one family. She was sure Luke would hate her once he found out.

The message hit her harder than she expected. She didn't owe him anything. But already he found a way into her heart enough for her to want to get better acquainted.

And here she was, a member of the team pressing his parents to sell their life's work. Luke would never believe she wasn't here on false pretenses. He might even think she was here to gather information about the place as she and her fellow lawyers built their case.

He's going to call me a liar. A traitor. Maybe the enemy.

She bowed her head and tried to get hold of herself. It was no use getting emotional.

This is business. I have no attachments here, beyond my responsibilities as a lawyer. I owe Luke nothing.

She sat, motionless, while her heart went to war with her brain. She couldn't say whether the battle lasted a few minutes or hours. It left her exhausted, her thoughts more muddled than ever.

Finally, she rose and stretched before turning back the covers on the bed. She had made no decision. Telling Luke would ruin the weekend. Keeping it a secret might be best for her boss and her client, even for herself.

The minute her head hit the pillow, round two of the battle of heart and mind began.

The question was how did she protect her heart? She remembered the way Luke looked at her in the cellar. She'd felt the warmth of his strong hands on her arm. The attraction was so strong, she couldn't deny how much she wanted to be with him.

Now she wondered if it would be better to keep some distance between herself and Luke. She sighed at the notion of pushing him away. She'd enjoyed their banter yesterday, their adventure in the cellar, their conversation this morning. When she met him—thanks to a tennis ball—she brushed him off as distracting. Now she found him hard to resist.

Even her opinion about the inn had changed. Her first impressions—weedy garden, faded colors—were now supplanted by her appetite for Henri's cooking and the excitement of finding the diary. To Mr. Lowrey it might be just "an old, once beautiful hotel." But she knew better. The truth was she had developed a fondness for the Broadview. And possibly for Luke.

Even if he might end up hating her.

Chapter Eight
Heart and Mind

Amanda stared at the ceiling, her brain refusing to shut down. She rolled over and turned on the meditation app that usually soothed her after a troubling day. No good. That only changed the rhythm of her thoughts. She switched it to Adele ballads and found herself listening to the words. She wasn't going to sleep. Not now, probably not all night.

Her conscience wanted her to be true to her client and boss. Her heart argued for Luke. Whom she hardly knew. What did her heart know that her brain didn't?

Even though it was past midnight, she heaved a loud sigh and threw off her bedclothes. Grabbing a sweatshirt, she padded down the stairs with her book.

Halfway down the steps, the crackle and pop from the fireplace made her flinch and pause. It was a sound that pricked at her anxiety since the day she lost her childhood home.

As hard as it was, she forced her feet forward into the parlor.

The orange and blue flames gave the room a golden glow, but seeing the fireplace unattended kicked her anxiety up another level. Putting a hand to her heart, she took a deep, calming breath. It worked every time she grew anxious about fire.

This house isn't going to burn down.

She stepped back and willed herself to drop onto the sofa. Sinking into the thick downy cushions, her heartbeat slowed. Curling her legs under her, she opened her book, hoping a few minutes of reading might quiet her mind. Sitting there in the stillness, her mood was already improving.

"Hey there." Luke carried a tumbler of something dark and

had his own book tucked under his arm.

The sight of him, so soon after reading Quin's email, forced Amanda to her feet, causing her to drop her book. Her heart beat wildly beneath her ribs. She felt so guilty, so traitorous and Luke looked so...friendly, trusting, open. She didn't know what to say.

"Didn't mean to alarm you." He held out his glass to her. "Would you like something to drink? I can give you mine and go make another."

What is it about his eyes? Such a cool blue but warm, as well.

"I didn't mean to take your place." She scooped up her book, lying on the cushion, but he shook his head.

"Stay. I'd like the company. Worries about the job are keeping me awake."

"You too?" Amanda accepted the drink he offered her and sat back down. She didn't want to discuss what was really bothering her, but she had to listen to what Luke had to say.

"I work for a construction company in Wilmington. I put together the reports that go to prospective clients, explain how we'll build their hospital or shopping center. They're pretty complicated and detailed. Anyway, my supervisor is looking over my latest proposal, and it's really important. My evaluation is coming up, and I'm hoping for a promotion."

He stopped talking and with a chuckle put his hand to the back of his neck. "Here I am with a pretty woman and what am I talking about? Work. I hate work. We should stop working."

"Then what would we do all day?" She sniffed the glass—*something spicy, maybe cinnamon. No, coffee.* "What is this?"

"A Black Russian." He shrugged. "Sort of. I had to substitute. It's Kahlua and cherry vodka. I couldn't find Henri's plain vodka. I think it's all right. Try it."

She took a sip and licked her lips. It was sweet and definitely tasted of coffee. She detected the cherry in the aftertaste. The overall effect was soothing. "Yum."

While he went to the bar to mix another, she leaned against a velvety cushion and enjoyed the sweet drink that warmed her as it slid down her throat.

It didn't take more than a few delicious minutes for her muscles to relax and her mood to mellow. *So that's why they call it a night cap.* She sipped the drink again.

"Looks as if I did all right." Luke returned, delight lighting his face as he carried a drink in one hand and a dish of mixed nuts in the other.

He laid the drink and the nuts on the table, plopped down right next to her on the sofa, and crossed his ankle over his knee. He sat close enough for their elbows to touch.

Awfully close. The chair by the fire would have done quite nicely. Amanda sat up stiffly.

"Relax. I won't bite." He briefly touched her sweatpants-clad leg. "It's just easier to reach the coffee table."

She tried to calm down despite his proximity. *What is it about him that jangles my nerves? As if I don't know.* She tried to erase any memory of Quin's email to focus on Luke. She wasn't supposed to discuss a case—and certainly not with a party who might be involved in it. *Might,* she emphasized in her thoughts.

Still, she needed to say something. Glancing around the room, searching for a possible topic, her gaze rested on the plain black cover of his book. "What are you reading?"

He held up the book in question. "I call it my sleeping pill. It's for work, and it's so boring I can't get through it. You'd expect a marketing book to have some zing to it."

"It can't be duller than a law book. My torts textbook had to have weighed ten pounds."

Luke smirked. "I hope that's a book about dessert."

She stared blankly at him until she realized his pun. Then she raised an eyebrow.

"Torts, tortes. Never mind." He scooped a handful of nuts.

Amanda groaned. "I got it. I wish I hadn't." She sipped her drink and thanked Dionysus for giving the world such delightful beverages. "This drink is wonderful. I love Kahlua, but I usually only put it in coffee."

"Henri knows his way around a bar. When he and his mother came to this country, he was a teenager. He needed a job and ended up—I bet you can you guess—in a restaurant. He bussed tables, washed dishes, and carried food before moving up to server. When he was twenty-one, he asked to learn the bartending side of things. Eventually, he found his way into the kitchen, the very place he wanted to be all along."

"Your father is a talented chef. It's a shame the restaurant wasn't overflowing with customers tonight. I'd love to see him in his element."

Luke frowned, and Amanda feared she had said something wrong. He stared into the fire for a moment as if he was deciding which words to use.

"It's only a public relations mistake. Word got out my parents sold the inn and closed the restaurant. Obviously, it's not true. With any luck, and a lot of online buzz tomorrow, the restaurant will be full again. I hope so, for Henri's sake. He's not happy if he's not cooking." Luke leafed through the pages of his book for a moment. "How was your trip to the waterfalls?"

Amanda was glad to talk about something else. Anything to keep her conscience from bugging her. She regaled him with stories of Hanna's toast, their first sight of Swallow Falls, and their delight with the picnic Henri prepared.

Amanda finally relaxed. She wasn't sure if it was the firelight, the cocktail, or the company that made it all so cozy.

Maybe Julie was right. Maybe it wouldn't hurt to indulge in some experimental romance.

"Tomorrow should also be fun."

Those baby blues of his smoldered with interest. "Tomorrow? What are you doing tomorrow?"

Yes, maybe Julie was right. Luke was darn attractive. "Tomorrow?"

He ran his hand down her arm. "You said…"

Her skin tingled at his touch. She told the sirens blaring in her head to shut up. "Fallingwater. Have you been there?"

"Not that I recall."

She breathed in his scent, like Ivory soap, clean and fresh. Maybe with a hint of something rich and robust, the coffee aroma from the Kahlua perhaps. How easy it would be to lean in a bit closer and take a taste. Just a little kiss. Would that be wrong?

All of her wanted to say yes, but Amanda's brain always overruled her heart.

She couldn't dismiss the email she read earlier. The one that told her this inn was part of the deal she was working on. The one that put her at odds with this handsome man beside her.

Even if she didn't know anything, she knew Quin's

client—whom she had never even met—wanted to buy this inn and tear it down. Since this was her case, romance with Luke was impossible. She wished it wasn't. She wanted to stay and see where things went. She was sure Luke's kiss was even more delicious than this sweet, strong Black Russian.

Her over-conscientious brain was winning, and it tore at her heart. She needed to go and started to push up from the sofa. "I ought to go to bed. We're planning an early start tomorrow."

When he gazed at her with those cool blue eyes, she stopped. He swept his fingertips down her forearm, and she froze.

Would it be bad to stay?

Yes, very bad.

She agreed with her conscience, and shook her head. "If I don't go now, I'll never be awake in time."

"Fallingwater is only an hour away, and it doesn't open until nine," he countered, his voice soft and dreamy.

How did he know that? Amanda jumped to her feet. "Wait. You said you haven't been there."

He smiled. "I haven't, but an innkeeper has to know these things. Don't you want to stay a little while longer?"

She came close to saying yes, but her brain won. It was late. They had a busy day planned tomorrow. Falling in love with Luke definitely wasn't a good idea, not right now, anyway.

Amanda wished him a pleasant evening, thanked him for the drink, then headed for bed. She glanced his way when she reached the stairs. His eyes might be beautiful, but she needed to keep a cool head. Now was not the time to fall for a man, especially Luke.

Chapter Nine
Decision Time

Even though their midnight meeting was almost perfect, Luke couldn't help his disappointment. His heart soared when Amanda entered the room and sank when she walked away.

After the quiet day, extraordinarily quiet for the inn on a Memorial Day weekend, Luke couldn't get his mind to settle. He found himself in front of a fire with drink in hand. Then she had sat beside him, leaning tantalizingly close for a moment, and now those memories would never allow him to sleep.

A faint hint of her floral fragrance hung in the air. He could still hear the ring of her laughter as she talked about Swallow Falls. He was happy she enjoyed the park as much as he did. In every season, the short stroll between waterfalls was often his go-to recreation with his fathers, then friends, and with every girlfriend…except Emily. Now he could picture Amanda there in his favorite spot. He wished he had been with her.

The trouble was he'd like to show her everything. He longed to take her to the Western Maryland sites he'd known nearly all his life. He suspected she would love a mountain bike ride down the slopes of the Wisp ski resort or a meander through the quaint craft shops of Penn Alps. She might like visiting the glassblowers at the Irish glass factory right around the corner. He knew paths through all the state parks that led to vistas of mountains and lakes and valleys.

It had been ages since Luke had any interest in sharing all his favorite places, showing everything important to him. He loved the idea of having someone he wanted to spend time with.

And it was killing him. How would he ever succeed at work and make a relationship work at the same time? He hadn't been able to do it with Emily.

He thought back to his conversation with his stepfather earlier that day. DeWayne must have noticed something was bothering him when he sat beside him.

"Have you heard from Frank?" his father asked.

"Yeah. He decided he couldn't come until tomorrow. Some work thing."

"Sounds like you, son."

Luke stared at his stepfather, who couldn't keep the smirk off his face.

"How many times have you been late—or not come at all—because of your job?"

Luke knew the answer. Lately, every single time he was supposed to come for a visit, something happened to keep him at the office. He knew it drove both his parents crazy when he didn't come home.

DeWayne grasped Luke's shoulder with affection. "It's what you have to do. We understand."

"Thanks, Pop." Even if work came first these days, Luke missed his time with DeWayne and Henri. "How about a game of tennis? You up for it?"

DeWayne, who taught him everything Luke knew about the sport, sputtered. "Am I up for it? Henri and I have been practicing every afternoon since the paint dried."

Luke grinned. He knew better. Henri enjoyed an occasional hike or paddle across the lake, but tennis wasn't his thing.

As they played, Luke wanted to talk about the hotel, but DeWayne kept changing the subject. The possibility of selling the place wasn't only causing a rift in the community. DeWayne's hurt expression signaled the issue was dividing the family as well. He considered himself one tough black man—and he was—but his face showed every emotion.

So Luke decided to change the subject. "I don't understand women." He tossed the ball high above his head and swung his racquet. Almost a perfect serve.

DeWayne smashed the ball across the net. "Anyone in particular?"

Luke was quick to volley it back over the net, softer than DeWayne's rocket launch. Luke wanted a friendly game, not a match good enough for Wimbledon. *"Not usually. I pretty much gave up on the opposite sex, until today."*

DeWayne took the hint and angled the ball Luke's way. "Aha. Amanda."

"Yes, Amanda."

As he mulled over his conversation with DeWayne, Luke stared into the fire. For a big guy, his father was an old softie with a romantic heart. A man of few words, he showed his love in quiet ways. He was a master at polite gestures of respect like holding the door. During school holidays, he dreamed up family outings. A careful listener, he made the person he was with feel as if he was the only one who mattered. His strength came through his heart and his soul.

His father taught him important life lessons. DeWayne was a good teacher, but Luke realized he had fallen behind in his studies.

Tomorrow, more like later today, he would try again with Amanda. He was still not clear on why he wanted to make her the center of his universe. He didn't trust his luck with powerful women like her would be any better than his past three failed attempts. All he knew was he needed to find out.

~ * ~

Luke woke with a start. Brilliant sunshine streamed through his bedroom window. He blinked at its brightness and turned to read the clock. One o'clock. In the afternoon. He groaned and fell back against the pillow.

He tried to remember what time he finally crawled into bed. Long after midnight was all he knew.

Puzzled, he wondered why he was allowed to sleep this late on a Sunday. Something Henri never let him do on busy weekends.

Luke hopped out of bed and considered his worn T-shirt and baggy gym shorts. Going downstairs in such an outfit was usually a no-no but with no guests except the bridal party, who were long gone by now, he figured it would be fine. Only Henri and maybe DeWayne would see him.

At the kitchen, Luke was surprised to find it empty. Neither father was anywhere in the house. He finally found the pair sitting out on the lawn overlooking the lake. Deep in discussion.

He usually didn't worry about interrupting his fathers when

they were talking. When he was a kid, he considered himself the center of their lives, so it never occurred to him to give them a few moments alone. Now, though, as an adult, he recalled the expression on DeWayne's face the previous day and asked himself whether he should leave them alone.

But Luke didn't want to. If they were talking about the sale, he should be there. Be part of the conversation. This was his house too. The developer's offer to buy might affect him the least, but he should still have a say.

Although spring was in the air, the atmosphere between DeWayne and Henri was closer to freezing. DeWayne gestured with big, bold moves as he argued with his partner. Henri looked away, a sure sign trouble was brewing.

Luke paused on the porch. He couldn't remember the last time he witnessed an argument between the two men. When they fought—and what couple doesn't—they kept it between themselves.

When Henri turned and spotted Luke, anger had taken the place of his usual joyful expression. His mouth was set in a thin straight line, meaning his father was unhappy.

DeWayne shook his head, but still stretched out his hands in an appeal to his husband.

Henri jumped from his chair and grabbed his son's elbow. "Luke, come talk some sense into this man."

This was not the place Luke wanted to be, in between the two most important people in his life.

Then he remembered Henri wasn't aware DeWayne told him about the possible sale. Luke decided he'd play it cool. Shoved his hands into his pockets and ambled toward them like it was an ordinary holiday weekend.

"What's going on?" He crouched between the two Adirondack chairs and looked from one man to the other. Things were icy, all right.

"It's time we told you." Henri shot a glance at DeWayne as he settled back in his chair. DeWayne put his hands up to signal the floor was Henri's.

"A local developer wants to buy our property, tear down the house, and build a mega resort. The neighbors have already sold. And they're mad at us for holding out." Henri spoke quickly as if the faster he got the words out, the less awful they would sound.

"And—" DeWayne crossed his arms and waited.

"DeWayne thinks it's a good offer, and we should jump on it." Henri turned his attention to the lake and bit his lip.

"And—" DeWayne scowled, then finished the thought, "And Henri can't imagine going on without the inn, especially the restaurant. He and I had both agreed it might be a good time to sell. Now he's changed his mind."

"We'll lose our family home, everything we've worked for. You won't have a place to come home to. I don't know what I'll do without…" Henri pointed to the land in question. "Without all this. This is all our family has left."

Luke understood. His father had been at his wit's end like this once before, an important moment in the life of them all.

At that time, *Maman* had been dead almost a year. Luke was in the fifth grade. As much as he missed his mother, he also missed the happy, crazy man who had nearly stopped acting like his father. In his stead, was a tired, distressed chef who left before the school bus picked Luke up every morning and came home long after Luke was finished with his dinner and homework.

DeWayne saved their lives. Maybe not literally, but if he hadn't come into their family, who knows what might have happened to the grief-stricken French chef and his lost little boy. DeWayne and Henri became friends after meeting on the subway, and from there developed a devotion that stood the test of time. Together they decided to make a life far from New York. They chose a place where they were certain Luke would be happy, Henri could feed people, and DeWayne could fish and hike when he wasn't hiring contractors or meeting with the chamber of commerce.

Having them at odds over the life they built broke Luke's heart.

Not quite sure of what to say, he decided the truth was a good place to start. "You found this place. Couldn't you find another place to make you just as happy? As much as I love the Broadview, I will be happy wherever the two of you are. By that, I mean the two of you." He looked at DeWayne then Henri, making sure they understood.

"I don't think I can bear to lose another home." Henri pressed a fist against his mouth.

"*Mon pere.*" Luke hugged his trembling father. Henri had lost three homes in his life. His family home in Paris. The home he shared with *Maman*. And the home in New York he made with DeWayne. No one ever mentioned the cruel words that drove them to leave the city.

"Papa, you and DeWayne are my home. DeWayne and I are your home. Wherever we are together, that is home."

"You're a good boy, Luke." Henri wiped an eye and squeezed his son. He sighed. "I'll think about it. I wish it were all so simple." He put his hand out to DeWayne, who clasped it with a smile. "It will be okay."

A familiar black Ford compact approached the inn. Frank had arrived. Before Luke rushed over to greet his friend, he paused. It was mid-afternoon, and he still looked like he just rolled out of bed.

Chapter Ten
Game On

"Looking good, my man." Frank shook Luke's hand and pulled him into a half hug.

He grinned from ear to ear, happy to welcome his oldest friend to his home. "I'm going for the record. How late in the afternoon can a perfectly healthy man spend in the clothes he slept in before someone makes fun of him?"

Frank, a tall, gangly man with bright red hair, a pair of ice blue eyes, and freckles that covered everything from his nose to his knees, wore his usual preppy attire. Khakis, bright blue polo, and his ubiquitous boat shoes. "You won't hear any criticism from me. I'm here to eat Henri's barbecue and take the kayaks out on the lake."

"Whatever." Luke waved off his friend's ridiculous comment. One thing not in Henri's culinary repertoire was barbecue. "You could have called to tell me you were going to be early."

Frank fished an old-style flip phone from his pocket. "Damn thing won't hold a charge anymore."

"Ah, that explains how the bride and the groom don't know they're staying at the same hotel."

"What?"

Before Luke could answer, Henri rushed across the lawn. "Here comes the groom. Hello, Frank."

With a quiet chuckle, Frank shook Henri's hand. "Nice to see you, sir."

"Ready for the big day? It'll be here before you know it."

He nodded. "Three more months. You got the save-the-date card, right? My fiancée is handling the list, and I'm not up on the details." Confusion clouded his face for a moment, but then his smile returned. "Tell me you'll be there."

DeWayne joined the group and answered for them all, "We certainly will."

"I've already closed the reservation book for that weekend," Henri said. "I'm telling everyone we're full and can't take any more. We would never miss the wedding of our boy's best friend."

Luke rolled his eyes. "Dad. We're almost thirty."

"That doesn't change a thing."

Frank chuckled. "Parents are all the same, don't you know?"

DeWayne wrapped his arms around the two younger men. "You'll always be our little boys."

"Pop." With a smirk, Luke picked up his friend's duffel. "Well, let's get you settled. Up for some tennis?"

"I guess. I haven't played since college. But first, Julie's here?"

Luke ignored him, enjoying the way Frank squirmed. Instead, he pulled out a racquet stuffed in Frank's bag. "Looks to me like you are planning to play."

"I knew you'd want to, but I'm not promising a thing. Luke…did you say Julie's here?"

"Yup. It seems you recommended the Broadview."

"Julie said they were going to some place in Pennsylvania."

"Water main break. Something you'd know if your phone worked."

Frank was still shaking his head when Luke left him to settle in his room before Henri filled them up with *omelettes au fromage*.

After eating, Luke switched his old shorts for tennis whites and waited at the courts, practicing his serve, and thinking of the last time he stood in that same spot. He had his mind on work when he swung his racquet and smashed that serve over the fence and into Amanda. She'd been a good sport, in spite of her injury. Her smile had been so bright. Her responses so witty.

Memories of Amanda slipped away when he spotted Frank trotting down the hill. His business casual attire was replaced by a faded pink T-shirt that looked like he picked it from the bargain bin at Goodwill, and his shorts, a grey plaid, hung loosely on his thin frame. His tennis shoes, if they could be called that, were shabby enough to wear mowing the lawn. The inn didn't require tennis whites on their courts, but Luke knew DeWayne would raise an eyebrow at Frank's attire.

He saw Luke's obviously critical look and blushed. "DeWayne already took me to task for my appearance. Hey, I didn't have time to do laundry. Do you care?"

"Course not. I'm glad you could get away from work."

"Me? Look who's talking? The man who never takes a day off for his best friend." Luke couldn't miss the hurt that crinkled the corners of Frank's eyes. "Not even for my engagement party."

"My bad, man." No use making excuses. Luke knew his old friend had a good heart and understood the demands of Luke's job. Frank had enough of his own, working for a nonprofit that helped homeless families.

With a steely-eyed gaze, Frank took his place across the net. "Shut up and serve."

An easy-going friend, he was also a fierce competitor. He let only a few serves get past him, and his return volleys were powerful.

As he raced to backhand a shot, Luke tried and missed it. Frank ran over and offered a hand which Luke grabbed with a scowl. "Hey, I thought you said you were out of practice."

With a sheepish grin, Frank bounced the tennis ball on the ground. "Muscle memory, I guess."

Even breathless, Luke was happy. He was glad to have his friend here. Not only to play tennis, of course. He needed to discuss a few things with someone who would understand, and Frank always was willing to listen.

After a few easy volleys, followed by a competitive set, he raised his racquet as Luke stood ready for the next game. "Time. I need a drink."

They sat on a bench by the court, gulping down bottles of water Luke had brought with him.

"Man, it has been months, maybe years, since I played." Frank wiped the sweat off his face and exhaled heavily.

"You weren't all that bad. Some of those serves were killers."

He tossed down his water bottle and crossed his arms. "You didn't put up much of a fight."

Luke spread his hands. "That's rich coming from someone with that forehand."

"Check the score." Frank punched Luke in the arm.

Game, set, and match later, Luke wiped his face before picking up a ball lodged in the mesh of the fence that surrounded the tennis court. "Man, where did you learn a backhand like that?"

As he zipped the cover on his racquet Frank grinned. "I've been catching you off guard with my swing since McNulty taught me in senior year."

"Yeah? I don't remember." Luke tucked the balls into his pockets and asked, "How about lunch?"

"Lunch? It's nearly five o'clock. How about a beer?"

"Good plan." Luke put an arm around his friend as they returned to the inn.

"Afterwards, we'll eat dinner. Henri's got something on the stove. Strange but it's only us tonight. Our only guests have dinner plans elsewhere."

"So I won't see Julie tonight?"

"No. She and the whole bridal party: Julie, Hannah, Marisa, and Amanda. They already had reservations at another place." Luke could feel the heat rising in his neck as he pictured the women who sat around the dining room table that morning, especially the last one.

His friend stopped on the lawn and put his hands on his hips. "I still can't believe she's here. I know she told me they were staying at some fancy resort in Pennsylvania."

"Well, they had to change their plans."

A faraway look crossed his friend's face and then faded. "Lucky me. Then I'll have to wait up so I can see her tonight."

"Hey, man. I thought you came to see me." While Luke appreciated the love between his friend and the woman he was ready to marry, he also needed time with Frank. Luke needed his advice.

"Of course I did." Frank wrapped his arm around Luke's shoulder, and they resumed the walk into the inn. "You say Henri's not feeding a crowd tonight? The dining room's always full. What gives?"

That was a topic Luke wasn't quite ready to discuss yet. He shrugged as he held open the door. "Rumors in a small town. People heard we were closed. I've updated the website and we've already got reservations for next weekend."

Setting down his racquet by the door, Frank headed into the sitting room to the bar refrigerator. He returned and handed a cold Heineken to Luke. "That's good. I can't imagine the lake without Henri and his barbecue."

Taking a seat, Luke shook his head. "You know Henri doesn't make barbecue, Frank."

"He doesn't? Well, whatever Henri cooks, I know it will be great."

Frank's comment triggered a twinge of heartache that left Luke at a loss for words. He wondered how much longer he could count on the view of the lake, a game of tennis, and dinner in the aged, but still elegant dining room. Even without barbecue.

As much as he said it wouldn't matter what decision they made in his speech to Henri and DeWayne, Luke was forced to admit—at least to himself—he'd miss the old place if they sold. It *was* home.

"Okay. What's up? The silence is deafening."

Luke glanced at his friend who appeared as if he could read minds. After years of talking to homeless mothers and fathers, he probably had learned to read faces—if not minds—quite well. "I could use your advice. Later."

Before he could explain, Henri called them to a family dinner around the kitchen table. While they stuffed themselves with roast chicken, fresh asparagus, and a Provençal rose, Henri grilled Frank on the details of the wedding, especially the reception menu.

It was moments like this when the Broadview wasn't just a hotel but the home Luke cherished. All his favorite people were gathered together, sharing a meal, enjoying each other's company. The idea that all this could vanish with the stroke of a pen on a contract left a lump in Luke's throat.

What could he do to save it? Luke hoped Frank's expertise might help. The minute Henri and DeWayne left the table, Luke rushed upstairs for his laptop. When he returned, he opened the webpage for the inn and spilled his story. He explained everything.

The offer to buy the property. The discord between his fathers. The lack of business when the place should have been bustling.

Frank held up his empty beer can and went to the bar for two fresh ones. "That's some dilemma. Even if the 'rents decide to sell the place, they still want to stay open for the season, right?"

Peeling back the pop top on the new can, Luke nodded. "That's the plan, as far as I know. Getting information out of those two has been a struggle."

Since Frank was a master at Facebook algorithms, Luke wanted his friend's opinion on the posts he planned to schedule, as well as web page changes already published about the upcoming Memorial Day picnic. The inn celebrated the opening of the summer season the same way every year. The whole town was invited for a day of games, conversation, and, of course, a sampling of Henri's fine cuisine.

Word of mouth created the inn's reputation. And the buzz had started with a picnic many Memorial Days ago. They went over the social media campaign and talked about messages all the way through the Fourth of July.

Luke frowned. "If we're still here on the Fourth."

"Think positively. We'll get traffic to your website, and people will be knocking down the door for a room or a meal."

"Thanks. I appreciate your help. Henri also has a meeting scheduled with the county tourism director, and DeWayne is going to visit the head of the chamber of commerce. We've even got a bunch of travel writers spending a few days in June."

Frank scrolled through the freshened-up webpage. "This should help. You need some new pictures. You could use a few stock photos mixed in with real life photos. But, nah, they always look fake. You need some real people." He glanced into the empty parlor. "What about the bachelorette party?"

"You don't fool me. You're looking for Julie. I told you, they're off having dinner somewhere else. Maybe we can get some pictures tomorrow."

"Pictures from the picnic would also be good."

"If people actually come."

"I told you to think positively." Frank clapped a hand on Luke's shoulder. "They'll come. Who turns down free food?" He paused for a minute, his gaze on Luke's laptop. "You've got some terrific ideas, you know."

He shrugged and thought of all the proposals he prepared at work. And all the criticism that followed. The rare word of praise. "I've gotten a lot of practice the past three years."

"Yeah, it shows. We have an opening at our office. We need a marketing director. You'd be great."

Luke put his laptop aside. "I bet it pays peanuts."

"There's no way I can match what you make at McDonnell-Douglas."

"*Windsor*-Douglas. My company is in construction, not airplanes."

"Right, my mistake. Anyway, I can't pay you what you make now, but the hours are probably a lot easier, and you'd be helping make the world a better place."

"Tempting as that is, I don't think so."

"What would it take to get you to say yes?"

Even though Luke was pleased by his friend's proposal, he didn't want to make a change. There were aspects of his job he really liked. Maybe not the criticism, but the pay was good, his coworkers were friendly, and the projects were challenging.

He was comfortable with his apartment too. Although it was pretty quiet, it was located near a waterfront park where he went jogging and close to a couple of good restaurants. He could count on a few friends to meet there every weekend. Well, almost every weekend. When they could get their schedules in sync.

Luke told Frank about his upcoming evaluations, the chance at a promotion, a proposal he needed to finish by next Friday, and an opportunity to travel to tour a project he helped the company get. "I'm flattered you would want me. But I like where I am. I'm even considering getting a dog."

Frank shook his head, obviously not convinced Luke was satisfied with his life. "Even though I've never been there, I can just picture your empty apartment in a beige suburb of Wilmington. I bet there's even a stack of empty pizza boxes and Gatorade bottles on the coffee table."

"Funny. Very funny." Luke finished his beer and held up the empty can. "That would be Heineken, not Gatorade. Besides, you're wrong. I've got a nice apartment in the cool little town of New Castle."

Frank cocked an eyebrow. "How long does it take you to get here—when you do get here?"

"About five hours, depending on traffic."

Frank leaned back in his chair and crossed his arms. "That's almost twice as long as it took me."

"Game, set, match." Luke threw his hands in the air. "When did you get to be so good at arguing? The answer is still no."

"I'd really like to have you on my staff. Besides, we have to get somebody spun up quickly. It's fundraising season, you know."

"Isn't it always fundraising season?"

Frank shrugged. "Seems to be. Let me tell you what I need. If you don't want it, maybe you know someone who would."

"But Frank—"

"Just hear me out."

The kitchen table became an impromptu office as they discussed responsibilities and goals, glanced over the charity's website, and even upcoming grant applications.

Luke wasn't searching for a new job. He kept repeating that fact, but Frank pressed on.

"Come work with me and you'd have more time to drive out and see Henri and DeWayne. You know, they'd like that."

"True. But now's not the time." Luke leaned back in his chair. "I'm about to move up in the company, become a more senior member of the staff. I'm looking forward to kissing my entry-level position goodbye. More money, more prestige, and a better office are about to be mine."

"Is that all?" Frank crossed his arms and smirked.

"With any luck, I'll get away from the popcorn smell from the kitchen that wafts by my desk at all hours of the day. Some of my colleagues have gotten promotions and stayed in their cubicles. I'm hoping I can move. My little cubby is nice enough, but I don't think I can ever eat popcorn again."

When his fathers bustled into the kitchen to start setting the dining room table for the next day's breakfast, Luke realized he needed to talk to them one more time. What if they did sell the inn? Had they weighed other options? Other jobs? Another place to live? He wasn't pushing for them to sell, and he wasn't pushing them to stay. Luke knew better than to side with one father over the other, but he did want to understand logically and rationally what they might do.

Even if he wasn't ready for a change, were his fathers? He had no idea.

Chapter Eleven
Masterpieces

"That's not where I expected to see the waterfall." Julie leaned over a living room railing for a better look through the glass panels covering a flight of wide stairs down to a swim platform.

Fallingwater, the mansion in western Pennsylvania designed by Frank Lloyd Wright, was poised right over the rapids of Bear Run. He'd even included the swim platform so the homeowners could plunge right into the cold waters.

The bridal party had decided to switch a second day of hiking for a trip to the famous house when tired mom-to-be Marisa confessed she couldn't take a second hike. Amanda had to remember to thank her later. This turned out to be a good idea.

"I can't imagine living on top of it." She shook her head. Although she couldn't hear the roar of the quick moving water through the glass, a surprise after the noise of Swallow Falls the day before, the idea the house sat right atop all that water worried her. She liked her houses firmly set on land.

"Or to say, 'Darling, let's go for a swim, and then dash down those stairs and jump right in.'" Julie giggled. "It would be fun, though, wouldn't it?"

Amanda nodded. While she preferred to spend her summers playing tennis, Julie grew up in her bathing suit. A swim team kid before she could doggy paddle, she still completed a mile of laps a couple of times a week at the Y pool. Even with her crack-of-dawn school schedule.

With Marisa and Hannah at the head of the tour group, Julie and Amanda took their time moving through the other rooms of the house. Amanda peeked out old windows to admire trees bending toward the house as Julie studied the windows themselves.

She admired the way the glass was cut to fit into the rough-hewn stone and how the panes met at corners.

"It's a nice house, but I wouldn't be comfortable here." Amanda ran her hand over one of the stone walls until a tour guide clucked in disapproval. "Too cold."

Julie scanned the room with a practiced eye, frowning at the windows, pursing her lips at the way the furniture was arranged. "You might be right. I'm not sure how insulated those windows are. We toured a hundred houses before we chose the one we're buying. This one does have some gorgeous views, but the commute would be awful."

Amanda laughed. "Where is your new house?"

She was embarrassed she didn't know. She needed to be better at keeping up on her friend's life. It wasn't like her to get so caught up in work that she neglected things like this. Especially before Julie's wedding.

As they followed the tour group, Amanda got all the details, from its location a twenty-minute drive from school, to its teeny mow-with-a-weed-whacker backyard. "We can't wait to move in. Settlement is in July. Then it needs to have work done."

From room to room, Julie talked on, describing paint colors, the wall they were knocking out between the kitchen and the dining room, the bathroom fixtures that needed to go.

Amanda's apartment consisted of two rooms, plus a galley kitchen and a bath. Only ten minutes from her office, she spent a fortune in rent each month, and could hardly describe any of it if Julie asked. The walls were sort of beige. The furniture came from her parents' storage shed.

Amanda and Julie had been devoted friends since high school. There was a time when Julie took French because Amanda took French. When neither had a date to the prom they went together. When they discovered they weren't accepted at the same college, they sat beside one another and cried. She and Julie were the kinds of friends who stood by each other after every heartbreak, every triumph.

Amanda wanted to kick herself now. She had missed so many important moments in the past few months. She couldn't even remember Julie's fiancé's name.

"Frank wants to do some of the work himself, but I needed

to put my foot down when he said he couldn't wait to demo the wall."

Frank. Amanda couldn't figure out how she kept forgetting a name as simple as that.

She needed to work harder to keep her best friend. She vowed not to skip even one more wedding-related event, to answer every single time Julie called, and to choose her friend over work whenever possible.

"One thing I do like about this house, the colors." Julie examined the red pillow on a chair. "Even though most everything is brown, there's a lot of red."

"You always did favor red." Amanda considered the handbag slung over her friend's shoulder. It was nearly the same rusty shade.

What Amanda liked was the vision that got this job done. The architect could have built the house beside the waterfall. He could have designed the rooms to make the waterfall visible from every window of the house. Instead, he turned an idea upside down and created a masterpiece. He studied and worked and stuck with his idea as crazy as it might have sounded to his clients.

She was going to remember this place, not only for its part in the bachelorette weekend, but for the model of exacting work and creativity she saw here.

Julie sauntered ahead of Amanda into a small room with low shelves crammed with books. Each piece of furniture, wall hanging, and knickknack inspired a new comment about how Frank and she were planning to decorate their own house. She described guest rooms and explained the compromise she made with her fiancé. She picked out a dining table big enough for Thanksgiving, and he chose the television for the living room.

"You won't believe it. I've been to cineplexes with smaller screens." Julie rolled her eyes.

Amanda didn't even own a television. She watched Netflix or Hallmark movies on a tablet if she could spare an hour. While her friend was planning a future, Amanda was laboring to create the present she wanted.

After the tour, they wandered along a path that gave them a terrific view of the house rising over the waterfall. Julie continued her assessment of the place. "I agree with you. It's beautiful, but I still wouldn't want to live here. It's cold, and no amount of sunshine will make it warm enough for me. Imagine having children here. I'd be afraid they'd fall on to the stone floor, or tumble down those stairs, or crash into the sharp edges of the furniture. And god forbid a small child plays in that water."

"You do have life figured out, don't you?" Amanda considered her friend with a new sense of awe as they strolled back toward the house.

Julie smiled with a confidence Amanda hadn't seen before. "The only things I've figured out are my job and Frank. I ad lib the rest."

"You're being overly modest."

Julie shook her head. "No, my plans weren't as grand as yours. I never wanted to graduate *summa cum laude* or make partner before I was 35. I only wanted to be happy. Maybe I'm not a very good teacher, but I'm getting better. Sometimes I forget to call parents or grade language arts papers. But I do love my kids even if they do get out of control every once in a while. I don't have enough money to buy the table I really want or afford the exotic honeymoon I dreamed of. But I love Frank, and if we have to eat off a second-hand table and spend our honeymoon in Ocean City, that's fine for me." She stopped on the path with a guarded expression. "Amanda, I have to say this. Please forgive me if I'm out of line."

Amanda couldn't imagine what her friend needed to say that could make her pause and take in a deep breath the way she did.

"I've been mad at you these past few weeks. I said it was fine when you missed the dress fitting and the engagement party. Then when you missed the shower, I realized it wasn't fine. I wasn't happy with you. I was pretty angry. And hurt."

Amanda's heart stopped at her friend's statements. She had been worried Julie secretly held some resentment toward her since she usually wasn't this direct about her feelings.

Now she knew her fears were valid. "Oh, Julie, I'm sorry. I should have realized you were upset with me. I should have been a better friend, but work has been so busy I was glad you understood. I didn't think—"

"I know you didn't. You never do. Work is Numero Uno,

no matter what else is going on." There was a rare steely tone in Julie's voice that made Amanda brace herself. When Julie wanted to make a point, she didn't mince words. "I'll bet other people in your office have lives outside of work."

Amanda crossed her arms. She didn't like where this was going. "They do but—"

"You told me about that guy who got married on the day he passed the bar exam. He got married. Imagine. Any children yet?"

"Yes." The guy was a machine. Came in early, worked until seven and most Saturday mornings. "His wife is expecting their third."

Julie crossed her arms in front of her. "She works too, doesn't she?"

Amanda stiffened. "Yeah, she does. There is a difference though. *He's* the lawyer, *she's* not."

Julie glared at her as if the distinction didn't matter. To Amanda, it made all the difference. "Either way, they're making it work." Julie started down the path again, a signal she made her point.

Oh yes, she did. Amanda's heart ached as if her friend jabbed a knife into it. Friends all these years, of course she should have understood how Julie saw the world. She had let her friend down.

Julie wheeled around. "Another thing." She put up one finger in front of her deadly serious face. "I decided to give you one more chance."

"One more chance? What's that supposed to mean?"

"This weekend. I decided if you came through and organized a whole weekend without rushing off to answer emails or talk business on the phone, then everything would be all right. I would forgive you."

"And?"

"And…well…" Julie hesitated, clearly searching for the words she wanted. "I want you to know I understand why you haven't been there for me. I understand how important your work is to you." She smiled. "You are my best friend in the whole world, a friend who would do anything she could for me—as long as it didn't interfere with 'the big case.'" She used those awful air quotes for the last three words. That was Julie in a nutshell. Angry one minute, ready to forgive the next.

"I'm sorry, Jules." Amanda put her arms out, and Julie stepped into them.

"You're doing the best you can. Sometimes, Amanda, I need you to be there for me. Like this weekend. It has been wonderful."

After a hug, she and Amanda turned to continue.

"There's Marisa and Hannah. I was beginning to wonder where they went." Julie pulled Amanda farther back on the path. "We better get going, but I need to say something more. I spoke to you this way because somebody has to. I doubt I'm the only person who misses you. You have to figure out how to have a life and a great career too." She paused then said, "I endured three excruciating days during spring break when there was no one to talk to. Frank was away at a conference. My parents were on a cruise. You weren't answering your phone. I worked like a dog: finished my lesson plans, including the hand-outs for the kids, graded papers, and wrote notes to parents. I admit I got a lot done."

Amanda was relieved her friend could understand what conscientious work meant to her. "See? It does feel great, doesn't it?"

Julie grimaced. "That feeling of accomplishment only lasted until I was forced to eat dinner alone, watch television alone, do everything alone. A bit of alone time is nice. I do have to admit, I missed Frank. But I also missed my best friend."

"Julie." Amanda wanted to explain, but Marisa and Hannah were on their way to meet them, packages in hand. Instead she squeezed her friend's hand. "I have been too busy for you and I'm sorry. I promise to be better."

Julie smiled. "I expect you to at least make an effort."

She turned and waved to her friends before facing Amanda again. "One last thing. For heaven's sake, go flirt with Luke. He's dying to get to know you."

Chapter Twelve
Manhattans and Romance

The spicy red liquid burned as it ran down Amanda's throat. Luke, although at first aghast that the bridal party would consider eating anywhere but the Broadview, recommended this spot. Amanda had to agree it was a good choice. The stone tavern a few miles from Fallingwater was established before the Revolutionary War and still had historic charm and an interesting wine list. She hoped the wine would rid her of the bile swirling in her gut. Maybe she needed to hear what Julie had to say—and she made a good point—but she wished Julie hadn't needed to say it.

Whatever. It came close to ruining a perfectly good day.

Amanda had looked forward to their dinner and the tavern's mountain views, but after her talk with Julie, including that crack about Luke, Amanda's steak and cabernet tasted like crackers and water.

When the conversation turned to wedding plans, she realized she was the only one hearing about the cut of Julie's dress, the location of the rehearsal dinner, and the play list for the reception for the first time. The other ladies had obviously discussed these things at great length and even attended the dress shopping trips.

Amanda had missed it all because she was stuck at work. As a junior associate trying to make partner, she had to get as many billable hours as she could. Partnership was still a few years away, years of exhausting hours and missed social events. Skipping happy hour to get a document finished was becoming a common occurrence. Missing Julie's pre-wedding events left her with a guilty conscience. She had to admit, however, that this weekend was succeeding at easing bad feelings with Julie and her own conscience. For the benefit of the bride, she had to forget about their troubling conversation, at least until dinner was over.

Hours later she was sitting by Henri's bar, still stewing over the question of balancing work and a home life. How would she ever do it?

Amanda held up her now-empty glass. "What did you say this is, Henri?"

"You mean what *was* it, dear?" He marched over with his mixing glass. "I could tell you were going to need two of those." He poured the drink. "Don't ask me for a third one. They're awfully strong for a sweet young thing like you."

"I can take care of myself."

"Oh well, if you're sure." Henri set bowl of cashews beside her forgotten book.

"You still didn't tell me what this is." Amanda took another sip.

"A Manhattan. It's my favorite. I'm sorry I couldn't find the cherries. This drink needs a good maraschino cherry to dress them up."

"It's wonderful even without it. Thank you."

"I was surprised to find you here all by yourself." Henri wiped down the oak bar.

She thought back to moments, both sweet and bitter, from her day with the bridal party. "My friends were exhausted after their day at Fallingwater. I couldn't sleep so I came down to read a little. I'm surprised you're still up. It must be well past midnight."

"I'm waiting for Luke. I don't like to lock the door until he's in."

Luke was out? Where and with whom? And why do I care?
"Aw, how sweet."

"I suppose I'm being silly. My little boy is nearly thirty years old."

Amanda was touched by Henri's devotion to his family. "Well, I can't remember the last time someone waited up for me. Probably senior year in high school. I was probably with Julie."

She nearly missed the bar as she put down her glass—Henri was right about how strong those drinks were. Emboldened by a bit of alcohol, she posed a question. "How do you do it, Henri? Run an inn, cook for a packed dining room, and raise a son as great as Luke?" Her cheeks heated when she realized what she said. She shouldn't comment on Luke at all.

Henri smiled and cocked his head. "Oh, so you *have* noticed my Luke."

The heat in her face burned some more. "That's not what I meant."

"Oh, well then. I have done what I needed to do. My family has to eat. So, I cook and run an inn to keep everybody together and my family happy." Henri's smile slipped away as a thin crease deepened between his thick black eyebrows. "It isn't always easy. It wasn't easy after Luke's mother, my wife, died. Poor boy had to make do by himself plenty of nights. Now, he's learned my work ethic but not the reason behind it. Pardon me for saying so, but I bet you're the same way. All work and no play?"

"My friend Julie told me the same thing today."

Henri leaned an elbow on the bar. "Your friend seems to have figured it out. If you'll excuse me for a moment."

As he bustled toward the kitchen, Amanda moved to a chair in the parlor and opened her book. *Henri is right. Julie's life is in order.* Yet here Amanda was, feeling sorry for her own unbalanced life, and mooning over a man she should avoid.

She looked up from her book at the click of the front door. Luke had returned home in the company of another man she hadn't seen before. A tall man with bright red hair and a freckle-filled face. She glanced at them, long enough to catch Luke's eye. He waved and pointed to his friend who didn't even stop chatting long enough to see she was there.

Amanda returned to reading but couldn't concentrate on it as they went through to the kitchen to chat with Henri. After a few minutes, the house was quiet again. She closed her eyes, though her mind raced with thoughts about work, her new case, and Luke.

When Henri strode in, she opened them to find he was staring at her, with an eyebrow cocked and a finger to his lips. "From the look on your face, maybe you do need another drink."

Without another word, he nodded as if he approved of his own idea, turned on his heel then went to the bar. Ice clinked against the crystal mixing glass as he hummed a song she didn't recognize.

He returned and set on the coffee table an old-fashioned

cocktail coupe and a mixing glass full of the amber elixir. "I've made you a double. Just in case. Now don't stay up late. You have a busy day tomorrow with your friends, yes? Good night then."

"Thank you, Henri."

Amanda returned to her so-so book, though she didn't really want to read it. She felt a bit jittery, sitting by herself. She didn't want another drink, either. Instead, she found herself staring into the dancing firelight. Fires still made her nervous, but she could see how a contained fire, like this one flickering in the fireplace, could be soothing. Maybe all she needed to do was learn how to relax.

After the past two days of walking, she should be exhausted. And even though physically she was, it didn't matter because sleep would elude her anyway. She couldn't quiet her brain long enough to chase dreams. Instead, she sat there grateful for the silence. It was rare she could hear, well, nothing.

The quiet closed in on her as she recalled her disturbing conversation with Julie. She didn't feel happy in her aloneness. It wasn't loneliness exactly. It was an uncomfortable feeling of working so diligently and letting people down. She left her book on the coffee table to pace around the room. Anything to take her mind off the hurt expression on her friend's face. Running her hand across the old, well-rubbed tables, she studied the knick-knacks that cluttered a surface here and there.

Strolling into the adjacent sitting room, she spied the corner cabinet with the small leather book inside. She reached for the key to take another peek at it. She still wondered if she'd missed a clue to the diary's owner inside.

A muffled noise stopped her before she could pick it up.

Luke entered the room and stood by the doorway. Smile lines crinkled beside those clear blue eyes. "I hoped you were still here."

Amanda glanced his way, her heart pounding frantically. *Was I hoping he'd come back? No, I couldn't be. I shouldn't have anything to do with Luke, not now that I know his family is a party in the case I'm working on. Still, it doesn't hurt to be nice.*

"I can't sleep. Too much fun, I guess." She fidgeted, not knowing what to do with her hands.

He pointed back to the parlor. "I see Henri made you a

nightcap?"

"He told me he made a double." She chuckled quietly. "I thought he meant I might need two before I could go to sleep. Maybe he had other ideas."

"I'm not sure my father is as devious as all that, but you never can tell. Can I pour you one?" He reached behind the bar for a second glass while waiting for her to precede him into the parlor.

No, no, no.

She turned off the alarms in her head, nodded then sat on the couch.

Luke sat beside her, stirred the cocktails, and poured them for Amanda and himself. The firelight played over the planes of his face. It reflected off his dark curly hair and shone in his eyes.

This is dangerous, her brain warned.

Not listening, her heart responded.

He didn't catch her looking until he handed her one of the two glasses. When he smiled, it was as if he smiled only for her.

She needed to get away. She couldn't do this. Much as she wanted to wrap her arms around Luke, drink in his warmth, she shouldn't.

Troubled, she stood up. "Going somewhere?" Luke raised a brow.

Yes, she should run far away from him. She couldn't stay, could she? *Nope. Nope. Nope.* Even as her heart thudded with excitement, this was not something she could encourage. It might cost her everything she worked for. Years of putting her life aside so she could make partner thrown away.

Her rational side lost. He was worth the risk. The warm aroma of whiskey mixed with the fresh scent of Luke. His blue eyes begged her to stay. She sat back down, every nerve tingling. He held up his glass. "What should we toast?"

Though it was rare, she found herself speechless.

"World peace?" she finally sputtered. *Groundhog Day?* A flicker of recognition lit his eyes. She was pleased he recognized her reference to the Andie McDowell-Bill Murray movie. "To world peace."

He clinked her glass and waited for her to take a sip. "Too much fun, huh? So Fallingwater met your expectations?"

"And then some." She turned off the alarm bells ringing in

her head and leaned against the soft cushion.

After all, it doesn't hurt to be polite when a handsome man sits beside you and asks how your day was.

"The house was lovely. Our well-informed tour guide clearly adored Frank Lloyd Wright. When someone asked a question about one of his wives, she cut him off and announced, 'We don't gossip here.' I have no idea what the story was, but now, I'll have to make time to look it up."

Amanda's frayed nerves calmed. Was it the drink? The hour? The company? She chattered on, unable to stop. "We stopped for dinner in that tavern you recommended. It was charming. More Colonial than Victorian like the Broadview. The food was more stick-to-your-ribs than French. We talked all the way through dessert and two cups of coffee. As soon as we came home, Henri made us a 'snack.' A wonderful cheese board. I'm surprised you don't weigh seven hundred pounds."

She was glad when Luke laughed. She liked the sparkle in his eyes.

"You and me both. He does know how to feed people. So, what else did you do?"

"After lunch we talked about going to another Frank Lloyd Wright house nearby, but my friends looked like they could use another diversion. We found an old fort."

"Fort Necessity?"

"Yeah, that's the one. How did you know?"

"Class trip many years ago."

She paused and sipped her cocktail. "It's a pretty part of the country."

"That's true. Not glamorous but solid, fresh and all-American."

"Yes. That's it. How was your day?"

"Not as exciting as yours." He told her about Frank's arrival, their tennis game, and even a few snatches of their conversation about publicity for the inn. He even asked if perhaps the group would pose for a few photos in the morning.

"Frank? What an odd coincidence. Julie's fiancé is named Frank."

"Mmmm hmmm," he mumbled as he took another sip of his drink.

She stared at Luke, wondering if he knew something.

"All right. I'll confess." He burst into laughter. "He didn't know she was here until I told him. Didn't Julie know he was spending the weekend here?"

"No. She'd have told me. I know she couldn't reach him. I don't know how many times she texted or called. She never got a response. She was even starting to get angry that he didn't answer."

"His phone died."

"That old excuse." Amanda rolled her eyes.

"You should see the phone. It looks like the one my father carried when I was in middle school. It never works. I don't know why he won't break down and buy something reliable. So, if Julie sent him a text, he probably never got it."

"You're sure we're talking about the same Julie and Frank?"

Luke nodded and reached for his phone to show Amanda a photo of the happy couple. Then he stifled a laugh. "He thought she was somewhere in Pennsylvania."

"Well, that was the plan until our reservation had to be canceled. Strangely enough, Julie found a brochure about this place Frank left, and that's why we're here."

"So Julie doesn't know he's here?"

"Won't she be surprised tomorrow?" A laugh bubbled up as she imagined Julie's reaction at seeing Frank. Amanda enjoyed sharing a lighthearted moment with the man beside her. Just for tonight, she shooed her worries away.

Even though she knew she ought to head for bed, she was unwilling to go. The room was warm and cozy. *It would be awfully easy to...*

"Amanda."

One single word, spoken gently, almost breathlessly, lit her up. Her heart pounded in her chest and a crackle of heat tripped through her veins. Her hands trembled, something that never happened.

The way he held her gaze, his lips slightly parted, made her wonder if he was waiting for her. Did he feel the same attraction that filled her? Would it be wrong to give in to something this strong?

Before she could debate the pros and cons of such a move,

something Amanda did quite often, he leaned in close. She caught a whiff of his fresh Ivory-soap scent. It wasn't exotic but it was honest and true. What was it the ads used to say? To hell with the ads. She followed his lead, brushed his bare arm with her hand then kissed him.

Hesitant at first, they hardly knew each other, after all. She had to admit this kiss wasn't like any other she'd experienced. It was warm, full of desire. Was it her hunger or his that she was feeling?

She relaxed in his arms after the kiss ended.

"I've wanted to do that since the moment I first saw you down by the tennis courts."

Amanda was flattered but surprised. "Is that why you hit me with a tennis ball?"

His laugh was a low melodious chuckle. "That's what happens when I take my eye off the ball."

"Then pay attention." She leaned toward him again.

"Yes, ma'am." The first kiss was good. The second sizzled the way the romance novels say they do.

When it ended, Amanda couldn't come up with a thing to say. Her thoughts were cloudy, suffused with alcohol and, she had to admit it, desire. No, she refined her choice of words. Manhattans and romance.

She could stay here all night. *No, I can't.* The haze dissipated as she remembered her meeting with Quin on Tuesday to discuss the biggest project of her life. *Why, oh why, did that have to come to my mind now?*

Time to be sensible. She straightened up only to gaze into those expressive eyes. She couldn't understand why this man made her want to forget everything else. Still, she needed to go.

His big, warm hand folded over hers. "Amanda. I'm not very good at this..." He stared at their hands, rubbing his finger over her knuckles.

"You could've fooled me."

He looked up at her and smiled. "I mean, I want to see you again."

"I'll be here until tomorrow evening. We're staying for the picnic."

"And afterward?"

"Luke, we live in two different cities." Amanda wanted to be—no, she needed to be—practical. Even though she gave into a moment of passion seconds ago, she couldn't plan on it lasting.

"Just go west on I-76."

Had Luke already considered this? "Let's discuss that tomorrow." She squeezed his hand before rising.

"It is tomorrow." He faced her and pulled her into an embrace.

She should run, flee, but her attraction to him was overpowering. She kissed him, reveling in the strong arms that encircled her. His heart beat against hers. When the kiss ended, she looked at him in wonder.

He laid a sweet kiss on her cheek. "Now, I'll let you go. Thank you for a wonderful evening."

"Good night." She let her gaze linger on his face for a moment more. She wanted to remember the cool blue eyes and the fire-lit glow of his face. Her lips buzzed from their kisses, and she could smell the Ivory scent on her hands.

Why did something so wrong feel so good, so right?

With a smile still on her lips and a burden of guilt weighing her down, she climbed the stairs. Tomorrow. She'd have to think about this tomorrow.

Chapter Thirteen
Second Thoughts

Amanda pushed open the screen door and headed out onto the lawn overlooking the lake. Morning was dawning fresh and bright. The rising sun gilded the gentle ripples on the water, the leaves on the trees and the cotton-ball clouds drifting across the sky signaled a brand new day filled with hope and possibilities. Breathing in the mountain air was all it took to fill her with new energy. She should be exhausted after her brief night's sleep but instead, the excitement of this beautiful Memorial Day exhilarated her.

She scanned the vista, absent-mindedly touching her lips, recalling what kept her up late the night before. The kiss. Luke's kiss. She sighed with deep satisfaction.

Then she trembled under the weight of what she had done.

There had to be rules about consorting with the opposition. Not that he was the opposition, but close enough. Encouraging him would be wrong.

Her fully awake conscience nagged at her. A hint of a headache pounded behind her eyes. She sighed then turned back toward the inn. She needed coffee to straighten out her troubled thoughts.

As she reached for the screen door handle, something caught her eye. The golden light of dawn lit a couple standing by the lake. Their arms entwined around each other as they enjoyed the luxury of an early morning kiss. She shouldn't stare, but they reminded her of Luke's embrace and kiss just the night before.

She awoke from her sentimental reverie when she realized she knew one member of the couple.

That flowing red hair, blazing in the sunrise, definitely

belonged to Julie. What was she doing? Who on earth did she find to kiss? Then she remembered. Oh yes, Frank was there.

Luke draped an arm over Amanda's shoulders. His gaze had rested on the lip-lock on the lake, and he sighed. "Ah love."

His sudden appearance made Amanda jump. She touched her chest to calm her pounding heart. "Looks like my friend found your friend."

He chuckled. "And so early too."

The couple turned toward the inn and waved.

Luke raised his hand and shouted, "Morning, Frank. Julie."

Julie pointed to the man at her side as they made their way across the lawn. "Amanda, look who I found. Oh yes, you haven't met."

Amanda cringed as Luke nudged her. "Sounds familiar. I caught the same kind of hell for not knowing my friend's fiancée."

She shook her head. "At last I finally get to meet the most wonderful man in the world."

"You'll love Frank. Salt of the earth kind of a guy. We've been friends since college."

Julie led her fiancé up the porch steps, her face glowing as she made the introductions. Frank's face was open and honest, his eyes piercing. He smiled a big goofy grin, the kind designed to put people at ease. It worked. Amanda forgot to feel nervous in the company of someone new.

"I hope I'm not spoiling your bridesmaids' weekend." The groom-to-be put his hand to his heart.

"No, of course not." She would never tell her best friend's fiancé he wasn't welcome. Especially since he left the brochure that recommended this little slice of heaven to Julie.

"To tell the truth, I didn't even know Julie was going to be here." He squeezed his bride-to-be who shook her head.

"I sent you a text."

"I didn't get it."

With a frown Julie pulled his battered cell phone from his hip pocket. "Now I know what I'm getting you as a wedding present."

"Aw, hon. That'd be so romantic." He kissed her cheek before turning his attention to Luke and Amanda. "My bad. I should have known. To tell the truth, reception out here in the mountains is terrible. Julie's right. I need a new phone. But hey, I'm glad things turned out this way." He held out his hand to Amanda. "Happy to meet the maid of honor at last."

"A pleasure." She added a smile to the handshake. Friendly and casual, he seemed a good choice for Julie.

"Funny how things happen. I expect my father will have breakfast ready by now." Luke held open the door and the scent of cinnamon and maple welcomed them.

Julie and Frank held hands as they crossed the threshold.

Before Amanda went inside, Luke closed the door. "I was wondering…"

"No, I haven't asked about taking photos for the inn yet."

He shook his head. "No, not that. I was wondering if you'd like to take a walk with me?"

"Now?" She smiled and stepped in close. He let go of the door which clattered on its frame and wrapped his arms around her. Luxuriating in the warmth of his embrace, she chose Luke's kind invitation over the sirens blaring in her head. "There's no better way to start the day."

They didn't speak as they sauntered to the edge of the lake. The day was calm. The water's surface reflected the brilliant blue sky dotted with great puffs of cloud.

"There is one better way to start the day." He leaned in to kiss her.

He was right. She turned off all those warning signals and closed her eyes.

One kiss turned into two. He held her firmly as she breathed in his fresh soap scent. They'd stopped for only a few minutes before Luke stirred from their embrace. "I guess we better get back. Henri will be on the porch tapping his foot."

She giggled softly at the image. "We can't disappoint the chef."

Hand in hand, they took their time wandering up the hill to the inn, savoring their moment together. Amanda didn't remember a day more beautiful or a Memorial Day more festive.

~ * ~

Before Luke's fathers finished their first cup of coffee, Henri began preparations for the annual picnic under the spreading branches of an ancient tree by the porch while DeWayne set up the tables and chairs. He hung red, white, and blue bunting from every window and railing. The inn's furniture gleamed from its last-minute dusting. And keeping with the family tradition they raised both American and French flags on the poles on each side of the entrance of the inn.

After breakfast, Luke rushed from father to father, helping whoever called him. In between he took photos to post to the inn's Instagram and Facebook pages, using Frank and the bridal party as models. Even on the last day of his holiday weekend, there was work to do.

On the porch. By the lake. At the tennis courts.

Luke grew hopeful the new images would bring customers back to the inn and restaurant.

By noontime, the table was laden with ham, salads, deviled eggs, and rolls. Pitchers of lemonade, iced tea, and mojitos stood ready. A chafing dish gently warmed a fragrant gallon of pork barbecue. In honor of the groom-to-be, Henri explained to Frank.

Henri raced past Amanda as she poured potato chips into a big basket. "He's going to wear himself out," she said to Luke. Since Julie was occupied with her husband-to-be, and the bridesmaids were still dressing, Amanda was happy to help with party preparations.

He nodded. "Henri loves this. I suggested he scale back since we aren't sure anyone will come, but he insists they will. Memorial Day doesn't draw the crowds we get on the Fourth. Because they aren't busy this early in the season, the neighbors and merchants usually join us."

She pointed to the parking lot. "Looks like this year won't be any different."

Cars started to fill up the empty spaces and families toted blankets and chairs, as well as bowls and steaming dishes to add to the buffet table.

Within minutes, Henri dashed from guest to guest carrying trays loaded with appetizers, and DeWayne served as the welcoming committee.

Luke was heading inside to refill a lemonade pitcher when DeWayne called him over.

"Luke, these fine people want a copy of the brochure and the sample menu I ordered a few weeks ago. They're on my desk."

His stepfather gestured toward a young couple.

Luke headed inside, swinging by the business office before going to the kitchen.

DeWayne obviously had done a quick clean-up before the party started. On a normal day, the surface of his desk was covered with various piles of papers. Now, the scratched but polished wood top was empty except for photos of Henri and Luke and a full "In" basket. Every piece of mail, note, and stray slip of paper had been swept into the low flat tray. The brochures DeWayne wanted were easy to spot, a short stack bound by a thin strip of white paper, fresh from the printer. Luke put his pitcher on a side table before sliding one from the pack. Underneath, he found the menus paper-clipped together.

As he retrieved them, a letter sailed onto the floor. He peeled off a menu and put the rest back. Then he leaned over to pick up the errant letter and returned it to the pile in the box. The plain simple sheet wasn't even worth a second glance.

He grabbed the empty pitcher and headed toward the door. But something about the letter stopped him. Something that nagged at the back of his mind.

Going back, he put the pitcher and papers down on the desk and reached for the letter, addressed to Mr. Beaumont and Mr. Wilson.

The name at the top of the creamy white paper, printed in a reserved unadorned font, screamed at him. Jones, Jones, and Taylor. "An unforgettable name," Amanda had quipped when she told him the name of the law firm where she worked.

It was unforgettable, all right. The question Luke wanted answered was, why did a lawyer from her law firm write to his fathers?

Curious, he scanned the dense type. Even with the legal jargon, he could tell this was a letter about the sale of the inn. Negotiations, closing details, deadlines. Information DeWayne already told him. He looked for the signature. Quin MacIntosh. An odd name, neither a man's, nor a woman's, and unfamiliar. Though Amanda's name appeared nowhere on the letter, he was still troubled. Was she aware of this proposal?

Luke put the letter back as anger surged through his veins. Betrayal turned his stomach. What had he gotten himself into? Had he been flirting with and kissing the enemy? Not the enemy exactly...but someone working on a project to tear down his home and build a big, flashy hotel.

He grabbed his phone and snapped a photo of the page. He wanted proof to show Amanda when they met before she went home. But now, Luke didn't imagine the shady spot by the lake, with a bottle of wine, the same way he did earlier. Or his plan to ask her to come to Wilmington the first weekend she could get away. None of that seemed to matter much anymore.

He needed to forget about betrayal and heartache and return to the party. DeWayne was waiting for him and some thirsty children needed lemonade. As Luke headed back, the joy that brightened his morning faded away. He pasted on a smile, for his fathers, resolved to look as if he was having fun, but in truth misery weighed him down like an anchor in the lake he treasured so much.

He loved this party. Henri always made it a celebration of both his adopted country and his native land. After feeding everyone and before the children's games, he led a short ceremony with the pledge of allegiance, plus a moment of silence for those who gave their lives during the Great Wars. He never failed to mention the historic links between the nations, or to express his gratitude for the freedoms each provided.

The crowd, already a proud, patriotic group, ate it up.

This year the lawn was filled with old friends and strangers who could become friends before the summer was over. The only people not present were their closest neighbors, the Masons, the Evitts, and the Browns. But that wasn't a surprise, the Browns never came. Mr. Brown still refused to speak to Henri and DeWayne. But Luke was disappointed the other families didn't show up. They had welcomed them as newcomers a long time ago.

Henri rushed over to Luke after putting a fresh pitcher of mojitos on the buffet table.

"Good crowd, isn't it?" Henri's face was flushed with pleasure. Luke couldn't imagine what his father would do without this place. "I don't mind admitting it now, but I was worried no one would come. Between the lack of reservations this weekend and the, um, difficulties with the hotel, I was afraid people were avoiding us. Your work on our social media accounts saved the day."

"*Mon pere,* I might have had my doubts, but you knew they would come. I think everyone woke up this morning and asked themselves, what will we do if we don't go to the Broadview for the traditional Memorial Day picnic? You've made this a party no one would dare miss."

"Mmmm hmmm." Henri put his hands on his hips and scanned the crowd. "Not everyone is here. Reese and Megan didn't come, and I haven't seen Tony and Jill—or their kids. I did hope they would come."

"Maybe they're on their way, Papa."

"Who's DeWayne talking to?" Henri shaded his eyes. "Oh, Bill and Penny. They recently opened a new shop in Oakland. I didn't expect them to come when I invited them."

"Everybody loves you, Papa. Of course, they came."

Henri shooed his son away. "Get out of here. I have work to do."

Luke found ways to keep himself busy. Frank was occupied with his fiancée—as he should be. Luke envied him his good fortune. It looked like his friend had found true love. He remembered the letter from Amanda's law firm and what she hadn't told him. Just when he thought he might have found someone to care for, that letter had proven him wrong.

Once he collected the empty cups, put new liners in the trash cans, and switched the god-awful classic rock for something decent on the sound system, he got busy replenishing half-empty dishes on the buffet table. Anything to avoid Amanda and the questions he wanted to ask her.

A burst of laughter made Luke look up. The bridal party was in high spirits, though Amanda wasn't with them. Earlier she had stuck close to him while they raced around getting ready for the party. It made the work, work he always enjoyed, even more fun. In a quiet moment, he set aside a chilled bottle of sauvignon blanc and asked her to meet him at the lake later. He didn't care if she was avoiding him now, did he? After all, that letter and her maybe-secrets ruined everything.

She emerged from the inn, her phone in her hand. Her face drawn, and Luke couldn't be sure, but he thought he saw tracks of tears trailing down her cheeks. He checked his initial impulse to go to her, wrap his arms around her. She didn't even glance his way, but instead, headed to the blanket where her friends were gathered.

He returned his attention to the bowl of coleslaw, the last dish in need of replenishment. What would he do next? Anything to look occupied until he got ahold of his emotions.

He felt like hell, although nowhere near as angry and hurt as the day Emily left. He'd thought they were happy. When she'd agreed to marry him, he was ecstatic, thrilled to plan his life around her. But on that day, she'd confronted him about her need to focus on her career. Then she walked out. More than a year ago now and it still hurt.

Amanda had gotten under his skin but so far all they shared was a couple of kisses. A couple of fantastic kisses, but still nothing more. Thank goodness for that. What if he'd—they'd— and then he'd found the letter.

He didn't want to think about it now. He'd have plenty of time alone in his apartment to wonder how everything went wrong. Again.

Henri took a seat beside DeWayne and a couple of the staffers from the county tourism office. Henri spoke with big gestures and even bigger smiles as DeWayne nodded the way he always did. Like DeWayne, *Maman* had always enjoyed the dramatic way Henri spoke with his hands. Luke missed her today. Well. Everyday. She was a tiny person, filled with an all-encompassing love. When Luke went to her for advice—like how to deal with the playground bully or a mountain of homework— she was ready with an answer. She'd know what to do about Amanda if she were still here.

"Hey, Luke." Frank jogged up to him. "The ladies are wondering if you'll be finished soon."

"Yeah. Sure. In a minute." Trying to avoid eye contact with Frank, Luke straightened two bowls on the table and repositioned the spoons. Maybe his answer was lame, but he didn't know what else to say.

"They have to leave in an hour or two, and I expect you want to spend time with Amanda. To tell you the truth, she looks like she needs your attention. Her boss just called her, and Amanda got reamed big time. She's a little bummed."

"That's too bad."

Frank frowned. "Something eating at you?"

Luke shrugged. "No. Yes. Um. I just got some disturbing news…I can't talk about it yet. It's nothing life threatening or anything. You understand?"

His friend slapped him on the back. "Come on over when you're finished whatever it is that you're doing."

"Will do."

The arrival of a big, dusty SUV diverted Luke's attention from Frank and the ladies. And Amanda.

Henri and DeWayne jumped up from their chairs to greet the newcomers. Even though one of the women carried a bunch of flowers and another held a bottle of wine, none of them looked like they were in a holiday mood. Their faces were grim with not a smile among them. Something was going on. These weren't ordinary guests. This wasn't a friendly social call.

Chapter Fourteen
More Than a Picnic

Leading the way was Joe Brown. Luke couldn't remember the man ever stepping foot on the property since the day Henri and DeWayne moved here. He held the elbow of the woman clutching the flowers. Henri rushed over to kiss Mrs. Brown on both cheeks in the French way of greeting. Behind them were Tony and Jill Evitt and the Masons, Reese, and Megan.

Mrs. Mason handed the bottle of wine to Henri with an embarrassed smile. Again, he kissed her on both cheeks. Mrs. Evitt stiffened next to her husband, clearly afraid of being the next to get kissed.

DeWayne shook hands with the latecomers, his business smile pasted on his face. Mr. Brown, a wizened septuagenarian with a shock of white hair and a face tanned the color of a walnut, frowned, and wiped his hand on his pants after the handshake.

Luke couldn't decide whether to join his parents or stay far away.

Henri was doing his best to be hospitable. He led them to an empty table, big enough for all of them. After they were seated, he glanced at Luke with an unspoken request for help. He knew that expression well enough. He grabbed some cups and a pitcher of lemonade and headed over to help out.

"We decided we should come together. Get this thing settled." Tony Evitt leaned his elbows on the table, his hands folded in front of him. He looked ready to cut a deal, not enjoy a picnic.

"What exactly do you want to get settled?" Henri sat straight in his chair, his hands knotted together in his lap. Luke hoped the early start and busy afternoon hadn't sapped the strength his father needed now.

Luke poured a glass of lemonade and offered it to Mrs. Mason. She shook her head and pointed to the bottle of wine. He put down the cups, the pitcher, then headed into the house for a corkscrew. From the sounds of the conversation, some alcoholic lubrication might help.

He went into the kitchen to find the corkscrew but came up empty. Drawer after drawer, he couldn't find a single one. Henri must own a dozen corkscrews so why did they all seem to be missing?

Luke grew jittery, worrying about his fathers facing the neighbors who were ready to sell and move away. They needed his support.

"Looking for something?"

He turned, and there she stood. Amanda. Her pretty curls now neatly brushed, her make-up refreshed. A smile replaced the drawn look she'd worn earlier. A filmy shirt hugged her curves. White shorts showed off her athletic legs. No, he didn't need this distraction right now. Not when disaster loomed in the yard.

"No. Well, yes. I need a corkscrew and can't find one anywhere." He tried not to look at her as he scanned the immaculate counters. Even with all the cooking and preparing, Henri managed to keep his kitchen ready for a visit from the Health Department.

"I'm trying to remember Sean Connery's line in that Indiana Jones movie. I loved it. Maybe you remember it?"

"Not now, Amanda. I'm in a hurry," he snapped.

"No, no. This works. He said, 'I find that if I just sit down to think...'" She sat at the kitchen table and put her finger to the delicious mouth he had kissed.

"Thanks, professor." He didn't have time for her joking around.

Her face lit up. "Did you try the bar?"

He rolled his eyes at her. "No." He rushed into the sitting room to find she was right. A half dozen corkscrews were lined up on the bar. He shouted his "thanks" and ran out the door.

By the time he got outside, the corkscrew was no longer needed.

Even from the porch Luke could hear Mr. Brown shouting

at Henri and DeWayne. He heard every word.

"It's now or never, gentlemen. I'm 74 years old. I've sold my horses. I've already put my deposit down on a condo in Fort Myers Beach and gotten my medical records transferred to my new internist. Next week, my kids are coming to help me pack. The only thing holding me back is the two of you. If the deal doesn't go through without your property, I've got my lawyer ready to sue you both." Mr. Brown jumped up and slammed his hand on the table. The cups and pitcher went flying.

Not only did the rest of the people around the table jump, so did everybody at the picnic. Luke hated seeing the whole town witness such an ugly confrontation.

DeWayne rose slowly, unfolding his impressive frame carefully from the chair to tower over Mr. Brown. He said nothing at first. Instead, he stared at the man until Mr. Brown grew uncomfortable under DeWayne's gaze. Mr. Brown's eyes flitted left and right as he wrung his hands. Finally, he cleared his throat and stared up defiantly at DeWayne.

"Mr. Brown. Mr. Evitt. Mr. Mason." DeWayne acknowledged each of them. His stern expression softened into a smile, though the coldness never left his eyes. "Ladies, I'm sure Henri and I appreciate your interest in the future of our establishment. I thank you for coming to our picnic."

DeWayne spun to face Mr. Brown, his hands on his hips as he stared down on his neighbor. "Mr. Brown, I do believe this is the first time you and I have talked face to face, in what, nearly twenty years?"

All around them, their neighbors waited. Conversation had come to a standstill. Plates of food were abandoned. Except for a few children cavorting by the lake, the crowd was quiet, listening. DeWayne had everyone's attention.

"My business partner and I, as well as Luke here." He put a hand on his son's shoulder. "Have yet to decide whether we will accept the hotel's offer. It's a good one. I agree with you. But my family enjoys it here, and we don't really want to move to Florida." He glared at Mr. Brown.

Mr. Brown found his voice. "I'm calling my lawyer in the morning. Come along, Karen. I've had all the picnic I can stand." He turned on his heel, nodded to his wife, then strode off.

The wiry elderly woman with the pixie haircut leaned in to say something to Henri.

Mr. Brown paused and snapped his fingers. "Now, Karen."

She straightened up and followed, giving Henri a sympathetic smile on their way out.

Mr. Mason stood, shifting from one foot to the other. "Well, Megan, we have to be leaving too. We drove the Browns over here. Tony? Jill? You coming?"

"Thanks again, Henri, DeWayne." Jill Evitt tried to smile but wasn't successful. Her look of apprehension transformed into more of a grimace. "We'll talk soon."

"It'll be all right," her husband said as he took his wife's arm to lead her away. "No hard feelings?"

Henri waved them off and turned his attention to the lake.

DeWayne crossed his arms. "No, no hard feelings." His gaze followed the three couples until they got into their car and roared down the gravel driveway.

Once the dust on the road settled, the crowd began to mill about. Their conversation muted, the sounds of laughter gone. One family picked up their blanket and folded their chairs. Another couple stopped to thank Henri and DeWayne for the lovely afternoon. The party was over. And it wasn't even three o'clock.

"I still have prizes for the children's games." Henri leaned an elbow on the picnic table and scrubbed his hand down his face. "What about dessert? All your cupcakes, Luke."

"It's fine, Dad."

"Maybe you could take them to your office tomorrow. I'd hate for them to go to waste."

DeWayne took a seat beside Henri. "Hey, don't worry about the damn cupcakes."

Henri, always full of hospitality, sat quiet and dejected like a wallflower at the junior prom. A line creased DeWayne's forehead, making him look as if he was itching for a fight. Luke hoped it wasn't with Henri.

Luke whispered to Henri, "Papa, don't worry. Go say goodbye to your guests. They came for you." Then he acknowledged their friend from the farmers' market. "Mr. Yoder, very glad you came."

The farmer doffed his straw hat and shook hands with

Luke. "You too, Luke. I expected to see that pretty lady with you today."

Luke smiled stiffly. "She's here somewhere."

"Sorry to see the place go, Henri, DeWayne."

Henri rose to shake Mr. Yoder's hand. "It isn't gone yet, David. I still have some fight in me."

"I wish the both of you luck then. Thanks for a nice party. The family always looks forward to it." Mr. Yoder put his hat back on his head and took the hand of the youngest of three children who waited with Mrs. Yoder a few yards away.

The smile faded from Henri's face. The expression of sadness that replaced it troubled Luke. It was the closest thing to the heartbreak they shared when *Maman* died. It made him want to protect his father even more. He nudged his papa. "Go. Circulate. You don't want everyone to think the Broadview's days are at an end. Rally the troops, Henri."

"What a wise son I have." Henri smiled, adjusted his chef's coat, and moved through the crowd.

"He is in his element here," DeWayne murmured as Luke sat beside him. "This is everything he wants. Convincing him to sell, even if it's a good idea from a business standpoint, would take that all away from him."

Luke sighed. "He was on fire this morning. Pots of water were boiling, the dishwasher was running for the second time. He got me out of bed at four-thirty to bake cupcakes."

DeWayne chuckled. "He woke me up with a feather duster."

"I was worried he'd wear himself out—and we weren't even sure anyone was coming."

"I can guess how it went." DeWayne's expression grew serious, filled with determination, as if he was mimicking Henri's. "It went something like this. 'We've been throwing this picnic for the town since the year after we came here. I'm sure they'll come.'"

Luke nodded. "Sounds about right."

A little crease appeared between DeWayne's eyebrows. "Yeah, he said the same thing to me when we talked last night. He also told me the party would be a signal he wasn't willing to give up our home, your home, and his livelihood. The family legacy."

Luke could see how heavily the issue weighed on his stepfather's mind. "So, you still haven't decided what to do?"

DeWayne shook his head and frowned, looking into the distance. "Part of me wants to take the money and run. Maybe it's time to go back to the city, find another place. The quiet gets to me sometimes."

"I didn't know that."

It was DeWayne who discovered the inn for sale all those years ago, who assured Henri they could make a success of it. DeWayne nodded as he fidgeted with his heavy gold West Point ring. Luke recognized one of his stepfather's signals he was worried.

Luke figured it had to be tearing him apart to have to decide it was time to go. "I thought this was your idea."

"It was once. You might remember I spent twenty years in the Army, working on military bases crowded with people. After that, and especially after the incident in New York, I needed to escape." He turned his gaze from the lake to Luke. A soft smile crept across his face. "I don't need to escape anymore."

"Maybe you should move to Wilmington"

"I suggested that to Henri. Even thought for a minute he was considering it."

"But?"

"You know Henri. He got caught up in the springtime activities here and—well, he wouldn't discuss it again."

Luke scanned the broad green lawn, his gaze stopping at the tennis courts where Frank and Julie were lobbing balls back and forth. Once he hoped he might enjoy a game with Amanda there. He sighed. "How about Baltimore, then?"

"What about Baltimore?"

Luke shifted in his chair. As much as he liked his present job, Frank's offer might give him a chance to help Henri and DeWayne. "Frank asked me if I'd like to be his marketing director."

"No, Luke. We don't expect you to do that for us. You like where you work."

"Oh, I do. I'm hoping for a promotion in July. If everything goes right."

DeWayne leaned his chin on his hand. "Then why—?"

Luke interrupted. "It would be a good opportunity."

DeWayne was onto him. "And..."

He tried to sound encouraging. "Maybe Henri would like to find a place in Baltimore. We could all move."

"You don't want to move back in with us." DeWayne's expression was that of an empty-nester afraid the chick was coming home again.

Luke laughed at the horror that widened DeWayne's eyes. "Fat chance of that."

"Oh, thank God." His chuckle was deep.

"But Henri might like a new challenge. A new business maybe, another restaurant. Maybe he'd be happy if we lived near one another again."

"It's a nice thought but neither Henri nor I would want you to give up everything you've worked so hard for. And Henri, he's dug his heels in pretty good. I'm not sure he can appreciate other possibilities. He wants to be here. It's home."

Yeah, Luke understood his fathers' dilemma. Amanda stepped on to the path headed straight toward them. It was time for a showdown of his own.

Chapter Fifteen
Conflict of Interest

Henri rushed past Amanda, wringing his hands, looking as if the world was collapsing around him. After that confrontation, perhaps it was. Her heart went out to him as he pasted on a smile and headed for another family packing up their gear to go home.

Amanda had paused on the porch as the meeting between Henri, DeWayne, and the latecomers broke up in anger. All six of them were strangers to her—until she heard DeWayne greet a man named Evitt and another named Mason. She'd seen those names on some of the documents on her desk back at her office. She was working on a contract for a Tony and Jill Evitt. Her fellow associate had mentioned Reese and Megan Mason. The name Brown didn't ring a bell, but she knew it could be another part of the deal. It was a big one, Quin said time and again.

Her heart dropped deep into her stomach as their presence here confirmed she was working on the project trying to bring these wonderful men, owners of the inn, to the brink.

It also occurred to her she was witnessing something she never understood. A project that looked wonderful on paper but affected people in very different ways. Up until now she witnessed only the smiles and handshakes after a sealed deal paved the way to something new and beautiful.

At her office in Pittsburgh, that's all she imagined. The excitement to work on a project like this hotel, with its spa, and restaurant set on a bit of waterfront property.

But here was the other side. A side full of anger and pain. Neighbors yelling at one another. The furrowed brows and frowns of families watching their world disappear.

As much as Amanda wanted to get in her car and drive

away without another word, she wasn't going to be a coward. She needed to talk to Luke—even if she couldn't come up with a single thing to say in her defense.

She dodged small children and big dogs as she circumvented the tables to find Luke.

There he was, sitting beside DeWayne. Chatting, as if neither of them had a care in the world.

Maybe she didn't have to worry. Maybe he would be fine after all.

How he was shouldn't matter anyway. They hardly knew each other. They shared a few polite conversations. A drink by the fire. A couple of kisses. Something her conscience would never let her enjoy again. Not after what she just witnessed. Knowing she was partially at fault for their troubles.

She waved away the memory of that moment of romance, hoping to bury it forever. Yet she did want to be kind. Even if tomorrow she might be on the other side of the table, today she was at this old inn, enjoying the owners' hospitality. She needed to at least show her gratitude for a wonderful weekend. She rehearsed what she planned to say, lifted her chin, and strode to their table.

Luke's laughing eyes set her at ease. Nothing to worry about at all.

Amanda ran her hands through her hair and took a deep breath. *Luke doesn't mean a thing to me. He is, at most, a new friend. That's all. Even if I did kiss him.*

She caught his eye. Something unreadable in his expression prompted her heart to thud against her chest. His smile disappeared as if he didn't trust her.

Could he suspect she was working on this deal? No, there was no way he could have found out. Just as her conscience prodded her to tell him, her nerve vanished. She couldn't. Did that make her a coward?

Honesty was overrated. Before she got more deeply involved, she was going to leave without a word about the deal or her part in it. Skip their meeting by the lake, and never kiss him again. It was for the best. Not only did she not need him, she didn't have time for him. A simple goodbye and good luck were all she needed to say.

Nervously, she turned to his father. "I've got to get going too. I've left my room key on the registration desk."

DeWayne stood and flashed his gracious smile. "So soon?" He put his hands on his hips and nodded at his son.

"Yes, it's time to go. It's been a great weekend, and the picnic today was amazing." She rocked back and forth on her feet, struggling to quiet her fidgety hands. "Anyway." She shook DeWayne's hand. "My boss called in a tizzy. She needs me in the office bright and early, and all good things must come to an end. I guess."

Luke rose from his chair, that troubled look deepening. He crossed his arms. "I guess so."

Now or never, Amanda. This was the moment when she should come clean. But she couldn't face him. *Coward.*

Instead, she'd find a way to tell him later why she decided to leave before they could have more time alone. An email might suffice. Once she was back in Pittsburgh when she'd never run into him again. There wasn't any reason to make a scene and ruin a lovely weekend.

"I hoped to stay later, but I have to get ready for tomorrow." *It wasn't a total lie.* It was close enough to the truth, but she hated herself for telling even a white lie.

DeWayne's smile never dimmed. "Sorry to hear you have to go. Do you need help with your bags? Luke will run and get them if you'd like."

In spite of the stormy look on Luke's face, DeWayne kept up the spirit of hospitality. Luke obviously hadn't shared whatever suspicions he held with his father.

She shook her head. "Oh no, no, no. I put them in my car already. I wanted to tell you how nice everything was. I raved about the food to Henri."

"Then you made him very happy."

"I hope so. Although it seems like those people have upset him."

"He'll be fine. Nothing to worry about at all." DeWayne's tone was light, but Amanda wondered about the turmoil he was hiding underneath that serene look.

Now was the time she dreaded. Saying goodbye to Luke. She could barely meet his gaze as she twisted her hands in front of her. "Well, then. Thanks. Luke? Very nice to meet you. Sorry we never got to play tennis."

His smile looked fake when he looked at her. "Have a good trip back to Pittsburgh."

His blue eyes looked so cold, so suspicious, she shivered. Though he said nothing more, she hated to withhold the truth from him.

All she could do was wave and walk away. She needed to search for Julie, who was still wrapped in the arms of her fiancé. Amanda stopped only long enough to hug her friend, kiss Frank on the cheek, and promise not to miss any more wedding events.

As she punched the key fob to unlock her doors, Luke called to her. "Amanda?"

She turned at the sound of his voice.

He stalked toward her, his eyes rimmed with anger. Afraid of the confrontation that might come, she planted her feet, ready to stand her ground. Work would always come before a man she hardly knew. She looked him square in the eye, ready for whatever he planned to say.

"You knew about the hotel sale when you got here, didn't you? Did you come here planning to report back that the place was falling on hard times? That the neighbors were against us? That our restaurant and hotel rooms were empty?"

It's clear he's fixing for a fight. Okay then. I'm ready.

"You think I'm a spy?" The car beeped as she relocked the doors. Amanda tucked her key into her shorts pocket and crossed her arms.

He huffed. "Don't act like you don't know what's going on. Your law firm is representing the developer who wants to buy the inn."

Before she could say another word, a phone jingled. His, not hers.

"Frederika. Hi, um. Yes." When he put up a finger asking Amanda to wait, she leaned against her car, relieved to have a moment to consider what to tell him.

He kept nodding though he said nothing until, "Yes, of course. First thing tomorrow. I'm glad you liked it. Oh. Sure. Sure. I should be able to make those changes right away. You need it tonight?" He sighed. "Yes. See you tomorrow. Goodbye." He switched off the phone, looking perturbed. "Thanks for waiting. It's always something, isn't it?"

"I know what you mean." While she waited, she lost her nerve. Telling him now would only hurt him more. "Look, I've got to get going. I have my own life to get back to. So, if you are done scolding me." She unlocked the car door. Again.

"Not so fast." He held out his hand to hold the door shut. "I think I deserve an explanation."

"There's nothing to explain, Luke. This isn't my case. I've done nothing wrong. Until I got an email from my boss Saturday night, I didn't have any idea the inn was part of the project."

The stony look on his face didn't budge. *Why didn't he believe her?*

"We shared a few wonderful moments, but now I need to go. I thought a workaholic like you would understand."

"That's not good enough. I saw the letter from your law firm." He flashed his phone with the pictures he had taken in front of her face. All she saw was a picture of a letter, impossible to read, but the letterhead was recognizable, something she saw every day.

She threw her hands up in frustration. "Don't you get it? Do you know how big Jones, Jones and Taylor is? We have five *hundred* attorneys in ten offices around the country. I couldn't possibly keep up with everything going on in the firm."

He studied the picture. "Who is Quin MacIntosh?"

"Quin? She's my boss. How do you know Quin?"

"She's the lawyer who signed this letter. So you don't know anything at all?"

Amanda had run out of patience. "Look, Luke. How many people work in your office?" She didn't wait for an answer. "Are you aware of what all of them are doing?" She continued without waiting, "Do you keep track of all the projects your own boss is overseeing?" Now she was worked up. "Quin has three associates working for her. We don't discuss what we're working on. We're up to our ears in legalese all day. When we come up for air, we talk about the terrible pitching during the previous night's Pirates game, what's on Netflix, which happy hour is the best. Maybe our families or our plans for the weekend. Not our workload."

While all of this was completely true, Quin's email and now this letter put her in an awful spot. *I have to tell him. What have I got to lose? He's already angry and hurt.*

She took a deep breath and stretched her hands in front of her. "I've been working on the sale of a couple of Western Maryland properties for a developer in Pittsburgh. He wants to build a hotel. Deep Creek is a big lake. When I came here, I knew nothing about plans to buy this inn. I came here because Julie suggested it. That's all."

His face hardened. "When did you find out your firm was trying to take our inn?"

Amanda's conscience pricked at her for betraying him. "I learned in a short email after I got here. This is part of Quin's project. Quin's project, not mine."

"Maybe so. You gotta admit though, you're working on it."

"You still don't get it. I work on a lot of transactions."

"No, you don't get it. You're working for the man who wants to take away my home, DeWayne and Henri's livelihood."

He made a valid point. "That's not what I'm doing. This is business, Luke. I'm not trying to hurt you."

Any of the softness left in his eyes disappeared. His features turned to stone, and he crossed his arms. "Yeah. Well, you did. You played me for a fool. Made me think you might care about me. All of that was a lie." He waved her away as he stormed off. "Have a nice life, Amanda Johnson."

So that was it. She smashed the fob button one more time. But this time she got in the damn car. She glared at him stalking away with hellfire in her own eyes. "Goodbye, Luke," she spit out only to her own ears.

She turned the key and tore away from the inn. She never wanted to see the place—or Luke—again.

~ * ~

It happened again. He let down his guard and got his heart stomped on. The blood in his veins ran cold as he watched her drive away from the safe vantage point on the porch.

Busying himself by picking up abandoned paper plates and cups, he fought an internal struggle of self-doubt and defeat. Why didn't he pay attention to all the warning signs?

Because there weren't any.

At first glance, Amanda was a nice girl with a head full of soft golden curls. Athletic legs he wanted to caress all day and all night. She was funny and sweet. When he'd told her about the long hours he put in as a business development assistant at a construction company, she'd understood. But none of that mattered because she worked for the people trying to take away the Broadview.

She knew when I kissed her.

Holding a cup over the big black trash bag, he froze. What an idiot he'd been, thinking she was different.

Cramming the cup in the bag, he realized she was just like Emily. Work was more important to her than anything else. Even him.

Amanda had done the same thing.

Once again, he'd found himself mooning over another pretty woman who never wanted him. He was certain, absolutely certain, she welcomed his kiss last night, but maybe she was just a good actress.

With each discarded cup or plate, he reviewed the events of the weekend. Nothing signaled a disaster was coming. Last night was sweet. She waited for him, sitting there by the fire. All that time, she knew. She asked questions, she looked over the place. Like a spy, she gathered intel for her client.

How was he going to tell Henri and DeWayne? They liked her.

Luke tossed the trash bag in the bin, ready to return to what was left of the picnic.

After the day they had, he didn't have the heart tell them now. He shoved his hands into his pockets and took a deep breath. Everyone was gone. DeWayne and Henri were packing up the leftovers, deep in a heated discussion.

They didn't look any happier than he felt. Henri's face was red with anger or hurt, Luke couldn't tell which. DeWayne, always the peacemaker, put down the aluminum foil to lay his hand on Henri's shoulder.

It appeared a full-blown argument was erupting in front of Luke. A rarity between his two fathers. Henri could be quite emotional, but he rarely lost his temper. Until now. He pushed DeWayne's hand away, said something to make DeWayne flinch, then stormed across the lawn into the house. The door slammed behind him.

DeWayne's gaze remained fastened on his husband's path until Luke came near.

"Pop, what happened?"

His father shook his head. "I told your father it's no use. We should sell."

The earth shifted under Luke. No wonder Henri was angry. The united front he and DeWayne always presented to the world was fractured. This was all the fault of those lawyers and the developer who saw their home as nothing more than a piece of lakefront property. Luke saw more than a home slipping away, he saw a future slipping away too. Maybe a family.

He didn't know what to say.

"It's difficult, son. Henri wants to protect the Broadview, but it isn't going to happen. Just imagine. Work begins on the new hotel, and suddenly we have trucks with those awful back-up warning beeps at six-thirty in the morning. Dust and debris cover the windows. Hammering going on all day. Traffic—not only cars, but dump trucks and semis with lumber and brick and stone—making it impossible for our guests to get here."

DeWayne put his hands on his hips and looked toward the lake. He sighed and returned his gaze to Luke. "They're going to win. We might survive another season, but that would be it. Even if we do, how can we ever compete with a brand new resort right next door? We're already seeing the effects of new development on the other side of the lake. Our little inn won't make it."

What he said made sense. He was always rational, always a realist. In the end, Henri would agree, Luke knew, but it broke his heart to see the same sadness that bedeviled his father whenever he faced loss. "Poor Henri."

Life as they knew it was going to change. The question was how could they make the best of it?

Chapter Sixteen
Legal Issues

Quin called Amanda into her office, a spacious room lined with bookcases and a floor to ceiling plate glass window. "I need you to get up to speed on this."

She never wasted time with pleasantries. The documents on Quin's desk were familiar enough. This was the first time, however, Amanda saw the drawing of the entire lakeside resort, complete with swimming pool, fire pits, and tennis courts.

She didn't want to know more than she already knew. "Aren't I already working on this?"

Quin smirked as she gathered the papers into a heavy file folder. "Yeah. The zoning hearing is Thursday. I was going myself, but I have a conflict. You've got to go. We've got local counsel to represent Ted Lowrey. Heath Charles—he's more knowledgeable about land use than anyone—will call you later. In the meantime, I need you to read up on the Garrett County code. You're ready for this. I know you won't let me down."

Her words sliced through Amanda's heart like a double-edged dagger. While she was thrilled at Quin's confidence in her work, it meant she was going to have to face Henri and DeWayne. And Luke. "You can count on me."

Quin glanced up and smiled before returning to the stacks of paperwork in front of her. "One of the owners is balking. We thought we made a deal but he, well they, might be changing their minds. Ted expects them to come around before the hearing."

Would they? Amanda wasn't so sure. She strode into her cramped dreary office lit only by her computer screen and sank into her chair. Her desk was already piled high with files, documents and assorted time sheets, office memos, and schedule reminders. And now the thick file on the Broadview Inn. With a long sigh, she pulled up the website with Garrett County's land use code.

Hardly two days ago, she had only an inkling that she was working on the project that was about to tear apart Luke and his family. Now, she held in her own hands a copy of a letter, probably the same letter he saw yesterday in DeWayne's office.

Amanda's heart sank as she scanned copies of agreements with the neighbors, correspondence with county officials and pages and pages of regulations and contracts. Everything was cut and dry, nothing out of the ordinary. Only now she could attach names to faces after yesterday's confrontation—especially the angry Mr. Brown.

Most unforgettable was Henri's face, and Luke's too, if she was being honest. None of this was ordinary to them.

Her gaze fell to the drawing again. With trembling hands, she picked it from the stack, spread it out and studied it. She marveled at how architects and landscape designers knew how to take four disparate properties and create a sweeping vision complete with hotel, spa, restaurant, fitness center, and a lakeside view.

She tried to imagine where on the map Henri's kitchen stood. Remembered how the present inn's porch faced the lake at sunset, in a location near the new spa. The expanse of rolling lawn that stretched to the tennis courts. She sat up in her chair as she studied the section beside the lake. Perched at the water's edge was the proposed restaurant.

If she had it figured correctly, the building close to the water's edge might be in a protected zone—one that would require an exception to environmental regulations. She jotted a note to check the setback requirements. That was the sort of thing that could get lots of people, from bureaucrats to environmentalists, hot and bothered. It could delay the project for months. She wasn't sure yet what she thought about that. Such a hold-up might be good for the innkeepers but not so much for her firm's client.

She couldn't help but admire the plans, though. The developer had thought of everything. Who wouldn't like to relax by a pool that overlooked the lake? Or have dinner watching the sun set? The tennis courts looked to be in the same place.

Where she met Luke.

Nevertheless, envisioning such a beautiful view without the old inn made her want to cry. Sure the place was old and creaky, no doubt about it. Yet it could be beautiful. Just as DeWayne had once meticulously painted the inn's railing in three shades of green, it could shine again.

She remembered the fishy-smelling diary and the entry detailing the president's visit. Perhaps it didn't give the inn any important historical significance, yet she remained convinced saving the place could be a good idea.

It reminded the world that a president and his young bride stopped there for a visit once. What a wonderful bit of romance, the very thing to draw customers for afternoon tea, wedding receptions, romantic dinners. A bit of history and a breathtaking view of the lake.

She put down the drawing, leaned back in her chair and stared at the empty wall where she had yet to hang a single picture. She was taking this more personally than she should. Still, she couldn't discount her own feelings of loss. With the fire, she lost everything in a single day. Without warning. It was different for Luke, Henri, and DeWayne. What would it be like to wait, knowing the moment was coming when you would have to leave and never enter your house again?

Maybe her weekend at Deep Creek Lake wasn't a total disaster.

An email alert from Heath pinged at the top of her screen. *Call you at ten?*

She dashed off a reply to the Garrett County attorney and hit the send button. She needed to stop worrying about what would happen with the inn and finish a lot of work to be ready for the hearing. It was only a few days away.

Another quick glance at the drawing made her wonder if she couldn't do two things at once—represent her client and find a way to preserve a two-hundred-year-old inn. Even if it wasn't eligible for the National Register of Historic Places, maybe she could convince Quin and Mr. Lowrey it was worth saving for Henri and DeWayne, for Luke, for the Deep Creek community.

To succeed, she needed to be all business. Don't think of the people. Henri and DeWayne, wonderful as they were, and

Luke, didn't matter. Her emotions could not be involved in this process. She didn't need a reminder that love and law don't mix.

If she could save the inn, she'd do it because it was the right thing to do.

She clicked on her desk lamp and opened the first file. She had a lot of documents to get through before her phone call with Heath.

Chapter Seventeen
Stuck in Between

"But Paul. You said yourself this was my best work yet." Luke couldn't believe all his efforts were now worthless.

A minute ago, he had sauntered into his supervisor's office and dropped into a chair, picturing himself in an office like this someday, maybe soon. He'd like a big picture window overlooking the Christina River. He'd walked in confident his promotion was assured. After all, he'd gotten nothing but praise during his performance evaluation the previous week. Then, after weeks of perfecting this report, his presentation had gone smoothly.

Now he was on his feet, anger coursing through his veins.

"It is. It definitely is." Paul handed the report back to Luke. "Unfortunately, the client wasn't convinced and went to another construction company."

"That's not my fault." Luke looked at two months' worth of work he could toss into the trash. Firm policy required he put it in an archive to use as a reference for other projects but all he wanted to do was scrap it.

"Will this affect my promotion?" As much as Luke hated to ask, he knew he should.

Paul shook his head. "No. That's already decided."

Luke reminded himself to breathe. "What?"

"I got Frederika's memo about promotions before the client's email." Paul frowned as he snatched a page from the printer. "No one got promotions this time around."

The report in Luke's hand felt as if it was leaching acidic poisons right through his skin. All those hours, all those missed times with friends, with his fathers in the mountains. He couldn't get any of that back. He'd kept his focus on his promotion. Coming in early. Staying late. His reports kept getting better and better with lots of positive comments from clients and the team.

Maybe he ought to throw more than the report in the trash can. What was he doing all this for if it didn't help him get ahead?

As if Paul heard his thoughts, he handed him a second piece of paper.

"What's this?" Luke scanned the page. The four percent raise was good news. The shares of stock added to his benefits package were a happy surprise. But was it enough?

"I hope that eases the pain." Paul was trying to be nice.

He was a good guy, as fair a supervisor as he could get. Still, Luke wanted the title bump. He was still a business development assistant at the age of thirty. By now he had counted on being a business development associate.

"Yeah, of course, it does. Thanks." Luke scooped up the paperwork and shook hands with Paul before heading back to his cubicle. He should be grateful. The raise and added benefits were generous. Even better than last year's.

As he filed the rejected proposal, the aroma of popcorn wafting across the hall from the kitchen assaulted him.

Luke tossed the salary increase memo in his "In" box and looked at the pile of papers scattered in front of him. None of it looked as interesting as it did a few minutes earlier.

His phone, sitting next to his keyboard, pinged twice. He glanced at the screen and found three message notifications. A voicemail and a text, from Henri. One text from Frank.

He clicked on Henri's voicemail and could immediately hear the relief in his voice. "The hearing for the project has been postponed again. Thank God."

Are you able to come home Friday night? his text inquired.

Luke chuckled. But there was no happiness in him. He didn't owe Windsor-Douglas any more late Friday nights. They could have Monday through Thursday nights for the time being, but he was reclaiming his weekends for Henri and DeWayne. The hearing had been postponed twice, keeping them in suspense over their fate. Okay then, the Broadview Inn would get his Saturdays and Sundays until they beat back the enemy. Or, remembering DeWayne's observations, they decided to surrender.

The enemy included Amanda. He pictured the first time he

saw her with her golden curls and her snappy comments about his tennis. Memories of their last, angry encounter wiped the smile off his face.

See you around eight, he typed. *Do you have reservations?*

Yes. Happy Fourth of July! Henri's response was immediate and punctuated with a happy face and American flag emojis.

First good news of the day. His social media campaign was doing its job, letting people know the inn was still open for business.

Frank's message lifted his mood. *Are you free for lunch Wednesday? I have a meeting in Philadelphia at three. I'll catch an early train and meet you.*

Hard to pass on lunch with an old pal. Luke texted back, then made reservations for his favorite seafood restaurant on the Riverfront, an easy walk for both of them. Baltimorean Frank would have to get over a menu without his favorite seafood seasoning, Old Bay.

~ * ~

"They refuse to give in. Or at least Henri refuses. DeWayne says he's ready to pack up and move on." Luke took another pull on his beer as he and Frank waited for their lunch to arrive.

He tried explaining his parents' situation to some of his coworkers, but they were aghast to hear DeWayne and Henri were stopping progress. That they were willing to pass up cold hard cash for a broken old hotel—even if they had called it home for the past twenty years. His construction company colleagues were always eager to tear stuff down in their rush to build something new. Luke was glad finally to have somebody to talk to about this.

"That leaves you stuck in the middle." Frank retrieved a travel-size plastic bottle of J.O. Spice from his backpack and sprinkled it over his fries and crab cakes.

Luke forgot what he was talking about. "What's that?"

Frank handed over the shaker. "Similar to Old Bay, but I like it better."

"I didn't think you'd ever give up Old Bay."

Frank shrugged. "They both make a crab cake taste like it's supposed to taste." He bit into his sandwich and smiled. "This is a little less salty but has the same great heat." After he chewed a minute and swallowed, he put down the sandwich. "What do your dads want you to do?"

"Come home. That's all. I don't want to get stuck in between them. I understand both sides. Henri loves the place and considers it our home. DeWayne says he's ready to try something new. He's always been a lot more flexible—I guess from all those years in the Army." The more Luke talked about it, the less he knew what he wanted himself. Going home didn't mean the house by the lake. It meant Henri. It meant DeWayne.

Luke was beginning to believe he'd be happy if they found a place closer to Wilmington. He'd be able to visit them more often. But he didn't want Henri's heart broken. He'd never forget the last time it happened. Luke was a child then, but as assiduously as Henri tried, he couldn't hide his misery from his son.

A man now always filled with laughter, he never smiled in those dark days. Even his good-mornings and good-nights seemed labored, as if he wasn't sure it would be a good morning or a good night. Luke never wanted to see that look again.

"So, what are you going to do?"

"For now, go home and fight for Henri." If he was ambivalent before, he knew he meant it the minute he said it. He bit into his fish sandwich and it tasted almost as good as Henri's.

Frank dipped a french fry in ketchup and smiled. "I'm here if you need me."

"Yeah?"

"Yeah. I think you knew it all along. I knew you weren't going to let some smart-ass lawyer get the best of your dad."

Luke thought of the leggy blonde lawyer. He spit out her name. "Amanda."

Frank shook his head. "Julie says she really didn't know."

"It doesn't matter when she knew, she's still one of the people behind the sale of the inn." Luke shoved his plate away.

Frank leaned his elbows on the table, looking Luke in the eye. "Julie told me Amanda was beating herself up pretty bad over the way Memorial Day turned out. She likes you, you know?"

He chuckled but he wasn't amused. "Likes me? She lied to me."

"She feels bad about the hotel."

"Why should she? It's just business, she told me so

herself." Luke's lunch burned in his stomach.

"Look, Luke. She's not acting like it's just business. She's been crying every night to Julie. She told Julie she hates having to choose between work and you, but she doesn't have a choice."

The Memorial Day weekend really was a complete disaster. Each time Luke recalled those terrible moments, his heart hurt as if Amanda was stomping on it all over again. "Amanda knew all weekend and never said a thing." She lied to him. She betrayed his family. All while she was flirting with him.

"Hey, man. I'm sorry."

Luke didn't want to think about Amanda anymore. Ever. She was nothing to him. He shoved the memory of their kiss or two into the deep recesses of his mind and forgot about them, or he tried. To him she was no one but a lawyer working on a case that might evict him and his family from the inn they worked so tirelessly to make a success.

Time to put aside his hurt feelings and let reason take over. "It's okay. I've got enough to worry about with the inn's business. I'm not going to get friendly with my parents' enemy or whatever she is. All I need is for Henri to learn I was siding with hotel people."

"Your dad likes Amanda."

"He wouldn't if he knew who she works for."

"You didn't tell him?"

Shaking his head, he ran a hand through his hair. "I couldn't. I was afraid the betrayal would be too much."

"Maybe it'll settle down, your parents will be happy, and then you can give her a call."

"Amanda?"

"Who else? Her boss?"

"Never gonna happen." Luke chuckled. "Even if she comes over from the dark side, she still lives two states away and works ridiculous hours."

"So do you." Frank gestured to the waiter for a couple more beers.

"No more for me," Luke said, putting his hand out. "I have to work this afternoon."

"So do I." Frank checked his phone.

"Hey, where's your old flip phone?"

"Like it? Julie gave it to me. An early wedding present." Frank read the time. "First, I have to catch a train. I have half an hour until then. C'mon. Give me another chance to hire you."

"I'm not interested."

"In the beer or the job?"

"I'll take the beer."

After ordering another round, Frank focused on Luke. "But not the job?"

"I just got that raise I was expecting. I'm not ready to move." When the waiter returned with fresh drinks, Luke picked up his glass and saluted his friend. "Thanks."

Frank lifted his own. "Why won't you even consider the job? You aren't happy at McDonald's."

"It's Windsor-Douglas. I'm disappointed I didn't get the title bump. But the raise was too substantial to turn down." Luke frowned for a moment and then swallowed a gulp from his glass.

Frank sat back and stared at Luke. "Look at you. Your current job makes you miserable."

"It's work. It's not supposed to be fun."

"You're in a bad spot. Go someplace else. Try something different. Maybe you will make less money, but you'll be happy overall."

Nodding, Luke laughed. "You mean come work for you."

Frank picked up the last of his french fries. "What a good idea."

"Yeah. No. I don't know. For one thing, you can't afford me. Besides, I got the raise. I got the benefits. I even have a cubicle that smells like popcorn."

"Living the life, huh?"

Finished with his beer, Luke signaled the waiter for the check. "Time to go." He signed the check and got up to put on his sport coat. Before his arm was through the first sleeve, he stopped. "What you said makes sense."

Frank shouldered his backpack. "Did I hear you right?"

"Yes, you did." After he shrugged into his jacket Luke slapped his friend on the back. "I'm tempted by your offer, flattered really. But with Henri and DeWayne flipping out at the inn, I can't announce I'm moving to Baltimore and, oh by the way, could you come and help me move?"

"I'd help."

Putting his hands on his hips, Luke looked at Frank. "Yeah. Right. You have a wedding coming up. I'm sure your fiancée has you plenty busy."

"She'd understand."

"Mmmm hmmm." Then he continued in a high voice, "'Dear, I'm sorry I can't help with wedding planning today. Luke needs me to help move his couch.'" Then he lowered his voice to its normal register as he said, "Like that would go over well."

"Didn't you tell me the apartment came furnished?"

Luke punched him in the arm. "You know what I mean."

"In any case, she would understand if I wanted to help my best man."

"Thanks, Frank. I appreciate the offer but I think I'll stay in Wilmington.

He and Frank stopped at the entrance to the train platform. Frank shook Luke's hand. "If you're happy, I'm happy. I won't ask again. I've got a good prospect coming in next week who may work out just fine. Thanks for lunch. Next time you're coming to Baltimore, man."

After waving goodbye as Frank got on the train Luke turned toward his office. His phone pinged with a text from Henri. *The new hearing date has been set. July 16 at 1. Can you come?*

That meant Luke had a week to come up with enough heavy artillery to fight a developer and his well-paid lawyers. Including Amanda.

Chapter Eighteen
Meeting in Oakland

Amanda waited by the printer for the last of her new documents to finish. After spending all night reviewing the case, she now had until one o'clock to get to the county courthouse in Oakland, Garrett County's capital, more than a hundred miles away. Quin was already in her office, on a call with Mr. Lowrey, going over the same paperwork. Even with the hearing only hours away, she continued to hammer out a proposal to save the Broadview. For now, though, it had to wait.

Thanks to so many late nights, Amanda yawned again and again as she nervously drummed her fingers on the top of the printer.

This was her first appearance at a hearing, even an informal one. If that wasn't enough to worry her, she couldn't imagine how she would face Luke, what she would say, if he was there. Laying her hand on her stomach, she begged the butterflies in there to settle.

Showing up to the hearing room was going to be horrible. Her name didn't appear on a single piece of paper, but that didn't stop Luke from blaming her. She wondered if he told DeWayne and Henri she was working on the project. Or as they would interpret it, working against them.

After she collected the paperwork, she put on her suit jacket and snapped the document case shut. Hurrying to her car in the garage, she rehearsed what she would say when she saw the innkeepers.

Maybe they would understand. It was her hope they wouldn't take it personally.

The icy stare Luke gave her on Memorial Day was hard to

forget. She dreaded seeing it again.

All the way to Oakland, she practiced speeches she hoped might make Luke understand. Nothing sounded right. There was no way she could come up with the right words to assuage his anger.

The zoning hearing had been delayed twice so that nearly two months had passed since that wonderful but awful weekend. Not once in that time had she spoken to Luke but now she was bound to come face to face with him and his fathers.

Though she'd known nearly nothing about the project back then, she'd studied all the documents so much she now knew everything. Including how much money Luke's fathers were turning down if they didn't sell.

After parking in front of the county courthouse, she threw open the door of her car. Thunder rumbled overhead warning her of an approaching storm. She reached for her umbrella just as the rain started falling in sheets. She'd be soaked by the time she got inside.

Holding her document case close enough to keep it dry, she ran across the watery street and slick sidewalk into the beige brick building in front of the ornate domed courthouse. She closed her umbrella and shook off the rain wilting her perfectly tailored suit. More pressing was the need to shake off the worries of seeing Luke again. Would he even acknowledge her?

Her colleague, local attorney Heath Charles, a stocky man not much older than her, stood out in a brown suit as he chatted with a cluster of men clad in charcoal gray and dark blue.

He glanced her way as she stepped inside, rushed over, and thrust out his hand. "You must be Amanda. I was beginning to worry you wouldn't get here in time."

"You said the hearing was at one o'clock. It's noon now." Amanda's cheeks burned as a trickle of perspiration slipped between her shoulder blades. She was not only fighting a case of nerves, but the stifling hot air of the narrow hall.

Heath's smile transformed into a frown. "There's already quite a crowd. I knew not everyone favored the project, but I didn't expect this kind of opposition."

"Oh no." Amanda pictured all her work heading for the recycling bin. She wasn't completely disappointed by the vision.

A fighting spirit lit up her fellow attorney's eyes. "You never can tell with these sorts of meetings. Once they look over the plans and hear how we'll deal with the traffic and the runoff, they'll change their minds."

One thing Amanda knew was that she was prepared for every argument. Until late last night, she had pored over each one of the environmental concerns and studied the land use plans. There wasn't a county regulation or land use code she hadn't studied.

A young clerk came up behind them. "Mr. Charles? I found a meeting room for your group." The woman's running shoes were a silent contrast to the heels that clattered across the stone tile floor as Amanda and the men followed her to a fluorescent-lit, windowless conference room.

The air was stale with the smell of sweat but at least it was cooler than the crowded hall. Amanda sat at the end of the scarred wooden table while Heath sat at her right. A tall, silver-haired man with a friendly smile and a hint of local twang stretched out his hand and introduced himself as Ted Lowrey and his employees whose names Amanda immediately forgot.

They huddled over their drawings and went over details. The development team had thought of everything. Pretty things like the walkways and gardens, nitty gritty details such as parking, drainage, and runoff.

One of Mr. Lowrey's men, an environmental engineer, shared with the group a series of graphs and tables outlining possible concerns about the lakefront restaurant. Even though the lake was artificial—created in the 1920s as the result of a dam built to provide electricity to the region—water quality was bound to be an issue.

Amanda ran a cool hand over her aching forehead. She didn't dare admit how tired she was after her all-nighter. She needed to keep her head in the game and show her client and fellow lawyers that she was up to the task.

Giving her strength was the knowledge she held an ace up her sleeve. She hoped her idea of preserving the Broadview would find a home if opposition to the proposal grew rancorous.

Aware it might be a tough sell, she glanced at the drawings again.

Before she could gather the nerve to make her counter proposal, Heath glanced at the clock over the door. "Look at the time. We have to wrap this up."

Stuffing papers into his document case, he leaned over to Amanda. "I don't want to frighten you, but they can be tough on big city attorneys here. Hold your ground if they try to 'town' you out. Quin assured me you have everything under control."

Even as she squared her shoulders and took a deep breath, the butterflies began a new dance in her stomach. Amanda strode into the hearing room, nearly full, with dozens of people already registered to speak about the project. As she scanned the faces, she wondered how many were here to oppose it.

She raised a trembling hand to her chest as a storm of emotions ripped through her when her gaze fell on Luke next to his fathers. He was leaning back in a chair with his arms crossed across his chest. Henri and DeWayne sat as motionless as statues, not speaking to each other. They didn't even look her way. Luke glanced at her as she put her briefcase on the table where the developer and Heath already sat.

Vowing to remain resolute, she marched over to him. "Hello" was all she could say.

He didn't respond, though to her relief, DeWayne caught her gaze and nodded slightly. Still, Luke said nothing. She swallowed and straightened her shoulders while she waited for him to speak.

When he finally did, he practically spat out the words. "Thought you were just a junior associate helping out the partner."

Amanda put her hands up in mock surrender and shook her head.

She wasn't going to make a scene. Not in front of Mr. Lowrey and Heath. Instead, she sat in the empty chair next to Luke, hoping to appeal to his good sense. "Quin asked me to come today."

"Quin asked you to come today." He slumped in his chair like a petulant child.

She wondered if he was going to echo all her statements. "I'm helping Heath."

"You're helping Heath. You do know who Heath is, don't you?"

"Would you let me explain?" Amanda paused to take a deep breath and settle down. "I'm sorry. I'm not feeling well today." She put her hand to her head. He didn't look even the slightest bit sympathetic, with his arms crossed and a scowl so etched into his face she wondered if it was permanent.

When she was a kid, she loved *Perry Mason* and always imagined herself arguing a case like they did. She wanted to be Elle Woods in the last courtroom scene of *Legally Blonde,* smart and knowledgeable—but without the pink dress.

If Elle or Perry didn't let an upset stomach get them down, neither could she. She straightened up in her chair and looked Luke in the eye. When he set his jaw, Amanda knew she had no chance of winning him over. That was when it occurred to her it didn't matter.

In spite of everything, this was a big day for her and a nerve-wracking one. It was important she make a good impression on her client, on the local counsel, on the board now filing in and taking their seats at the bench marked with the county seal. Even though she was a young associate, she had a big job today. Quin, Mr. Lowrey, and his staff were counting on her.

"Quin asked me to fill in for her. Heath is local counsel. Do you know him?"

Luke nodded, the corner of one side of his lip twisted as if he was remembering something distasteful. "Everybody knows Heath. He was a big shot senior when I was a high school freshman."

"Oh, you do. He seems pretty well connected. When I got back to Pittsburgh after Memorial Day, Quin handed me the file—the whole file for the new resort—and told me to get up to speed on the project. Next thing I know, she's sending me to Oakland."

Amanda paused to see if she was making any inroads with Luke. He wasn't the one she needed to win over. Not today anyway. If anything, he was the guy on the other side of the case keeping this project from moving forward.

Those blue eyes, now looking worried and skeptical, had once invited her to get to know him, had asked her to allow him to hold and kiss her. Even if her head didn't want to remember, her heart did. For a wonderful moment in front of a fireplace, she once believed maybe she found love. Even in a nondescript county hearing room, her heart tripped at the sight of him.

Maybe she no longer had a chance to win over Luke. She intended to be sure the case was handled fairly, that Henri and DeWayne got a fighting chance to save their inn, and—most importantly—that her client got his project approved and built.

His expression still stony, he leaned on the arm of his chair and glared at her. "Look. Do you know what this has done to Henri and DeWayne? They're barely speaking to one another. Don't you dare let me see even a hint of triumph on your pretty little face." He pointed at her as if he was holding a weapon.

"Luke, no matter how this goes, I don't want you to lose your home."

"Yeah. Right." The skeptical edge to his voice was razor sharp.

She flinched, knowing there was nothing more to say.

"You go take care of your *big* case, Amanda Johnson. Don't worry about my family. We can take care of ourselves fine." Luke practically spit out the bitter words and then looked away.

His anger left her weak, unable to fight back. Yet if the damage was done, she could nothing to make things right. She sat there, uncomfortable in the silence.

"I'm sorry." She struggled to speak the words above a whisper.

"Yeah, a lot of good that will do." He got up as if he needed to get away from her and dug his hands into his pockets. "My poor Papa can't imagine what he'll do next. Hope you're happy."

He dismissed her with his gaze. Once so beautiful, his eyes were cold and cruel. Blood surged in her temples as she left to take her chair beside her client.

The zoning board chairman gaveled the hearing to order.

"Mr. Beaumont giving you a truckload of grief?" Heath's sympathetic expression surprised her.

Amanda shook her head. "Luke? Nothing I can't handle."

Chapter Nineteen
Pros and Cons

Luke stared at Amanda throughout the whole zoning hearing. The pretty woman he met Memorial Day weekend was now his opponent, and it made him furious.

She had the same head full of bouncy curls, the same full mouth as the woman he fell for, and yet something was different. She ignored him all afternoon, except for that brief, unpleasant conversation as soon as she entered the room. Instead of sweetness, she was all business. Instead of the friendly girl next door, she was a big city lawyer taking care of her powerful client.

It frosted him when Heath sat next to her. Luke remembered Heath and his take charge manner during school assemblies at Southern Garrett High School. When Luke was a freshman, Heath was the senior class president. After law school, he returned to the county to work at his father's law firm and made a name for himself quickly. A local big shot, he even reserved a regular table at Henri's restaurant.

Luke knew he shouldn't take Heath's attendance personally. He was an expert in these kinds of cases. Still, the way he leaned over to talk to Amanda, touching the sleeve of her blue jacket, was driving Luke crazy. Just another layer of betrayal.

Realizing he was torturing only himself, he chose to focus on the testimony of friends and experts, rather than the lawyers, opening his notebook to scribble note after note.

He was heartened as many questions arose about the project. Some people were skeptical. Some completely opposed the construction. Luke rejoiced with every new speaker. In the past few days, he asked a few questions of his own and made sure he talked to people around the community who tended to get excited by change. Even so, he didn't expect such high emotion.

A lepidopterist took the microphone to inform the panel that the section of Deep Creek Lake where the hotel would be located was one of the last pristine inlets on the thirty-nine thousand-acre reservoir. He described how the lake was the habitat for a striking yellow butterfly, *Papilio appalachiensis,* or the Appalachian Tiger Swallowtail, and warned runoff would endanger the ancient hemlocks at nearby Swallow Falls State Park.

Take that, Amanda. Luke didn't dare look over at her table.

Mr. Brown was sitting with his wife and the two other couples who already agreed to sell to the developer. His expression was dark with resentment. Opposition to the project might affect them too. It might even kill the whole plan before they received a single dime for the sale of their properties.

DeWayne watched his neighbor as the testimony continued. The man would be surprised to find out DeWayne was on his side. At breakfast earlier in the day, DeWayne tried to explain to Luke and Henri why they should sell. He held up a folder filled with the newspaper clippings he collected over the past year. "I don't want to stop progress. I'm not against building the hotel. It's just that, Henri..." His expression pleaded with his husband, who looked more stubborn than ever. "I do believe selling might be our best option."

Henri sniffed but said nothing and DeWayne went on, "Our friends are excited about the new hotel. They're looking forward to more customers at their own businesses. There are bound to be plenty of new jobs. How can we oppose that?"

Henri shook his head. "It doesn't matter. We shouldn't have to sacrifice everything for others. If that's what it takes to save our house, our family's legacy, then so be it."

DeWayne threw up his hands in surrender. "I don't see it the way you do, Henri."

Now, even as neighbors seemed to be rallying to their side—so many rose to talk about traffic and noise and pollution—the chasm between Luke's two fathers continued to widen.

Like Henri, Luke wasn't ready to admit defeat. Amanda's expression showed her own desire to win. He was glad they never got the chance to meet across a tennis net. Her game face—surely the face of an almost-Olympic athlete—was fierce.

She straightened her suit jacket the way Emily always did. Holding a pencil to her lips, she was ready to jot a note as each person rose to ask a question or make a statement. Nothing fazed Amanda. Her expression didn't change. She never looked away from the people testifying.

"The restaurant's location is sure to cause damage to the lake," an environmentalist explained.

Luke sat back and drank in the man's words as he continued on about water quality and harm to the aquatic life. The developer grew animated, leaning over to speak sharply to Heath. Even if Luke couldn't hear a word Heath or the developer said, the opposition's words had obviously touched a nerve.

Henri tapped Luke's elbow, his face glowing. "You know that restaurant is supposed to be built on our land."

DeWayne leaned forward to look at both of them. "Don't get your hopes up yet. The developer can go back and make changes after this meeting."

Henri's head swiveled in anger. "Don't say that. We've got to have hope."

"I wish I did." DeWayne glanced over at Luke and shook his head. He understood. One father was already packing his stuff. The other was digging in his heels.

Luke couldn't wait to get out of there, a wish that was soon granted. After the environmentalist finished, the meeting was adjourned until mid-August.

The developer stood to shake the hands of his attorneys. "Good work, Mr. Charles, Miss Johnson. I'll be in touch after I talk to my team tomorrow. Looks like we have to make a few changes."

Though Luke expected the man to wear the distraught expression of a loser, he didn't. Nor did he look like the enemy as he stretched his hand toward DeWayne and Henri and introduced himself. "I want you to know I understand how you feel about our plans. When I offered to buy your land, I thought you'd jump on it. Same as your neighbors."

Henri vaulted to his feet, his face red with ire. "How could you know anything about us? We've never even met before today."

Ted Lowrey chuckled. "That's true. We haven't. To tell you the truth, I didn't know you had reopened the old place."

DeWayne stood and put his hand on Henri's shoulder. "You've got to understand, Mr. Lowrey. This has been Henri's life's work for twenty years. This is our home."

"When I was a small boy, I used to go there with my parents. It was their favorite place to celebrate family milestones." Lowery pulled over a chair from the lawyers' table, sat down, and leaned his elbows on the armrests. "I grew up in this town. Learned to swim and sail in the lake. These are my neighbors and friends too. I saw an opportunity to build something new on your part of the lake. A good place to visit and a good place to work. I'll be honest. I want your property. It's a beautiful spot. But if you don't want to sell, I'll build the hotel on the other lots and let you be."

Next, he rose and buttoned his jacket. "Even so, I'm hoping you'll reconsider. I want you to know I'll do what's right for Deep Creek. These people raised plenty of objections, and I will make sure we don't build anything that will cause harm to the lake."

Henri shook Mr. Lowrey's hand. "I'm sorry you want to tear our inn down but I do appreciate your honesty."

DeWayne nodded. "We'll discuss it and be in touch."

Henri waited until the developer was out of earshot before he blew up at DeWayne. "Discuss it? I will do no such thing. There's nothing more to discuss."

As they left the hearing room, Henri handed the keys to Luke, marched through the blinding rain to the car, then climbed into the back seat.

DeWayne clenched his jaw so tight Luke could almost hear him grinding his teeth.

How was he ever going to bring them back together? This was bad, maybe the worst he'd ever experienced.

By the time they turned onto the road to the inn, rainwater was rushing across the pavement and filling the roadside ditches. A gust of wind bent trees low to the ground until branches yielded and broke, a flutter of leaf and wood scattering on the street.

He pulled the car onto the inn's driveway and stopped short. The corner of the porch roof lay smashed around the building, a branch of the ancient oak on top of it.

Henri leaned over the front seat and joined them in staring at the damage.

DeWayne sighed heavily. "I've been meaning to have that

old tree looked at. I knew it might be trouble." He ran his big hand over his face. "It's going to cost a fortune to fix that porch."

To Luke, it didn't look like repairs would require more than some wood, nails, and paint. "Maybe we can do it ourselves."

"We can make the porch look nice, but I'll need to call in an arborist. That branch may be only the beginning of our trouble with that tree. We might have to have it taken down. I can't imagine what that will cost. But I'm sure it's something we can't afford."

They dashed from the car, through the rain, and into the house. Henri went for towels and DeWayne stared out the window at the damage, a look of worry stretching his face. Luke stood beside him and wiped rain from his hair.

Henri handed them each a towel and then joined them. "It won't be difficult to repair."

"Henri, this is bad. It's everything, the roof, the columns, even the floor. And then we have to look at the tree. We need expert help, and we haven't got the money."

Speechless, Henri stared first at DeWayne then at Luke before staggering to the sofa.

DeWayne turned away from the window to sit beside him. "I was going over the books this morning. Even without the storm damage, we are struggling."

He paused long enough to make Luke worry. DeWayne was a plain-spoken man who rarely minced words. What he planned to say must be bad.

He looked at Luke and Henri then put his hand on his husband's shoulder. "This might be the final nail in the coffin, Henri. We can't afford to keep the inn open."

Henri recoiled as if he'd been bitten. "What are you saying?"

"We've been losing money, Henri." DeWayne sighed, and his broad shoulders slumped as if he was admitting defeat.

"But last year…"

"The inn just about broke even last year. We didn't raise our rates although costs went up. Then we had to replace the water heater and get you a new stove. You remember what that cost."

Henri nodded, opened his mouth to speak but stopped himself.

"This year's only been worse. An empty inn on Memorial Day and the following weekend cost us plenty." He tapped Luke's arm. "Your work on our website helped, son. But it wasn't enough."

Luke didn't want to believe it. "But Henri told me reservations are up."

DeWayne shook his head. "We've gotten a few more. The truth is, Luke, we aren't getting business like we used to. Even dinner reservations are way off."

Henri's face creased with sadness. "It's going to rebound, DeWayne."

Scrubbing his face with his hand, DeWayne then shook his head again. "No, I'm afraid it won't."

Such a dire assessment left a sour pain in Luke's stomach. He sank onto the chair across from his fathers, trying to understand. How could it be that bad? They worried they wouldn't make it to the Fourth of July, but they did. Surely there would be plenty of business between now and Labor Day. Then the fall, with all the leaves changing color, was always busy. His mind went into overdrive as he considered how to save the inn. If he could.

First, he needed to know something. "DeWayne, how bad is it? Really."

"We aren't going to make it past summer. There are outstanding bills for the tennis court remodel, and the heating system needs repairs. Raising menu prices isn't an option in this economy, even though food and fuel prices are skyrocketing. Every weekend, we're losing money. Now this."

DeWayne leaned back and sighed. "I looked in the faces of everyone who came to the hearing today and saw a few supporters. Mr. Yoder, and some of the others have said they want to help us. But the rest want the big hotel with all those guests. They're seeing dollar signs."

Henri clasped his hands in his lap. "They're convinced we're as good as stealing money from them." He searched his husband's face. "You don't have any hope at all, do you?"

DeWayne smiled a sad smile. "I know you can't imagine life without your kitchen."

Henri closed his eyes and waited.

"Henri, I'm willing to try to keep it open, but I want you to remember we may not make it."

Henri nodded at DeWayne. "*Merci*. I mean that."

Luke realized he hadn't taken a breath since DeWayne delivered the bad news. Even if the inn's future was in doubt, even if it was hemorrhaging money, he held onto a hope the old place had some life left.

"I'm glad those environmental guys said all those things," DeWayne added.

Luke was puzzled. "You are?"

"They raised some pretty big questions. Better to find answers now, rather than after the new hotel is built and trouble starts."

"You're already talking as if the hotel is going to be built no matter what." Henri stood. "I don't have time to worry about that now. I have guests coming tomorrow and dinner to plan for the weekend. Maybe we're going to be here for only a few more months, but until we're gone, I've got work to do."

He raced toward the kitchen. But instead of the usual sounds of clattering pots and pans, the room stayed quiet.

"I better go talk to him." DeWayne rose from the sofa and ruffled Luke's hair. "He's probably in there sobbing like a baby."

Until that moment, Luke had almost been sure they could win. The environmentalists and their neighbors raised so many questions. Their concerns, he hoped, might stop the project or at least delay it. Even the developer admitted he was willing to leave the Broadview alone and build on the land he already was buying.

Now, though, it looked like none of it mattered. If DeWayne's figures were right, the inn would soon be shuttered. Maybe it was time to face facts.

Luke didn't like it, but Amanda was going to win. The idea didn't remind him of the pretty girl with the golden curls. Instead, he remembered Emily in her trim blue suit, tossing her ring on the kitchen counter, a curt goodbye ending their engagement. The cold pierced him just as it did that day.

Chapter Twenty
A Liar and a Traitor

Listening to the sounds of the spirited conversation building in the kitchen was painful. The sense of loss deep in Luke's soul couldn't be worse if a moving van arrived at their front door. From everything DeWayne said it was only a matter of time before the truck really did show up and take their stuff away.

Frozen in his seat, Luke couldn't get used to hearing DeWayne and Henri argue. It was harder to take than the possibility of losing their home. To his relief, it didn't last long.

"Fine." DeWayne shoved open the kitchen door so hard it slammed into the wall.

Henri followed after him. "Watch it. While we still have reservations on the books, we need the house to be intact."

DeWayne threw up his hands and stormed upstairs as Henri returned to the kitchen to mutter and rattle cabinet doors.

Luke moped alone in a quiet, frosty parlor. This was not what he expected. Or hoped for.

He went behind the reservation counter and looked at the books. A couple of rooms were reserved for the weekend. The dining room would be full on Saturday. People were coming back. At least for now. He looked ahead and found healthy bookings for August. Maybe DeWayne miscalculated. The leaf-peepers always came in droves in late September and October. They'd be booking soon. Maybe, by then, the future would look brighter.

Except DeWayne sounded like he was ready to close up the place.

Luke collapsed onto the sofa and stared into the cold, dark fireplace. It troubled him to imagine DeWayne and Henri moving away. Even if DeWayne's dire predictions were right, he was sorry the situation was driving a wedge between the two of them.

Luke's conversation with Amanda at the farmers' market echoed in his thoughts. She surprised him when she said the power of money changes people. Sure, he got that when he looked at Mr. Brown and the other neighbors who now saw DeWayne and Henri as hindrances to their fortunes.

Was money changing the two men he loved the most?

The phone in his back pocket vibrated. Expecting a call from work, he cleared his throat and sat up.

Instead, it was a text from Amanda. *Can we talk? I'm on your front porch.*

Luke leapt off the couch. The last person he wanted to see. His breath became ragged, and he considered dashing into the kitchen and hiding, anything to avoid her. Henri must need his help. Or should he go talk to DeWayne? Luke should get his laptop, answer the emails piling up since the morning, finish looking over his to-do list.

He knew he was going to do none of that. He was caught. Amanda was waving at him through the big front window.

There was no way he wanted to talk to her. Even so, he pasted on a smile and gestured for her to come in. Better to listen to whatever she wanted to say—it wasn't going to be good—and send her on her way.

She entered, stopping to examine the damage to the porch. "What a mess."

"Tell me about it. It just happened."

She strode toward him, her hand outstretched. "Thanks for seeing me."

Reluctantly, he shook her hand, but he decided he wasn't going to notice how beautiful she looked in her business suit. He refused to look at her long, strong legs, or gaze into those expressive eyes.

"Luke—"

"Amanda—"

Both started to talk at the same time, and Amanda giggled nervously.

"You shouldn't be here." He took advantage of the pause as she gathered her thoughts, or maybe her nerve. "You've done enough already."

"I don't blame you for hating me. I look like a liar and a traitor." She held out her hands, palms up. "Please, listen to me."

"This should be good." He gestured to a pair of chairs by the front window, carefully avoiding the sofa by the fireplace. He'd gotten in trouble with her there once already. Why did she have to look so beautiful? Why did he have to remember how wonderful her kisses were? He clenched the arms of the chair, trying to steady his heart.

Her hand trembled as she drew a stack of papers from her briefcase. He was glad she was nervous. Maybe it was a sign she was afraid of losing this case.

Good.

Perhaps his anger was misplaced. Even so, the woman sitting beside him represented everything bad happening around him. If he had to be angry at someone, and he did, it was going to be Amanda.

"I'm sorry we're in this position. I want you to know that. Even if you don't believe me." She spread a copy of the architect's plan for the new hotel across the coffee table. There were all kinds of notations on it. In a spot near the western edge of the site—at present, their property—she had drawn in a big square near the proposed site for a spa and pool. It looked as if she drew it right where the inn now stood. "I know your parents haven't decided to sell. If they do… Well, let me show you what I've been thinking about."

As if she could do anything once Henri and DeWayne sold the inn. She wasn't an architect, just some low-level lawyer. He was even more steamed, his patience sorely tested. Though he didn't want to see any more, he set his jaw and waited.

"One of the objections the conservationists have to this project is how close this part of the project is to the lake." She pointed to the proposed restaurant.

"So? What's your point?"

"I have an idea. But I need your help if we're going to save the Broadview."

"Save it? What for? That won't do us any good once we aren't living here, now would it?"

She shook her head. "I don't know. When you took me on a tour, you showed me how beautiful this place is. We can still save the inn. I came by now because I wanted to talk to you but also, I wanted another chance to look at the diary."

"Sure." He waved his hand. "Go ahead. I have to warn you though, if Henri and DeWayne decide to sell—and it looks like, oh lucky you, they are going to—they won't care what happens to the inn. Tear it down, burn it down, keep it. They'll be gone, twenty years of dedication reduced to a memory."

Amanda sighed. "Oh, don't be so dramatic. They'll be millionaires able to live anywhere they want."

"They will be homeless with no income."

She perched on the edge of her chair and rolled her eyes at his ridiculous remark. "Work with me, Luke. You have a viable business here. With a well-deserved reputation and a lengthy history of success. I don't know if Henri would want to work for someone else, but I hope, maybe, he'd consider it."

"I doubt it." So now the hotel was going to trade on Henri and DeWayne's success. Luke didn't understand why she was bothering to tell him this.

"I haven't talked to anybody else about my idea. Quin has been so preoccupied she hasn't had time to listen. Heath put me off when I raised it after the hearing today. But I believe Mr. Lowrey will be interested. He's the developer. You met him."

"He's only looking for ways to make a profit."

Amanda huffed. "I heard him tell you he wants to do the right thing. This community is his home too, you know."

Luke was running out of patience. Whatever she was planning still left his family without a home. "Well, it will only be ours for a few more months."

She stretched her hands toward him across the table. Even if she pleaded, he wasn't softening. "Luke, this could be our chance to save the inn. Your home."

No, he wasn't going to yield, but he might as well listen to what she had to say. After all, she was trying to prove that underneath her proper, well-fitting suit was a woman with a heart. He was forced to admit that it did matter to him that she wanted to do what was right.

He also needed to defend his parents. "And this will benefit Henri and DeWayne, how?"

"If the inn is declared to have some historic significance,

its value could increase which would make it worth saving. Right now, please forgive me for this, it's no more than an impediment worthy of being demolished."

Ouch. That hurt.

"There are still a lot of ifs, but if we can get approval, if the building is structurally sound, if there isn't a lot of asbestos, maybe we'll have to get the kitchen up to code and figure out bathrooms, electrical upgrades, sprinklers, and smoke detectors, if—"

"That *is* a lot of ifs. Where are you going with this?"

"I told you. I'm going to propose to Mr. Lowrey that they restore this beautiful building."

"Wait. Isn't this a little above your pay grade?"

Amanda laughed. "It's not in my job description at all. It has nothing to do with real estate law—but it has everything to do with helping my client."

"Oh." Now he knew who she was standing up for.

Fed up, he made a move to stand, to walk away from her crazy proposal. Then she captured his gaze with those big eyes of hers, as if to plead with him to let her finish. He re-settled in his seat.

"The environmental review is probably going to mean the lakeside restaurant will have to move. If that's so, then the inn won't have to be torn down. They could turn it into a museum—that's why I want to see the diary—or a honeymoon or family cottage or…I don't know. That's far above my pay grade."

Her gaze trained on him, he didn't want to admit she might be onto something. He was speechless.

"I'm not getting paid to do this. My job is to prepare the paperwork in my briefcase. I fell in love with this inn on Memorial Day weekend." A blush bloomed on her cheeks, a beautiful contrast to the all-business look she was going for. It was enough to make him smile.

"You really didn't know my home was part of the case you were working on?"

"Honestly, I didn't. I never saw this drawing until Quin called me into her office when I went back. I've been working on contracts for the sale of your neighbors' property. Even though I knew our client was planning a big project, I wasn't aware of the whole scope until I went over it all with Quin. If she hadn't mentioned it in an email while I was here, I would have come and gone blissfully unaware of my own involvement. I wanted to tell you on Memorial Day but, how could I? I didn't intend to lie to you or betray you." She rose and walked toward the corner cabinet. "Now, may I take a look at the diary? I want to see if I can find any clues about the girl who kept it."

What could it hurt? He went to the cabinet and opened it for her. The smell of the old journal assaulted his nose right away.

"It doesn't smell any better, does it?" She wrinkled her nose and held the leather book at arm's length.

Its new home in a drier, brighter location had changed the book. The pages now seemed more brittle and curled more at the edges. Fragments of ancient paper fluttered away as Amanda opened the diary.

Leafing through, she stopped at the entry about President Cleveland. "I couldn't wait to look again. I was beginning to think I dreamed it existed at all."

She resumed scanning the book. Was it curiosity or was it attraction that made him want to get closer to her? Even if the diary smelled like rot and age, Amanda smelled fresh and floral. He breathed in her scent as though he couldn't get enough of it.

Pay attention. The pages looked too water-damaged or faded for Luke to make out a thing worth mentioning. She worked to tease the last pages apart and a few yielded their secrets, but none of the entries were as interesting as the one about the president.

Except perhaps the last one. Amanda gently nudged a page stuck on the back cover. It tore at the corners but then pulled away, revealing a curling, girlish script that trailed down the page.

"Hey…what's this?" She studied the handwriting and then giggled.

"What's so funny? It's only names."

"It's something little girls do all the time. Even I did it when I got a crush on a boy. No, you wouldn't get it."

"Get what?"

She read the names on the page. "Mrs. Alexander Prince. Rosalind Smith Prince. Mrs. Rosalind Smith Prince. Mrs. Rosalind S. Prince. Mr. and Mrs. Alexander Prince." It was even decorated with curlicues, hearts, and flowers.

"Don't you see?" She leaned toward him with the open book. "Now we have the name of the girl who wrote about the president. Plus another name."

"So?"

When Luke looked at her with confusion, Amanda chuckled. "Little girls dream about their weddings and their married names. Back then, every girl took her husband's name and sometimes they would practice writing them. Apparently, our little Rosalind was in love with a boy named Alexander."

"Nope. Sorry, still don't understand what you're getting at."

"A young girl named Rosalind wrote in this diary. Maybe she wasn't a child. She might have been a teenager or a young woman when she wrote these last pages—maybe even when she saw the president. I wonder if she married Mr. Prince and lived happily ever after. Maybe we can find her—or at least her great-great-granddaughter. It's a stretch but it might be worth it."

Luke wanted to believe it was something. Even so, the image of his fathers' pain and worry—not to mention the way they stormed off in opposite directions earlier—made that nearly impossible. Should he be lured into what might be a wild goose chase? With Amanda?

If it could help Henri and DeWayne, yes.

She laid the diary down, brushed dust off her fingers, then straightened her jacket. A simple gesture, unimportant unless the person observing it was Luke. It was a habit of Emily's, a simple adjustment she made to punctuate a statement. The last time he saw her do it, she broke their engagement. Before she turned on her sensible two-inch heels and strode to the door.

His heart thudded in his chest. He couldn't trust the pretty woman with the yellow curls standing next to him. She was only another of the high-powered women he fell for and lost.

"It sounds like a good plan, but I don't see a place in it for me. Or my fathers." He stood as if he was ready to go. He wanted to be the powerful one this time. "Take a picture of the diary pages if you want. I'm not interested in your idea." He held out his hand. "I wish you luck."

She looked puzzled, hurt. "I was hoping…well. Yes, I understand." She nodded and snapped a photo of the page full of fantasy signatures and another of the entry about President Cleveland's visit. Then she took her time gathering her papers, folding the drawing, and tucking everything she brought back in her briefcase.

He waited until she clicked the case shut, stood, then smiled. He wished she hadn't done that. The business-like smile of an executive, it meant the end of everything.

"What's that smell? It's wonderful."

"Henri's cooking dinner. We still have a business to run, at least tonight."

Amanda recoiled, as if his cold tone burned her. He steeled himself, trying to retain his anger. Now was not the time to weaken.

"Oh, of course." She glanced at her watch. "I better go. I have a long drive ahead of me."

"Safe travels." He held the door open until she maneuvered her car onto the driveway and sped away.

The room was quiet now, but her fragrance, light and flowery, filled the air. He had kept his cool, stayed strong. Yet he felt as empty as the room, unsure what he had proven to her or even to himself.

In the kitchen, Henri dropped a pan and swore. It was enough to remind Luke he needed to protect his family. He better go find out if his papa wanted his help.

He found Henri staring out the window, an ear of Silver Queen corn in his hand.

"What do you see, *mon père?*" He leaned against the counter next to his father and followed his gaze. The view wasn't remarkable. A narrow patch of grass, thin and weedy, and a tall stand of evergreens.

Henri shook his head. "Nothing, really. I was thinking about how many times I have looked out this window. Your swing set used to be right there where I could watch you."

Luke knew his father mixed up his memories when he was feeling low. "No, it wasn't. After we came here, you decided not to get one. You said I was too old for a swing set by then. I was. I wanted a skateboard."

"Oh yes. Did I get you one?" Henri responded without taking his attention from the view.

Luke wrapped his arm around his father's shoulders and grinned. "Oh, Papa, you must remember. When I asked, you said, and I quote, 'On these mountains? Over my dead body.' Thank goodness for DeWayne. He finally talked you into it."

Next Luke knew Henri was going to say Ana would sit on one swing watching him go higher and higher on the other. That did happen but at the park in New York City. Since he loved the New York swings, Henri planned to put one beside the inn—until he realized his little boy was growing up.

Henri chuckled. "Yes, that's right. Funny how I have this memory of you on a swing set, your mother sitting beside you." Tears came to his eyes, and he pinched the bridge of his nose to make them stop. He always did that too.

"Papa, I remember. At the corner park near our apartment. I remember."

Henri collapsed into his arms. "I shouldn't feel like this. I wish I felt the way DeWayne does. He's ready to move. All I can think of is how sad I will be at seeing an important part of our family legacy bulldozed away."

He stopped talking long enough to sniffle. Then he braved a smile for Luke before picking up his knife. Dinner would be simple tonight. Local tomatoes and corn and roast chicken. Without guests to feed, Henri put aside his elaborate menus.

Finally he continued in a stronger, braver voice, "I know it all makes sense. I'm sure everything will work out. We'll find a place closer to you. Start over. Start on a new adventure."

Luke took his place beside him to shuck the corn. "Do you think you'd like to come to Delaware?"

Henri shook his head. "It's a nice area. Lots of tourists. Maybe we can find an inn to run in the Brandywine Valley. I'd like that."

Luke was proud of Henri even as he struggled to look beyond life at the Broadview. The world they built was coming apart, and there he was rinsing strands of silk from ears of creamy white corn.

Luke found it difficult to believe there was little time left for the inn. In the few weeks that remained, the inn would be busy, thank goodness. One last busy autumn, when Deep Creek Lake, and the Broadview, looked their best.

After that, if DeWayne's numbers were right, the inn would close for the season.

And maybe forever.

Henri put the chicken in the oven and hugged his son. "You're a good boy."

"What prompted that?" Luke held his father at arm's length, sad his father didn't have his usual smile.

"When you were a toddler, Ana told me how you liked to stay close to her. She often was afraid of tripping over you, to tell the truth. You always wanted to help. She'd let you dry the tops of pans, open the junk mail, and stir the lemonade with the big wooden spoon."

"I don't remember that."

"You don't? Come to think of it, how would you? You must have been two or three. I was standing here watching you with the corn, and I thought of Ana. And the dear sweet boy she never saw grow up."

He stopped, trying to brook the tears that threatened. "Papa…"

"She'd be very proud of you here now, *mon fils*."

"I always hope so."

"I am proud of you too." He pulled Luke into another bear hug, and Luke, breathing in the warm cooking smells that always enveloped his father, hung on tight. He wished with all his might he could take away Henri's heartache.

"*Je t'aime, Papa.*"

"*Je t'aime, Luc.*"

"Can a non-Frenchman get in on the love?" DeWayne leaned against the door jamb, a tentative smile on his face.

"*Mais oui, mon amour.*" Henri held out a hand to his husband. "You are an honorary Frenchman always."

The three of them hadn't taken part in a group hug in quite a while. Once common when Luke was a child, he refused to join in when he turned into a stubborn teenager. Today, Henri needed it. Maybe DeWayne needed it too. Luke knew it made him feel better.

Chapter Twenty-One
Return to the Falls

Amanda had expected Luke to see it her way. Wiping her cheeks and sniffling, she took off down the driveway as if she couldn't get away from the inn fast enough. She refused to look in the rearview window even once until she turned back onto Route 495. She'd been a fool, and she cringed at such humiliation.

After Amanda drove onto Route 219, she realized she was going the wrong way. Though it wasn't a big deal, it was sure evidence she was losing her cool. She slammed her hand on the steering wheel and maneuvered the car off the road to check her GPS. That's when she saw the sign for Swallow Falls.

She couldn't drive back to Pittsburgh now. Her head was pounding. Her hands were shaking, and she couldn't stop the tears.

Seeing Luke again was a bad idea. Even though her attraction to him was strong, even overpowering, her job made it impossible to be near him.

She didn't want his family to lose their home. She didn't want to take away Henri's kitchen. More important to her, though, she needed to do her job. She had to represent the developer who hired her.

If that meant losing her chance with Luke, so be it.

Amanda leaned on her steering wheel and cried bitter tears. She hated seeing those nice people lose their house, their business. It shouldn't matter to her. She had a responsibility to her client, to the law. That needed to be her first priority.

Seeing Luke again had left her troubled. He resented her, with good reason, and maybe even hated her. Those blissful days in May when she wondered if she'd found the man she might like to spend her life with seemed like a dream. Yet, as angry as he was, she yearned to find a way back to him. Maybe saving the inn would do it.

For a split second, she considered resigning from the firm. Laying a cool hand against her hot forehead, she closed her eyes and realized how insane that would be. It had taken years of long hours to get where she was.

Maybe this moment was awful, but she'd forget. She'd move on. So would Luke. They'd both find happiness somewhere else. With someone else.

Yes. That's what would happen.

Taking a deep breath, Amanda wiped her cheeks and put her car in gear. Desperate to calm her frazzled nerves, even if she couldn't fix her wounded heart, she steered toward the park.

A stroll in the cool dark forest would help. She yearned for its serenity.

It only took a few minutes to get her back to the tall green hemlock forest. Even this late, even after all the rain, the park was busier than on her last visit. The parking lot was full of cars. Groups of people clustered around the rustic tables for late afternoon picnics. Beyond the chatter and the laughter, the waterfall thundered in the distance.

Though the hike to the falls wasn't far, after the thunderstorm the path was bound to be muddy. Even if she couldn't change from her blue linen suit, her pumps would have to go. She tossed them in the back seat and snagged the sneakers from her gym bag. They were a lot more sensible, better for climbing around roots and jumping over puddles.

Focusing on her feet might be silly, but it did distract her from thoughts of Luke and the inn. She wiped her tears and turned down the path to Muddy Creek Falls. It was cool under the trees, quieter than she expected, almost empty. Only a few birds twittered above her. The sounds of other visitors faded away as she neared the falls. The roar of rushing water grew louder, drawing her to it.

Amanda gulped in the clean air that soothed her pounding heart. The last time she was here she was celebrating with friends, even worrying needlessly that she might lose her friend once she was married. Today she was aching over something she had lost. Luke. She didn't have a claim on him and yet she hoped as she stood on the inn porch, they might have a future. Her solution wasn't perfect, but it would preserve his family's home. It would always be a place they could come to and remember.

That was important, wasn't it?

While she leaned over the railing overlooking the waterfall crashing down the rocks, a hint of wood smoke reminded her of that terrible day when fire took her childhood home. Perhaps she should have told Luke about it, though how could she? In the midst of such grief, who wants to hear someone else's sad tale of woe?

This time, however, the memory made her think of the Broadview. Even though Luke and his parents weren't witnessing a fiery blaze taking everything from them, it had to be as painful.

Amanda resolved to find a way to convince her client to save the inn and spare Luke, Henri, and DeWayne such pain. That would be something.

She strolled down the same path she walked with Julie and the bridesmaids. What a happy group, as they giggled from Muddy Creek Falls to Swallow Falls. Hannah's toast to Julie, so sweet, echoed in Amanda's thoughts. 'May she find peace and love in the arms of the man she has chosen.' Someday, she hoped, she'd have what Hannah wished for the bride.

This time Amanda thought of Luke, as she stopped to look back at the falls and dried a new round of tears.

In spite of his angry expression, she'd told him she had fallen in love with the inn. Maybe Luke didn't want her help, but the inn itself needed her.

Yes, it needs me.

Imagining the place as brightly colored as DeWayne and some past owner once painted it, she pictured the Victorian beauty serving as a bridge between the new modern resort and the old fashioned days when tourists came by rail.

A president decided to bring his bride there during their honeymoon. Shouldn't the inn be part of the future instead of a shadow from the past?

Amanda quickened her pace. With or without Luke, she needed to put together a presentation that made the Broadview part of Mr. Lowrey's plan. How? Why? She didn't yet have the answers. So she still had a lot of work to do. A. Lot. Of. Work.

She wasn't tired anymore. Instead a new energy flowed

through her.

Luke doesn't need me? Well, then, fine. The inn does. Someone has to speak up for it.

That someone was Amanda, and she was going to give it everything she had.

~ * ~

Quin clicked through the presentation for a second time. Amanda smoothed her slacks and shifted from foot to foot. Her toes ached inside her pointy-toed stilettos, making her wish she had worn flats today. Quin was famous for her keen eye and sharp critiques, so waiting for her comments was nerve-wracking.

Amanda took it as a good sign when Quin went through the slides a third time, stopping at the photos of the diary entry.

She studied the picture for a few minutes before looking up. By then, Amanda had calmed herself. "Are you sure this is true? It might be no more than a little girl's flight of fancy."

"We don't have any firm records to confirm the story. It does fits into the history." Amanda was not going to be deterred. "Grover Cleveland got married at the White House and took his bride to Deep Creek Lake for their honeymoon. The inn was nearby—and who knows how Grover and Frances spent their days? It's not impossible they went to afternoon tea at the Broadview Inn. Maybe they met friends there. Besides, what little girl imagines a president coming to visit? If they were anything then like they are now, they'd be more likely to imagine fairies or princesses than presidents of the United States."

"True." Quin chuckled. "Tell me, though. Why go to all this trouble?"

Amanda took a seat in front of Quin's desk. She told her about her overwhelming grief when her childhood home burned. "I hate how sad the innkeepers are at the prospect of losing their inn."

"Have you talked to them?" Quin removed her reading glasses to listen.

"I spoke with Henri and DeWayne's son, Luke. He wasn't much interested. Though he did let me look at the diary again."

"It's an interesting idea. But I'm not sure if Ted will go for it. It could mean a lot of expense and delays."

"I hope it will be worth it in the end. Something Mr.

Lowrey said at the meeting convinced me he might like this idea. He said he wanted to do the right thing for Deep Creek Lake. He talked about how he grew up in the area and cared about the lake. I admire him for that."

"Ted is one of the good guys." Quin looked through the presentation one more time and grinned. Amanda breathed a long sigh of relief.

"It's a start, anyway." Quin's assessment encouraged Amanda that she might be on the right track. "We have a meeting in a few minutes. After we talk, I want you to show him your presentation the same way you showed me. It might solve our problems." Quin smiled. "Except one, of course."

Amanda wondered what she forgot.

"The owners still haven't agreed to sell."

Oh, that. That *was* a big problem.

Two hours later, Mr. Lowrey shook Amanda's hand. "Miss Johnson, your presentation is very well done. It's a good idea. But I don't believe it's the right idea. It's expensive, and my plans really have no use for that old barn of a building." He clicked through her presentation again. "I'm really not convinced. Your argument for the inn's historic value is flimsy at best."

"Thanks for considering it, sir." Amanda put on a brave smile even as her heart thudded to a stop. "I was in that inn recently, and it would be a shame to lose it. Especially with its history."

"It's a lovely spot but its time is over, I'm afraid." Mr. Lowrey shook her hand before turning to Quin to discuss next steps.

With disappointment filling her, Amanda collected her laptop and notes and rushed from Quin's office. Tossing her things on her already messy desk, she slammed the door and threw herself into her chair. She turned away from her failure of a proposal and closed her eyes.

Maybe I'm wrong. Maybe I should give up. But I still think there has to be a way to save the inn by the lake.

Chapter Twenty-Two
A Time for Change

Monday morning, eight-thirty. The normal starting hour. And today, the traditional hour to get fired. Luke held his head in his hands.

"It's not a good fit anymore," Paul had told him.

What the hell did that mean?

Luke needed to get away as quickly as possible. Paul had already packed his stuff for him. It wasn't much, a couple of pens, a dark green mug with "Deep Creek Lake" printed in gold letters, and a book on graphic design. He couldn't take his laptop, not even take copies of his proposals with him.

Paul shook his head when Luke asked. "They're company property, I'm afraid."

"Even though it's all my work?" Luke needed something to show at interviews.

Paul shrugged.

Might as well get going. With a piercing ache between his eyes, Luke picked up his box of stuff—not much for three years of sixty-hour work weeks—and trudged to the back elevator. He was less likely to meet his colleagues there. The thought of facing them was humiliating.

His colleague Joe tapped his shoulder as Luke carried his few belongings toward the elevator. "Sorry, man."

"Word's already out?"

That was fast. Too fast.

He knew why he was fired. Even though he managed to get every project in on time and with the usual Luke Beaumont flair, Paul and Frederika began commenting on how often he disappeared before six on Fridays or wasn't available on

Saturdays. He was forever answering texts and emails from Henri and DeWayne as they took on the difficult process of sorting through a lifetime of belongings. Paul, especially, must have noticed how distracted he was.

Luke made sure he explained the crisis in his family and promised it was only temporary. It didn't matter. With a new crop of college graduates coming on board, they weren't interested in accommodating him.

He passed an empty trash can, looked at his box of stuff and tossed it. Then, changing his mind, he retrieved his mug. He'd owned that mug since—actually, it wasn't his. He gave it to Henri for Christmas when Luke was in middle school. He'd better take it home.

He leaned impatiently against the wall while he waited for the elevator—for an inordinate amount of time.

Three months ago, he was on top of the world. He liked his job and was good at it. He was even hoping for a promotion. Three months ago, he was looking forward to the end of summer when he planned to celebrate his best friend's wedding and, afterward, go on a vacation of his own. Where, he didn't know, but he had already put in his request for time off. Another good idea shot to hell.

He couldn't afford a vacation now. Or his apartment. Not only was he now unemployed, he might soon be homeless.

Luke couldn't imagine how he was going to tell Henri and DeWayne. They were going to want Luke to come home. Really, did he have a choice?

He carried the mug to his car and yanked at the sticking door—now both doors were sticking—and he couldn't afford to get either of them fixed. And he sure couldn't afford to trade the car in. Not that he would, he loved his Jeep. He climbed in, put the mug in the cup holder then stared at the dashboard.

Monday morning at eight-thirty-five. Luke didn't have a thing to do. *When was the last time that happened? Probably never.* Henri and DeWayne gave Luke chores at the inn until he was old enough to get his own summer job, instilling a serious work ethic.

He couldn't imagine what to do on Monday morning without a job, so he went home. He packed his kitchen stuff and crammed his clothes into his only suitcase and a couple of kitchen trash bags. The apartment came furnished and he was glad he didn't have to figure out how to move couches, chests, and beds. He unplugged the Xbox and the TV.

After calling the cable company to turn off the internet, he called the landlady with the bad news. He was breaking his lease. A brand new lease, renewed only in July. She told him she'd keep the security deposit and to send her the three months' rent she was due. She didn't care he no longer had a job. They'd made a deal.

Then he picked up the router. He needed to return it.

Luke stared at his stuff. Everything fit in his car. He was glad. He was never coming back here.

~ * ~

Frank leaned back on the two rear legs of his chair on the Broadview's porch and took a gulp of his beer. He'd surprised Luke by saying he was coming out Friday evening. He'd arrived only a few minutes before and already the two of them were watching the sun set.

With so much of his life upended, Luke found solace in his friend's presence. "Glad you could come, man."

"Julie is busy with wedding stuff, and since we didn't get out for the Fourth of July…"

Luke shrugged. "We were pretty busy. I'm surprised you could come visit now."

As he peeled the label off his empty beer bottle, Frank chuckled. "The wedding is taking over my life. Julie told me months ago everything was done and all I needed to do was show up at the church on time."

"That kept you busy on the holiday?"

"No, there was some family thing on the Fourth. Parade, picnic, fireworks. All her relatives get together. Julie never even mentioned it before."

"Sounds like fun."

"It was—but all we discussed was…the wedding. Julie can describe the cake for twenty minutes. This weekend is all about centerpieces. Did you know women collect ideas online and share them? I needed to get away from the wedding planning. Julie, her mother, and Amanda have gone into overdrive."

Luke froze at Amanda's name. He didn't want to think

about her, another powerful woman out to ruin his family's life. It didn't help when he remembered her sweet smile or her quick wit on the tennis court. He'd never forget who Roger Federer was again. Or how giddy she got in the wine cellar when they found that smelly old diary.

"Sorry." Frank's voice was full of regret. "Julie told me not to mention her."

Attempting to brush off any appearance of hurt feelings, Luke scooped up a handful of bite-sized pretzels. He didn't want to discuss her or, for that matter, anything right now. He was still feeling sorry for himself.

"It's fine. Really." What else could he say? Frank meant well. There was no denying that in a few weeks, Luke was going to have to walk down a church aisle with Amanda by his side. It made him cringe, but it was just another thing to get used to. "How is Amanda?" Part of him was curious.

"You know Amanda. Oh wait. You know exactly what she's working on. She's always talking about it with Julie. It makes her late and crazy all the time. Julie has to send her a couple dozen reminders so she doesn't miss stuff."

Luke needed to change the subject. "So, how's the new marketing director working out? You said she was not only talented but beautiful too."

Frank laughed. "She's doing a terrific job."

"Oh, man. That's great."

"They keeping you busy at Buildings R Us?" Frank asked.

"That's Windsor-Douglas, the finest construction company in the mid-Atlantic. Never better." Luke spent so much time the past week whining to Henri and DeWayne, even he was sick of his own complaining. Frank didn't need to hear any of it.

"Come on, Luke. Henri told me."

"I should have known. Henri keeps calling my boss 'that man.' Every time, I have to correct him. Her name is Frederika."

Frank snorted. "So what happened?"

"Beats me. One day I'm on top of the world, getting the best raise in the department. Then Frederika has Paul packing up my things before they toss me onto the street."

Frank straightened up his chair and leaned toward his friend. "You didn't do anything?"

"Not one thing. A hundred little things. Stupid stuff. Leaving early on a regular basis is a big no-no. They were used to me working until seven every night and showing up Saturdays if a project was due. I still got the work done. Good work too. I'd show you, but they wouldn't let me bring any of it home."

He was especially proud of his last project, which was a lot like the resort that would soon replace the Broadview. Pretty spot on the ocean, not a lake. With a beach front hotel, a pool and spa. He was hoping he'd get to visit it once construction began. It was in Hawaii. Now he'd never get there. He'd never even find out if the company's proposal was chosen.

Frank leaned his elbows on his knees. "In other words, you stopped meeting your department's expectations."

"Yeah, I guess. Something like that."

"I could've hired you a couple of weeks ago."

Didn't Luke know it. Yet he was glad he didn't accept Frank's offer. Now he had the flexibility he needed to help Henri and DeWayne. Whatever happened, he and his parents had each other. His family might be fractured at the moment, but they would ultimately pull together. They always did.

Before he could respond to Frank, DeWayne arrived with two frosty glasses and laid them on the table. "Hey, Frank. Henri asked me to deliver these. I forget what's in them. Did you talk some sense into him yet?"

"I don't think so. This boy is stubborn."

Luke smirked. "What? Is everyone but me in on this conversation?"

"Yup." DeWayne pulled up a rocking chair and sat next to Luke. "Henri and I discussed it and decided to call in reinforcements. We thought you might need your old friend. You've been down in the dumps these past few days."

"Sounds like…what's the movie?" Luke could envision a hint of a scene with Rob Reiner.

"This is usually your father's expertise, but I believe it's *Sleepless in Seattle*." DeWayne paused in a dramatic way. "'What do they call it when everything intersects?'"

Luke knew the answer to that one. "The Bermuda Triangle.'"

Frank looked perplexed. "You guys watched that movie?"

"No. Yes." Luke shrugged. "Just until the *Dirty Dozen* scene."

"Oh of course. That's a classic." Frank turned to DeWayne. "So how are things?"

"Not bad, considering." DeWayne took the last of the pretzels. "We have a full house this weekend. More reservations than we can fit in the dining room. Henri's planning on adding extra tables and chairs in the sitting room. He said he'll feed everybody who wants to come. He might put tables here on the porch too."

"That's great."

"It's positive for now. The newspaper reported on the hearing the other day and that was good publicity for us. I suspect everyone decided this was their last chance to come to the Broadview."

"That's bad."

DeWayne jumped up. "It's all good. We're playing it by ear for now." He ruffled his son's hair. "Let's say we're waiting to hear what Luke decides to do next."

Frank waited while DeWayne strolled back into the house. "He does that all the time, doesn't he?"

"What?" Luke smoothed his hair.

"That. The hair thing."

With a chuckle, Luke shook his head at the memory of the first time DeWayne did that. "He's done it ever since I met him."

"It was cute when you were a kid."

Crossing his arms and wearing a frown, Luke assumed a mock-defensive tone. "Hey, you're talking about my father."

"Chill, man. It's still cute."

"Yeah. That's what I want to be known for. Cute." Luke tasted the drink in his hand. "I saw Henri experimenting with this the other night. It's weird but I like it."

"Yeah? It's iced tea." Frank took a taste and then another. "Oh, no it's not. There's bourbon in my iced tea."

"He makes it with gin too. It's not bad, is it?"

"Not bad at all."

Luke was taking another sip of his cocktail when his phone buzzed. "I don't recognize this number." He showed his phone to Frank.

"That's a Maryland area code, but I don't know it either."

Luke punched the green answer button. "Hello?" Then he frowned. "Oh, hi, Amanda."

Chapter Twenty-Three
Going to Pittsburgh

Amanda hoped by now the sound of Luke's voice would have little or no effect on her. She was wrong. The minute he spoke, her pulse quickened, and perspiration bloomed on her lip.

This was not the time to let her emotions get the best of her. She needed to make this call as businesslike as possible. She sat taller behind her desk and took a deep, calming breath.

"I found her, Luke." No, that's not how she should have started. She tried again. Calmer, dispassionate. "I called to tell you, I found Alexander and Rosalind Prince. It took hours, but I did it."

"So?" The bitterness in his voice quelled Amanda's hopes of reconciliation. She should have known when Julie promised her Luke would be happy to hear from her that it wasn't going to be all hearts and flowers.

"Rosalind is the girl who wrote the diary. Alexander was the boy she met the summer the president came to the inn."

"That was over a hundred years ago. Where did you find them? In a cemetery?"

He was being difficult. Amanda was sure she told him she was going to look for descendants, someone who might remember the story. Or at least remember the girl who wrote the diary. If the first calming breath didn't work, maybe a second one would. She paused, disappointed he wasn't as excited as she was.

After all, this might be the key to convincing Mr. Lowrey the inn was worth saving. "I scoured the internet. Facebook, and those people finder sites. I found an obituary for one of Rosalind and Alexander's children, and it mentioned her survivors. You probably don't want to hear about the rabbit holes I went down. Anyway, I found Alexandra Prince O'Neill."

"So?"

Amanda persisted, "I picked up the Pittsburgh telephone directory—do you know how many pages of O'Neills there are? There was no Alexandra, but I found a W.J. and A.P. O'Neill. Figuring it was worth a chance, I called, and it was Alexandra Prince O'Neill."

When Luke made no response, she continued, sure she'd get him to pay attention at some point, "Mrs. O'Neill didn't recognize the name of the inn, but she was aware of the president's visit to Western Maryland. Her great-grandmother had told her the story many times. Only, the name of the inn was lost in the fog of memory. She was quick to add, though, that she owned a photograph taken when Rosalind was sixteen. The year she met Alexander, whom she would marry the next spring. Remember, she mentions meeting a boy in the diary. And she wrote his name in the back."

Hoping for a response, she waited. When he said nothing, she went on. If the inn was to be spared, it was important he hear what she was saying.

"She was amazed we found the diary. Her great-grandmother never mentioned it. I only hope it's Rosalind's." Pausing to gather confidence, she searched for the right words in hopes that Luke would agree to her next request. "Luke, I have the pictures on my phone of the two pages, but Mrs. O'Neill would like to see the real thing."

He sighed before answering her, "I guess you can come and get it."

That would be fine, but it meant four hours of driving. Even though she was anxious to get this all settled as soon as possible, she wasn't sure how she felt about seeing Luke again. To calm herself, she closed her eyes and cleared her throat. Then she used her attorney voice.

"I am proposing a trip—together—to visit her here in Pittsburgh. Could you bring the diary and meet me at my office? Since we found the diary together and in your inn, you should hear what she has to say too." She softened her voice, almost pleading as she said, "I need to do this, Luke. I feel terrible about what's happening at the Broadview. The diary gives us a chance to save it."

"How can that smelly old book save my fathers' inn?"

Luke's resistance was wearing down the triumphant elation that had bubbled up in Amanda after talking to Mrs. O'Neill. But this had become a mission, and Amanda wasn't giving up. She exhaled slowly as she carefully chose her words.

"It can't. Not really. The president and first lady's visit didn't change the world. But it does recall a time when this was a place so special presidents came to call. It's an opportunity to remember the magic of that moment, to savor it, then to build on it. You know all those places that say, 'Washington slept here?' They aren't significant either, but they are places touched by history."

"So?"

Why doesn't he see?

"Frances Folsom Cleveland entranced the nation. She was young and charming, the first bride in the White House, the youngest first lady—she was only twenty-one. And when President Cleveland lost the election for a second term, she told the White House staff they'd be back. She was right. Her husband won a second term four years later. I think tourists would like the connection between your inn and this interesting woman. The diary entry relates how excited everyone was to see the president and first lady. Even a sixteen-year-old girl."

When there was still no response on the other end of the call, Amanda forged ahead. She'd tried to be patient but now her fighting spirit had been aroused. She laid down the phone, clicked on the speaker icon, then folded her hands to try again.

"Look, Luke. I proposed to both Quin, my boss, and Mr. Lowrey, my client, that they should preserve the inn. Quin liked the idea as did Mr. Lowrey. But he ended up by turning the idea down. He just wants the land. If I can prove the property has some historical significance, he might be convinced otherwise."

"What's the point in saving the inn if Henri and DeWayne aren't there?"

Amanda winced to hear such bitterness in Luke's voice. She softened her tone, hoping he'd understand she was trying to help both her client and him, as she said, "Even if the inn can't be saved as your fathers' business, it wouldn't be torn down. It would still be there for you to visit."

She hoped that would convince him, knowing how painful it was to lose the family home. "It also may answer all the concerns people brought up at that meeting."

"Wouldn't that be lucky for you?" His voice sounded resentful.

Another person might have given up but not Amanda. "You have a choice here. It's more important for you than me. We can visit this woman together, or I can come get the book and go on my own." She paused. "Or maybe I should forget the whole thing while the inn—your family home—turns into rubble."

"It doesn't matter anymore. We'll be gone by November."

Amanda already knew; Julie had told her. Even though Amanda understood the bitter tone in his voice, she remained hopeful her news would help ease the pain.

At least, she needed to try. "Come to Pittsburgh and listen to what she has to say. It's a good story. I hope it's enough to save the inn. Please? Say you'll come."

This time, the pause on the other end of the line offered Amanda a little hope. Maybe, she had reached Luke's heart.

Then he sighed. "All right, Amanda. You win. When?"

She remembered his job kept him as busy as hers did. "I told her I'd meet her Monday. But if you have to work, we can reschedule."

"No, I'm already at Deep Creek. Monday works just fine."

She told him the address of her office and asked him to meet her at eleven. As she clicked off, she silently hoped he'd want to stick around and join her for lunch.

~ * ~

Luke switched off his phone and ran a hand down his face. A hint of a headache pulsed behind his eyes.

"You look like you just scheduled your execution." Frank crossed his arms and wore a knowing look that made Luke pause as he reached for his drink.

"Feels like it. You already know, don't you?"

Frank fluttered his eyelashes and pressed his hands over his heart. "It's so romantic." Then he grinned. "Of course I do. Julie and Amanda have talked about it nonstop. The only thing they discuss more is the wedding."

"What's the big deal? Is it true Amanda's trying to

convince her developer client not to tear the inn down?"

"I'm not sure. Maybe. Look, Amanda is trying to be business-like, but Julie says it's an act. Would it be so bad the woman you want to hate is doing everything she can to save your home?"

"But she isn't. She's just trying to ease her own feelings of guilt. We are still losing our home. I'll give her one thing, though. She's tenacious."

"Julie said it's important to her. Did you know Amanda tried out for the Olympics? And finished at the top of her class in college. And law school. When she wants something, she's not giving up. Guess you'll have to ask why she cares when you go to Pittsburgh."

"Wait. I didn't tell you that. Am I so predictable you already knew I'd say yes to her trip?"

"'Fraid so."

Luke stared at a couple of sailboats skittering across the rippling surface of the lake. What would be the point of her attempts to save the inn, when his family wouldn't live here anymore? Should he even care?

Frank leaned toward the screen door and called into the house. "Henri, he said he'd go."

"Shit. Are you saying they know too?"

"Oh yes. The only one I wasn't supposed to tell was you."

"This is unbelievable. My family and my friends are conspiring against me."

Frank snickered. "It's self-preservation, man. Julie told me if the maid of honor and the best man aren't on speaking terms before we head down the aisle, she was calling the wedding off."

"She wouldn't do that."

"I hope not. But what am I supposed to do? The wedding is less than a month away. She's always announcing she's calling the whole thing off. My sweet, level-headed Julie is a bag of nerves."

Once Luke was foolish enough to be as sure he had found the woman he wanted to marry as Frank was now. He thought of Emily and the ring on the kitchen counter only long enough to shudder. They never got a chance to set the date.

"I get it. Really, I do. It's only I don't want to keep playing this game with her. Why should I? You know what those men inside are doing, don't you? Henri keeps on behaving like the place will run forever. DeWayne is going through the business office, deciding what to throw away and what he needs to take when he leaves."

Frank raised an eyebrow and looked at his friend before calling into the house. "Henri! DeWayne! Did you hear me? He's going to Pittsburgh."

Only Henri responded, coming through the screen door like a locomotive. "Sorry, I was up to my elbows in bread dough." He sat on the edge of a rocking chair, looking expectant. If Luke wasn't sure before, he was now. He couldn't let his father down.

"I told Amanda I'd go take the diary to see whatever-her-name-is."

Henri sprang from his chair and hugged his son. "Oh hooray. I was afraid you might say no."

Luke pulled away to see his father's expression. "You want me to go?"

Henri's expression became serious. "Indeed I do." He put a hand on Luke's shoulder and scanned the blue water lapping the edge of their property. "I would prefer to stay here forever, but DeWayne has talked some sense into me. We're out of money. We don't even know how we're going to pay off the loan for the storm repair."

He returned his gaze to Luke who saw the love and regret in his expression. "I've loved this place for a long time. Wouldn't it be great if it survives? Even if we aren't here anymore it will always be part of our family legacy."

Luke couldn't help but nod. His father's voice held a wistful note.

DeWayne stepped on the porch, brushing dust from the rolled-up sleeves of his button-down shirt. "Did I hear my name?"

Henri squeezed Luke's shoulders. "He said he'd go to Pittsburgh."

With a smile, DeWayne put his hands on his hips. "That so?"

"You think I should go too?"

Nodding, DeWayne rested a hand on the railing. "We worked hard to keep this place going. I think it's great you want to save it."

Well, now it's my mission is to save the Broadview. Even if it meant sitting beside Amanda for an hour to talk to a total stranger, he needed to go to Pittsburgh.

For Henri and DeWayne.

Chapter Twenty-Four
Alexandra

Alexandra O'Neill led Amanda and Luke into a bright, well-lit parlor that looked like it was recently renovated. The furniture appeared to be new too, surprisingly modern for an old Victorian. The black-and-white and sepia-tone photographs that hung on the walls, and faded and chipped knickknacks that sat on the table and mantelpiece, hinted at her family history.

Alexandra, a sixty-ish year old woman in navy slacks and top with a multi-colored scarf tied at her neck, was soft-spoken as she invited them to take a seat. Even thick lenses in her glasses couldn't hide the excitement in her eyes.

She settled on the edge of her chair between the fireplace and a window and looked at the two of them. "I can't tell you how surprised I was by your call."

"I was really happy when you said you'd talk to us." Amanda wanted to reach for the diary but held down her impatience while she got through the pleasantries first. "When you said you had a photograph of Rosalind, I knew I found the right person."

Luke leaned his elbows on his knees. "How are you related to the girl who wrote the diary?"

"She's my great-grandmother." Alexandra adjusted her glasses and looked over their heads as if she was doing a little figuring. "I was born in 1950. My mother in 1924. Her mother, my grandmother, was born in 1904. Her mother, we called her Nana, is the girl in my picture."

Amanda held her breath as Alexandra stretched to lift a photograph from the wall and hand it to her. "I knew her only briefly. She died when I was six or seven."

A young, hope-filled face of a thin girl stood next to a tall solemn boy. She was exactly as Amanda pictured her. She wore a white dress with a high collar, her hair cascading down her back in ringlets, a flowery hat perched precariously on her head.

"And the boy is Alexander?" Amanda asked.

"My great-grandfather, yes."

For a moment, Amanda was quiet, studying the face of the girl who hid her diary in the Broadview's wine cellar. "Did she ever mention a diary?"

Alexandra shook her head. "I wish she did. She didn't talk about herself much. Not to me anyway. I would love it if my mother was here to tell me more. She always said she was Nana's favorite. They spent lots of time together. This was her favorite photograph, but Nana never said where the picture was taken."

Luke looked at the picture and smiled. "It was taken at our inn at Deep Creek Lake. The porch still looks a lot like this. I was sitting right there yesterday when Amanda called me."

Goosebumps rose on Amanda's arms. "Thanks to DeWayne. You told me he went to a great deal of trouble to repaint the railings to look the way they used to look." She turned to Alexandra. "Luke's father has restored the exterior of the house. It was painted white when they bought the place, but now it's beautiful with green and red trim and the siding is a sunny yellow, almost the same color as your living room."

Alexandra took the photo from Amanda. "It's not all that far from here, is it?"

"No, it's only about two and a half hours. It's at the far southern edge of the lake. You should visit."

He shook his head. "You better hurry. One of Amanda's clients is about to tear it down."

"What?" She and Alexandra replied together. Amanda couldn't believe her ears. He made her sound like the villain in this.

"That's not exactly true." When she shot an angry glance at Luke, he repaid her with a smirk—one of those smart-alecky expressions common among know-it-all boys. She wondered how he could be so annoying. Didn't matter, she reminded herself as she put her smile back on her face and prepared to explain.

"The reason I'm here—" Amanda paused when Luke

cleared his voice. "The reason *we're* here is to save the inn. The developer, my client, did want to bulldoze the inn. It's old and needs a lot of repairs." Luke shot her a dark look and cleared his throat again. She ignored him and continued, "My client said it might be worth saving if we can prove the president was there. Your great-grandmother's diary is the only record we have."

"May I look at it?"

Amanda held her breath as she handed over the book. Not only was the odor still appalling, she knew this was a make-it-or-break-it moment. Luke looked as nervous as she was, clenching his hands.

Alexandra smiled a bit as she gently leafed through the pages. Amanda wondered how she'd ever be able to read the childish scrawl or make out any of the words in the water-damaged pages neither she nor Luke could decipher.

Her expression grew dazzling when she reached the notation about the president's visit. "She *was* there. We always suspected she made it up. What would the president of the United States be doing in a little inn so far from the White House? She didn't remember the inn's name, only that it was near the Deer Park Inn and they got there by train. One time, many years after she was gone, my mother went looking for proof. She discovered the president who stayed at the Deer Park Inn. When she compared her picture with the inn, she knew it wasn't the right place. There weren't any newspaper or diary entries for another inn where the president might have visited. Until now. This says he and his new wife stopped for tea at the Broadview." Alexandra held up the book with a smile. "At your inn. Are you certain this is the same place?"

Luke nodded. He went through the photos on his phone he had taken for the summer social media posts. In the one he showed them, Amanda and Julie stood together on the porch, in the same location where Rosalind and Alexander once posed for their picture.

Amanda remembered when he took that photo. He was cute that day, maybe a bit nervous around her after their first kiss the previous night. She pondered then if they might find love together. In the photo, there was hopefulness in her eyes. Now she knew better.

"I wonder if my mother knew about this diary." Alexandra studied page after page until her fingers finally rested on the inside back cover. She chuckled again. "Even then Nana was thinking about marrying my great-grandfather. I wish I'd known him. He died quite young, way before I was born."

"You're sure it is your great-grandmother's handwriting?"

At first, Amanda thought Luke's question was impertinent. Of course it was hers. Then she remembered how skeptical Mr. Lowrey was. This could be the proof necessary to save the inn. Historians like evidence.

The question didn't seem to bother Alexandra at all. She crossed the room to a delicate oak drop-leaf desk. The drawer screeched open to reveal a bundle of letters tied together with a thin pink ribbon. "Nana wrote these letters to Granddad. My mother found them in my grandparents' attic, tied with the same ribbon. She never told her mother she carried them home that afternoon. It's a good thing she did. Lightning later struck the house, and those letters might have been destroyed."

She gave them to Luke who leafed through them as if they were a pack of playing cards before handing them to Amanda.

"There's not much in there. They're filled with nothing more than the silly lovesick scribbling of a teenage girl. She had fallen hard for my great-grandfather. Look at the signature. You'll see it matches what's in this diary." Alexandra encouraged her to open the letters.

Then, she looked at the book one more time before gently closing it to return to Amanda.

Amanda tried to push it back into her hands. "Why don't you keep it? We have copies of everything we need."

She shook her head. "Oh no, it's too valuable. It's enough to have seen it. Thank you. It almost feels as if she was in the room again, although this time as a lovestruck young woman. You don't often think of your elders that way, do you?"

~ * ~

Luke wanted to shake his head at the two women bent over the picture and the diary and the letters. He forgot how sentimental people could be when they were looking at old things and considering olden times.

DeWayne was the same way. Big, strong, and sentimental

as hell. It was DeWayne who had found the inn. He'd taken the time to research the original colors and then was the one who climbed onto the window ledges to paint the trim.

Even as he talked about finances, movers, and new opportunities, he supported Amanda's effort to preserve the inn. Was it only yesterday he had pulled Luke aside, far from where Henri could hear him?

"Do what you can to save the Broadview," DeWayne told him. *"Not for me. I'm ready to move on. For Henri."*

Luke knew what DeWayne meant. Henri was having a tough time keeping up his happy-go-lucky appearances. He kept reminding them all, *"This is the last Fourth of July here. This is the last summer here. I'm going to miss the sunsets over the lake."*

It broke Luke's heart. DeWayne was brave, but his eyes betrayed the same sadness so evident on Henri's face. DeWayne might say he was ready to move on, but both he and Henri were already mourning the loss of the home where they'd become a family.

The women continued murmuring over the diary before they aimed their phone cameras at faded photographs, pages of the diary, then each other. While they were documenting the past, he recalled a quote from his favorite old movie, *Back to the Future*, "Your future hasn't been written yet. No one's has. Your future is whatever you make it. So, make it a good one."

A few months ago, Luke's future was assured. His parents were settled. He was doing great at a job he kind of liked. He'd just clapped eyes on a blonde woman with muscular calves.

Today, everything was different. The Broadview was slipping away, leaving his parents in limbo. He didn't have a job or a house. Or even someone to love. What kind of future would he have if he didn't do something?

"Luke?" Amanda was snapping her fingers in front of his face. "Earth to Luke, come in please."

He laughed and quoted his second favorite movie, "Just when I thought I was out, they pull me back in."

She laughed. "At least you didn't use the mattresses quote."

He stared at her. "You know *The Godfather*?"

"I've seen it a few times, and I love that quote. I first heard the mattresses quote in *You've Got Mail*."

What was he thinking a minute ago? *No future, huh? Here she is, trying to save the Broadview Inn. And quoting movies. Do they make women any more attractive than that?*

"Anyway," she continued. "We need to get going. You ready, Luke?"

He rose and smiled at Alexandra. "Please come to the inn. DeWayne and Henri would love to meet you and see that photograph. You're welcome anytime. We'll save a room for you. Is there a Mr. O'Neill?"

Alexandra blushed like an ingénue. "There is, indeed."

"Come for the weekend. Henri would be happy to cook for you." He shook her hand.

"I'd like to do that sometime." She walked them to the door. "Amanda? Luke? Thank you for showing me the diary. It means a lot to me. I hope our meeting helps save your inn."

She waved one last time as Amanda skipped down the steps to the car at the curb. She wheeled around and threw her hands over her head. "Wasn't it great?"

Luke, opening the driver's side door for Amanda, had to agree. "Maybe. The question is, is it enough for your client to decide against tearing down the inn?"

"It has to be. We have her signature, the picture, the diary. I can't believe it all fits together so nicely. It's like Kismet."

"It is. Not like the Bermuda Triangle at all."

She stopped before getting in and frowned. "What?"

"*Sleepless in Seattle*...I thought we were remembering old Meg Ryan movies. Never mind."

As Luke clicked his seatbelt, he turned to Amanda and wondered what she expected him to say. Something filled with gratitude, probably. Instead, he had a question.

"Amanda? Why are you doing this? It doesn't make any sense."

Chapter Twenty-Five
The Value of Old Things

Amanda could have answered Luke's question in one of several ways. She fiddled with the mirrors and kept glancing back as if pulling out into traffic on this quiet suburban street might be tricky. In her excitement, she could hardly remember which way to turn.

Finding the diary that first day thrilled her. Should she tell him how much she loved historic buildings? How eager she was to see this one preserved? How many times did she have to tell him? He must know by now. So that didn't seem to be enough to satisfy him.

Should she reveal the guilt she suffered after discovering how her client came between Luke's family and their inn? Even if it sounded plausible, it wasn't entirely true. No matter what he believed, she didn't know she would have any part in it.

Did she love him? She was beginning to believe she did. That wasn't something she could tell him now, not while the hotel deal wasn't settled. It didn't feel right.

It was time to tell him about her house, the one she lost.

"Why am I doing this?" Echoing his question, she hoped to buy some time to steel herself before she answered. "Why *am* I doing this?"

"That's what I asked."

"Well, Luke." Amanda kept her focus on the road, staring at the cars ahead of her and hanging onto the steering wheel like it was a life preserver. "I need to tell you a story." She took a deep breath, exhaling slowly. "I told you how much I love the beach?"

"Yes, but…"

"We were at the beach when my family's house burned

down."

There she said it. It didn't hurt a bit. Except for maybe that ache in the pit of her stomach, so much like the pain that she suffered on the long drive to the home firefighters were trying to save.

Luke nodded but didn't say anything. So she went on, "I sat next to my brother Chase and held onto our dog, a little ugly mutt named Cheerio, I loved until the day she died. I kept thinking how glad I was I'd convinced Mom and Dad to let me bring her."

Amanda swiped away the tears that stung her eyes, hoping he wouldn't see them. "What if she had died in the fire? Thank God she didn't. I can't tell you how awful I felt driving home that day. It was midweek so the traffic across the bridge wasn't bad at all. If it had been Saturday, the back-up would have been much worse."

Remembering the torturous drive to Baltimore was still hard, all these years later. "I tried to concentrate on my book but couldn't. My brother and I didn't dare say a word. We didn't even have the radio on. Dad said he couldn't pay attention to the road if it was playing. Even in the silence, Dad beat out a rhythm on the steering wheel, a nervous habit he still has sometimes." She sighed and glanced at Luke. Finally, she had his attention.

So she went on. "Occasionally, our neighbor, Mrs. Ward, called with updates but each bit of news made the three-hour trip feel like it stretched on for days. My mother was the only one who broke the silence during the entire drive home. She wondered if the piano her aunt left her would survive. She fretted over lost photographs, souvenirs, gifts from family and friends."

Then Amanda paused, surprised at herself and the things she still missed.

"I thought about my room going up in smoke. I was too old for its bright pink color and the toys scattered about. But even if it had been years since I played with my dollhouse, I was upset it might be gone. My dad made it for me when I was three or four."

It grew quiet then until finally Luke asked, "What happened?"

"When we got home, there was nothing left. The front of the house was faced with stone. That survived, but it was nothing without windows and the bright red door. The rest was no more than ash. Even the tire swing was gone."

"I'm sorry, Amanda."

The sympathy etched on his face somehow helped soothe the painful memories.

"My mother cried for days. My father, when he wasn't on the phone with insurance people and whoever else he talked to about getting the house rebuilt, took a leave of absence from work to stay with Mom and us. It was as if he was afraid if he went away, he might lose us too."

Amanda tried to explain how painful it was to realize everything they had lost. Everything but her family and Cheerio. "The funny thing, well it wasn't funny at all, was how often I went into a drawer, looking for something I lost in the fire. My favorite book, a necklace, a sweater. Then I'd remember. I began thinking of things as 'before the fire' and 'after the fire.'"

Luke turned his body to face her as she explained. His face was softer now, the resentment all but gone.

"Losing my childhood, little bits of it anyway, made me ache for you when I discovered you might lose your home. It wasn't any of my business whether your parents sold it or not. But I can't look at this transaction as just another legal agreement. As much as I need to take care of my clients' interests, I can't watch your family home get torn down."

Luke sighed. "I appreciate your story, but it's not the same as mine. You can't save our family home. Soon, it will be just an old building where we used to live."

She stopped as the light turned red, glad for a moment to look at him. "But isn't that something? I want to protect that inn. Your inn. Now we have proof of the president's visit. Maybe now I can convince Mr. Lowrey not to tear it down."

Luke's smile was sympathetic as he wiped away one of her tears. Amanda was glad she told him. She couldn't remember the last time she told anybody that story. Julie knew, of course. When you don't have mementoes from your past, you have to explain.

"Maybe that's why you treasure old things." Luke laid his hand on her arm.

"What?"

He shrugged. "You don't have anything old. Everything you own is new and has been since your house caught fire."

She chuckled. "I never thought of that. It's true though. I love old buildings like the Broadview. I was thrilled to find Rosalind's diary. I did love being in Mrs. O'Neill's house today with all her old photos and knickknacks. My parents don't even have their wedding album anymore. I always thought that was sad."

The light turned green, and she looked back to the street. "I know what it's like not to be able to walk through the rooms where you grew up. I didn't appreciate that until I became friends with Julie. Her family's house is cluttered with old stuff. She's almost as bad as her mother. I looked over everything on the walls and on shelves and tables, packed into drawers—there were all those memories. I realized we never would have that again. Well, we would have to start over anyway."

"Just as my fathers will have to do."

Luke's remark cut deep. He was right. She hadn't done anything to help them yet. All she had was an inkling of an idea, a smelly diary with a fairy tale. She had one thing more, proof of the Broadview's bit of historical significance. *Is this enough to save the place?*

"Not if I can help it. Or, better yet, not if we can help it." She shot a glance at him before turning on her signal.

"You have that look in your eye."

"Damn straight. We have a chance to demonstrate how the inn has made its mark at Deep Creek Lake. I'll rework my proposal with the new information."

"To what end?"

"I don't know yet but we'll think of something."

"Whatever you come up with, it's not going to keep us from having to move out."

"Don't give up yet, Luke." Amanda forced herself to keep her attention on the road, unwilling to see skepticism in his expression. She was going to have to work harder to win him over. "Henri and DeWayne have given twenty years to that place. It's where you grew up. It's where I met you. I love that old place."

"That's not enough."

"No, it isn't." Even though Amanda knew Luke was right, she wasn't backing down. "We still have time to convince Mr. Lowrey history makes the inn worth saving."

"For what, if not a country inn?"

"I told you before. A museum or maybe a honeymoon cottage. We'll be back to your car in twenty minutes. By then, we'll think of something."

Chapter Twenty-Six
Turn the Page

In the days after Luke and Amanda met with Alexandra, DeWayne and Henri sat together in the kitchen every morning. Luke kept his distance, knowing they needed time together to decide their future and repair the division between them.

It was the same routine every day. DeWayne went over the books, studied the latest bills, examined the bank account one more time. Then he and Henri would talk over their options. Henri still held out hope they'd find a way to stay while DeWayne argued for a move.

Everything changed when the traffic began. Surveyors knocked on the door asking for permission to come onto their property. Utility workers marked up the lawn by the road. Men in hard hats brought laser distance measurers, maps, and plans.

When the doorbell rang for what had to be the sixteenth time, Luke poked his head in the kitchen to inform his fathers of the latest arrival. They called him in to sit with them.

"We've signed the papers." Henri looked tired. "It's all done."

Before they said a word, Luke already knew. "The numbers don't add up, do they, DeWayne?"

Both men shook their head. DeWayne held up a sheaf of bills. "We got the arborist's estimate for taking down that oak tree. That and the insurance deductible for the porch repairs…" Instead of finishing, he only sighed.

Henri picked up the thought. "As painful as it is to say, we can't stay here anymore. We have to face the facts."

"But, Papa. Pop," Luke spread his hands toward them both. "I told you about Amanda's plan. That's why I went to Pittsburgh.

With your blessing."

"It isn't only the numbers." DeWayne folded his hands in front of him. A furrow in his usually smooth forehead deepened. "We're going to keep seeing people like the ones who were just at the door. We can't stop change."

Already, there were orange ties around trees on the Evitts' property, a sign they would be cut down. Spray paint to mark underground utilities and culverts covered wide swaths of their former neighbors' lawns.

"Even if we stay, nothing will be the same." Henri shook his head.

"But Amanda—"

"No, son." DeWayne shook his head, a deep frown across his face. "Amanda is taking care of her client. This activity all around us is a clear sign the project is moving ahead."

When the high-pitched beep of a dump truck interrupted him, DeWayne raised his eyebrows and cocked his head while he waited. "All of this made us realize if we hang on, we'll eventually be pushed out. We think so anyway. Imagine all the dump trucks and cranes and people who will be here during construction. You know how that is."

Even though Luke had worked for a construction company, his focus was always on the end result. The building after it was completed with the parking lot freshly striped, the non-glare lights, trees and bushes dotting the freshly-graded landscape. He rarely gave a thought to the actual process of building. Obviously, DeWayne did.

"We aren't sure how long construction will last, but it's got to be at least a year. A year without any business here. No one would want to stay next to a construction zone. It's loud and dusty. It's stressful. If our business is slipping now, imagine next summer. All those back-up warning signals from dawn to dusk, the hammers and power tools."

Henri glanced toward the window over the sink. "Yesterday, I was staring out the kitchen window at a bunch of men in white hard hats staring at a plan. Or maybe it was a map. Either way, I decided I didn't want to be stuck in the middle of all this anymore."

Even though he smiled, his eyes still looked sad. "I hate to move. I've hated it every time. It always means saying goodbye. To France. To Ana. To my restaurant. Now to the inn where DeWayne and I have worked with such devotion." He reached for DeWayne's hand. "But just as it was important to start over every other time, it's time for us now to turn the page."

"Are you sure?" Luke pursed his lips, anguished at the news. "Amanda said she thinks the developer might be convinced. You know how she cares about this place."

Henri smiled as he used to smile at a much younger Luke. "We know she cares about you, *mon fils*. As for this drafty old place…"

"But we're working on a plan. I told you."

"It's too late." His papa laid a comforting hand on Luke's.

The room grew silent. Rays of sun splashed golden across the floor.

"Let's go watch the sunset." Luke spoke quietly.

The sun, now an orange disk, had sunk almost to the tops of the trees on the other side of the lake. Its light splashed pink and purple across the clouds of a mackerel sky. A few low-flying birds, dipping their wings to the lake, disrupted the colors' reflection on the mirror-like water.

Henri put his hand to his heart. "I never get tired of this."

DeWayne stood beside Henri and draped his arm over his shoulders. "Me neither."

The men's voices were filled with wistfulness. Sunset usually meant the end of another successful day, the yearning for a restful night, the anticipation of another morning.

Tonight was different. Tonight it meant goodbye. Though no one said a word, Luke lingered with his fathers in silence, waiting for a tomorrow far different from what they knew so well. Luke hoped his efforts—his and Amanda's—would stop it from coming.

~ * ~

After a sleepless night, Luke rose before dawn to take another look at the inn's webpage. Maybe his fathers were ready to give up on the Broadview, but he wasn't. He was taking the fight to the world wide web.

Besides, he couldn't just wait around while Amanda tried to get the developer to save the inn.

Staring at the pictures from their meeting with Alexandra, he recalled bits of conversation from their last time together, not only the excitement over the diary, but also Amanda's retelling of her family's house fire.

He put his fingers on the keyboard to weave a history for the inn. Until today, the webpage had ignored the past, focusing instead on the present and future. Now he had a rich story to tell, one of romance and elegance, a teenaged girl, and a presidential visit.

Luke was putting the finishing touches on the new page when DeWayne knocked on his door. "You have a visitor."

When Luke came down the stairs, Alexandra jumped from the chair by the fireplace. "I hope you don't mind."

"Why would I mind? Please, have a seat. May I get you a cup of tea or coffee? A glass of water? It's too early for anything stronger." He waited until she was settled before taking a seat of his own.

"No thank you. I'm already putting you out by barging in unannounced. I hope you don't mind me coming so soon. You see, I dreamed about our conversation last night and couldn't get it out of my head. Finally, I got in the car and asked Siri to find the inn. You must drive a lot faster than I do. It took a good three hours."

He laughed. "It helps to know the shortcuts, I guess."

She glanced around the room. "It's how I pictured it when we spoke yesterday."

Luke shook his head. "It doesn't look the same as when your great-grandmother was here. Outside may be similar but inside the previous owners got into the Laura Ashley craze so it looks like 1980s English countryside."

"I like it though. It fits the area."

"Thanks. Would you like me to show you around?"

"Yes, please. That's what I came for. I've always wondered where that picture was taken. I've looked at it my whole life. Do you have photos like that?"

He had plenty of them. One was a photo of his father as a little boy standing with his own *maman* on a street in Paris. Luke often promised himself he was going to go there someday. He told Alexandra about it before showing her where they kept the diary.

"It's not there now, of course. Amanda still has it. She's

got a meeting with the developer today. Cross your fingers and pray. We're hoping he decides to restore the inn."

Alexandra studied the picture he had put in the place of the leather-bound book. It was a terrible picture, but the phrase about the president visiting was clear enough. "I'm really glad to learn the story is true."

"You and me both." He led her into the dining room where tea might have been served on the day of the president's and first lady's visit, then into the kitchen. "This looks very different. The Health Department would have a heart attack if Henri tried to cook in a nineteenth century kitchen. Come to think of it, *Henri* would have a heart attack if he had to do that."

She responded with a polite titter.

Luke opened the door to the wine cellar. "Do you want to see where she hid the book? It's dark and a bit smelly, and you have to watch for spiders."

"A few spiders don't worry me. Lead the way."

It was as dank and damp as the last time he was in the cellar. This time, though, it wasn't an adventure that concluded with finding treasure. This time, it seemed more like a pilgrimage, a visit to a sacred shrine. He kept quiet and let his visitor look and think and remember.

She touched with reverence the wine bin where the book had spent the last century. "I wonder how it got here."

He shrugged. "I wondered too. Maybe she waited for Alexander down here. Seems a little creepy now, but we'll never know, will we?"

His guest returned to the sitting room with a wistful expression.

"Let me get Henri and DeWayne. They'd love to meet you." Luke raced off to round up his parents—DeWayne up to his ears in paperwork in his office, Henri scrubbing a pot at the sink.

"You go on. I'll be right there." Henri shooed him from the kitchen. "Don't keep her waiting."

With a manicured finger on her chin, Alexandra was scanning the room with a dreamy smile as Luke sat down across from her and introduced DeWayne.

"I'm so glad I came. Sitting here I almost sense the shadows of people who were here on their summer holidays that day. My great-grandmother is over by that window, scribbling in her diary. Maybe she just met her future husband, and she's trying out his name in the back of the book. Do girls still do that? We did."

Luke wasn't used to middle-aged women letting their imaginations get away from them. Yet, he was curious to hear more. "What else do you see?"

"It's a hot, sunny day. The breeze off the lake is making the lace curtains flutter though it's not enough to cool the room. The ladies who are dressed in their high-necked Victorian finery are waving fans in front of their faces. It's nearly tea-time, and they have dressed and gathered here to chat while they wait to be called."

She turned toward the door as if she heard something. "A carriage pulls up. And someone near the windows gasps. She says it looks like the president. They probably would have known he and his new bride were staying nearby on their honeymoon. It must have been reported in the newspapers, which they read that morning."

Alexandra pursed her lips for a minute. "I can't imagine how they would react. Would they rush to the window? Or stay right where they were? Either way I imagine they held their breath, tugged on their lace sleeves then straightened the brooches at their throats as they waited for the famous couple to enter the sitting room. It must have been exciting. Maybe they clapped, or curtseyed. Or maybe they waited for him to speak to them." She smiled. "It gives me chills to picture Nana being in this room with Grover Cleveland."

Luke waited a few seconds before responding in case she might say something more. "I think you have imagined it all perfectly."

"Silly, I suppose. But I feel her here. And all the ladies with her who met the president and first lady that afternoon. I can imagine the respect the president used to get. And I can't help but wonder at the young love of a bride for her husband that must have touched everyone there."

"You are a hopeless romantic, my dear."

She jumped at the new voice, the one with a French accent. Henri was leaning against the dining room entryway, a towel in his hand. She chuckled. "Maybe an old fool."

He came and sat in a chair near her. "Your story is wonderful. It makes me look at this old place with new eyes. My son here will have to include it on our website with the photos of your great-grandmother's diary and her picture."

Luke urged her on. "Please say yes. Maybe it will help save the inn."

"Well, go ahead then. You know this stuff better than me, I suppose." Alexandra rose from her chair. "I've taken enough of your time, gentlemen." She scanned the room one more time. "It's been delightful. Thank you."

She held her hand, first to Henri and DeWayne, then Luke before she floated out the door.

He picked up his phone. "Alexandra? May I take your picture? To go with the story?"

"Oh, no. I'll break your camera."

He laughed at the old joke every middle-aged person seemed to use. He asked her to pose on the porch, right where her great-grandmother had once been. Perhaps unconsciously, she rested her hand on the railing exactly the same way Rosalind had done it all those years ago. A perfect coda to his story.

Chapter Twenty-Seven
Her Story

"Call her." DeWayne crossed his arms and stared at Luke. "I mean it, Luke. It may make a difference. You heard her. It was as if Alexandra was going back in time and remembering an event now lost to history."

"Yes, you must." Henri's tone was pleading.

"Papa, you called her a hopeless romantic. She was telling a wild story with no basis in fact."

"We have the diary. The photos and proof the president was here at our inn." Henri spread his hands. "What more do you want? No one had iPhones that day to take Grover's and Frances's picture. Too bad. Hearing Alexandra describe what she imagined…it was perfect."

Then he shook his head. "If you don't call, I will. I want Amanda to hear everything before we forget a single detail." He flipped his fresh white towel over the shoulder of his chef's coat and turned toward the kitchen.

"No, wait, *mon père*. I'll do it. I'll call her."

Henri bustled over to his son and patted him on the shoulder. "Good boy."

Luke scowled. "Henri."

Then he punched in Amanda's number. Henri was right. Luke knew she'd like to hear the story. Maybe it would help the crusade to save the Broadview.

When it went to voicemail, he switched off his phone. He'd finish the page on the website and send her a link. Seeing the photos and reading the text would be more helpful than a phone call anyway, right?

Luke clicked a file and posted the new picture of Alexandra

next to her great-grandmother's on the web page. Side by side, he couldn't help but notice the resemblance. They had the same eyes. The same mouth. It was spooky, seeing two people so much alike and hearing one imagine scenes as if she'd been there herself.

Writing the text to accompany the photos, he tried to recall everything she said, from the lace curtains fluttering to the sound of the carriage and the sweep of the ladies' fans. Alexandra's great-grandmother had written only a few lines about that day. Yet it excited Alexandra, Amanda, and the developer, even Henri.

Luke pasted the website's address into a text to Amanda and attached a copy of the new photo. "Alexandra O'Neill stopped by today," he wrote. "Go to our website and see what she said. I'm sorry you missed her. You would have been entranced. I am attaching a photo from her visit too."

His forefinger paused over the send button. Should he say something more?

"Come back to Deep Creek Lake soon..." He shook that idea away. Maybe he wasn't angry anymore but he still didn't trust her. For now, they'd reached an uneasy truce, a kind of working relationship. Strictly business only. That's what she wanted anyway. If once he had a chance he'd tossed it away.

Damn. He looked at his watch. He wondered if Henri needed help with dinner.

~ * ~

A message pinged on her phone just as Amanda was about to finish her appeal for saving the Broadview. Irked, she put down the old diary to turn off the ringer. Then she glanced at the text and forgot about silencing it. She smiled at Quin and their client, sitting in chairs borrowed from Quin's office.

"Mr. Lowrey, I'm sorry, but do you mind if I look at one last thing?"

Amanda didn't wait for an answer. Instead, she woke her computer and went to the Broadview Inn's website.

Chills ran up and down her arms as she looked at the two photos of Alexandra and her great-grandmother posted side by side. The faces shared many similarities, especially the dark expressive eyes. Seeing the two of them standing in the same place, on the same porch, a century apart, assured her saving the inn was the right thing to do.

Amanda laughed quietly before sharing her amusement with Quin and Mr. Lowrey. "I'm sorry. I just got a text from the innkeepers' son. He says the woman I was telling you about visited today. He posted pictures of her visit on the inn's website."

She swiveled the monitor to enable the two of them to see what got her excited.

"This is the great-granddaughter of this child?" Mr. Lowrey held the copy of the picture Alexandra had given her. "It's uncanny. I mean, this new picture is a much older woman, but there's no mistaking they are family. If I didn't know better, I'd think it was the same girl."

He stopped and read the text on the webpage. Amanda and Quin craned their necks to read along. Amanda wanted to swoon. It was beautiful, evocative, a charming reminiscence of a forgotten day in the life of a president and his new bride. Oh yes, perhaps, it was only imagined. That didn't matter if it made her own heart melt. Imagine how it would inspire romance in the resort's guests?

"This is so sweet." Quin's face lit up with unusual delight. The tough partner might be a romantic at heart. Would their client be as sentimental?

Mr. Lowrey was quiet as he studied the webpage. Then he looked off into the distance as if he was trying to remember something. "I heard about that visit when I was a kid. There were people who recalled it when they stayed at Deep Creek Lake. I guess it got forgotten over the years. Pretty as the story is, I'm afraid it doesn't change my mind. I do appreciate your efforts, young lady."

"Thank you sir." The glimmer of hope that sparked in her heart fizzled in disappointment.

What else could she say to convince him? Whatever it was, she'd have to think fast. He was checking his watch and closing up his briefcase.

Then her chance was gone. He rose, put his straw boater on his head, grabbed his briefcase, then paused at the door. "I'll tell you what. I've already got the inn and its property. If you can find another good reason to save that old place, I'll consider it. I'll give you until the hearing to convince me. See you at the courthouse." Then he swept from the office leaving Amanda and Quin staring down the corridor.

Quin turned to study the webpage again. "Amanda, I can't believe this didn't do the trick. It's a wonderful piece of history."

With a sigh, Amanda sat at her desk and leaned her cheek on her hand while a million ideas whirled through her thoughts. What other reason would convince her client? At least Mr. Lowrey had given her time.

"I'm not ready to give up yet. I do wish I had been at the inn to hear Alexandra talk about it."

"First, you have to focus on the hearing. Remember who you're working for. It isn't the owners of that broken-down inn."

Amanda moved to object, but Quin smiled as she closed her laptop. "I respect your tenacity, Amanda. I hope you think of something. Even I'd like to see you succeed."

"Thanks, Quin. You know, I never pegged you as an old softie." Amanda cocked her head.

Quin laughed. "That'll be the day." She picked up her file and laptop. "Next time we hold a meeting, we use my office. Yours is way too small."

"Next time, we won't have a smelly old diary stinking up the room."

"Right. That's the only reason I said we'd meet in here. Why don't you find a safe place for that, um, book until you can get it back to its owner?" She didn't wait for an answer but left for her own spacious office.

The day hadn't turned out as she planned. Amanda had been so sure Alexandra O'Neill's pictures and the bundle of letters would win Mr. Lowrey on her idea. But they didn't. And neither did Luke's beautiful web page, which made the inn sound like a fairy tale come to life convinced him.

After one more look at the Broadview's website, she turned off the computer, tidied the pile of documents on her desk, then watered the drooping greenery that desperately needed sunlight but was denied a window.

The diary needed to be sent back to the Broadview. Amanda wrapped it in a dark cloth that only softened the odor before she tucked it into a FedEx box. Sealing it shut, she felt a little wistful.

As she gathered her things to leave for the day, her phone buzzed. Although she quickly juggled her bags to retrieve it from her pocket, she was too late.

Seeing she'd missed Julie's call, she hit the redial button. "Julie? What's up?"

"I just looked at the Broadview Inn's website. Did you see it? I was telling a friend about the place, and when she said something about going there, I looked it up for her. You have to check out the photos."

"Luke emailed me the link. It's wonderful, but it didn't convince my client."

"Are we talking about the same thing?" Julie sounded confused.

"The story about the diary and the president visiting the inn…"

"No. That's not what I meant. Go to the Events page."

"I have to get my computer. Hold on. Tell me what made you call. You're scaring me."

"Oh, it's not scary. It's kind of cute."

Amanda laughed nervously. "Cute? I'm looking now. What am I looking for?"

"The Events page. Do you have it? The pictures of us during the bridesmaids' weekend. You look adorable, by the way."

Amanda was relieved. "That's all? I'm going there now."

"No, that's not all. I must tell you, I'm loving this opportunity to torture you."

The webpage came up, featuring a gorgeous sunset view from the back porch.

She clicked on the Events page. A happy group was celebrating the holiday. The bunting was festive. The faces were full of smiles. She realized not all of these photos could be Luke's. He was in a couple of them, and she was in one, taken during one of their last happy moments. She was sure they were alone as they snuck away before breakfast to stroll by the lake. Luke had leaned over for a quick, awkward kiss. She'd been surprised but touched. They'd kissed twice, there, and late at night by the fire. Such sweet memories, they'd often found their way into her thoughts though she pushed them away to focus her attention on her work.

She stopped breathing for a moment.

Who could have been there to take that picture? How did Luke get it? Whatever possessed him to put it on the inn's webpage?

She slammed the laptop shut and stuck the phone into her pocket. Her hands shook as she stuffed the computer into its bag, threw it on her shoulder then dashed down the hall.

As she waited for the elevator, Amanda kept remembering that image of her kiss with Luke. When the elevator doors opened, she rushed in and punched the G button. She wasn't sure whether she was angry or confused—or delighted to see it.

Julie must have taken the picture. That was why she called. She must have seen the picture on the webpage and thought it would make Amanda happy.

Did it? Does this picture mean Luke hopes for something to develop between us, even now after all this?

Her phone buzzed in her pocket. "Hello."

"Amanda, are you okay?"

She had forgotten about Julie. "I'm sorry. I didn't mean to leave you hanging. That picture surprised me and...I'm sorry. I must be losing my mind."

"I thought you'd like it. Especially since everything is going well. If you don't, I'm sorry. Frank and I-I'll tell Frank to get Luke to take it down."

Deep in the garage, the phone connection died before Amanda could answer her friend. Julie was right. Amanda liked the photo, didn't mind its appearance on the inn's website. What bothered her was the feeling she'd lost something she'd never get back. That inn wasn't just a relic of the past. No, it was where she'd glimpsed the future.

She unlocked her car, tossed in her bags, then leaned her hand on the sedan's roof to steady herself. During that weekend at the inn, when she shut out the alarms warning her to stay away from Luke, when she let herself fall into his arms, she thought for a fleeting moment she had found her place, a home she never wanted to leave.

I'm so close to finding an answer. I want that future.

Amanda climbed in her car and backed out of her parking space.

Chapter Twenty-Eight
Memories of the Broadview

DeWayne pushed back from the breakfast table and unfolded a slip of paper sticking out of his shirt pocket.

"Oh no, DeWayne. No to-do lists today." Henri jumped up to gather the dishes. "We haven't had a summer break in years. I don't want to think about all the things we have to do before November."

"All right, Henri." DeWayne dropped his list on the table, took the plates from his husband's hands, then placed them in the sink. "Sit down and tell me what you want to do."

"No, no. We should get some of those things done." Henri perched on the edge of his chair as DeWayne retrieved his lengthy list.

A lot had to happen in ninety days. The second zoning hearing was now only a few days away. Then, before November was over, twenty years of their lives had to be wrapped and boxed while they looked for a new home, new jobs, a new life.

In the meantime, interest in the inn meant they'd stay open for at least a few more weeks. Not the whole place, but some choice rooms with views of the lake, many of which were already booked for the colorful fall weekends. Henry was happy to see the dining room's reservation list grow as news of its closing spread through the county.

While Henri and DeWayne talked, Luke decided to clear out. He needed to update the website or check the inn's email, something far from these two men getting ready to argue over how to spend a perfect summer day.

He pushed back his chair. "I have work to do."

"Okay. Fine." Henri waved him away with a smile.

"Have you started looking for a job yet? We won't be here much longer," DeWayne called as Luke headed up the stairs.

Not yet, but I should.

But before he could log onto LinkedIn, he noticed an email from Amanda. Fearing more bad news, he almost deleted it. Then he reconsidered. *How could things get any worse?*

Two hours later, Luke found himself staring at the inn's website, far from LinkedIn and the job search sites, thinking about what Amanda had written. So far, neither his efforts nor Amanda's had convinced Mr. Lowrey to preserve the inn. But Mr. Lowrey offered them one more chance. Slim though it was, Luke had to grab it. For Henri who longed to see the place saved as part of their family's legacy.

Perhaps it would help if Luke tweaked the history of the inn. Add some romance. Enhance the magic. Alexandra's story had both. People on vacation liked romance, magic, a pretty story.

He wanted the inn to be remembered for all the romance it gave to Deep Creek Lake. It wasn't enough to remember the elegance of a century ago. Through the years, the Broadview had been the setting for so many stories of love and celebration.

Even in his own memory, the inn had witnessed so many important moments. His first kiss in a canoe on the lake. Friends crashing at the inn after a school play, the senior prom, graduation. That snowy Saturday when Emily first saw the inn and he realized he loved her. And then, there was Memorial Day weekend. Yes, there was pain but there were moments of immense sweetness.

His hands hovered over the keyboard. His work was instrumental in the increase in bookings and restaurant reservations. Now, he had one last chance to tell the story that would convince his neighbors of the value of the Broadview. He would remind them of what the inn had meant for them.

Opening the bottom desk drawer, he found a box of old photographs. Among the dozens of family pictures were the pictures he was looking for. So dated now, and some a little faded. Even in the fuzziest of them, the smiles were unmistakable.

He found photos from early Memorial Day picnics, back when he was small, when Henri didn't have as much gray in his dark hair. Many of the boys laughing on the front porch remained Luke's friends. The girl with the straight black hair went with him to the prom. In the photo, she stood shyly next to him in her floor-length pink dress. Emily's intense dark eyes reminded him how happy he had once been.

Did he dare tell his own story?

He studied all those faces. Almost all of them were Deep Creek faces. They were part of the inn's story too.

"Once upon a time," he had begun the page telling Rosalind's story of meeting the newlywed presidential couple.

Now, he keyed in a new headline, "Since then," and added old photos that told the story of a family—his own—whose history was intertwined with the inn's final two decades.

Then he finished the page with a comment form.

What do you remember best about the Broadview Inn? When did you find joy here?

Romance. Magic. Happiness. My family found all those things here by the lake. Please share your own stories.

All day long, Luke posted photos and requests for stories on the inn's Facebook page, on Tumbler, Instagram, Twitter, and made a Snapchat story. Was it enough? What did he hope it would accomplish? At best, it would prompt a groundswell of support for the Broadview's future.

If all he did was provide an opportunity for neighbors to remember a day the inn mattered to them, that would have to be enough. He tucked the photos back into his drawer and closed the photo app on his laptop.

Now that everyone had a chance to remember the Broadview, he turned to job search sites. With the past taken care of, it was time to consider his future.

He was rewriting his resume for the third time when a text pinged on his phone. It came from Amanda. *Romance. Magic. Happiness. This changes everything!*

~ * ~

The second zoning hearing was much shorter than the first, lasting a mere thirty minutes. This time, few people attended. No angry neighbors. No engineers or environmentalists with charts and graphs. The Masons, Evitts, and Browns were there, squirming quietly in their chairs in the back row.

Not even the whole panel showed up. The chairman and one other zoning board members listened intently as Mr. Lowrey's staffers answered questions raised at the last meeting about water quality and traffic.

They leaned forward to look at the easel where an architect displayed the updated plan with the restaurant relocated from a new building at the lake's edge—the one the environmental engineer had opposed—to the Broadview Inn.

The room was silent as Mr. Lowrey stood and buttoned his dark gray suit jacket. "Gentlemen," he then nodded to Amanda, "and ladies. As you see, we have made a last minute change to our plans. We think it will eliminate any lingering environmental concerns."

Then he walked over to the easel and with his shiny silver pen pointed to the location of the resort's new restaurant before continuing. "We've come to realize that tearing down the old inn would be a mistake. Many of us here have fond memories of special days spent at the Broadview. Even me. My wife reminded me only yesterday of how she treasures her own recollections of the place. I'd forgotten how important it was to the both of us."

Nodding to Henry and DeWayne, he slipped a hand in his trousers pocket and addressed the panel. "Since Mr. Beaumont and Mr. Wilson have agreed to sell the property, we will proceed with rest of our proposal—with the changes that have been requested. Furthermore, we've decided not to build a new restaurant. Instead, we're electing to restore the current inn as the hotel restaurant. We plan to call it 'Henri's.' This all happened so quickly we're still putting all the pieces into place. We're hopeful the second floor will continue to be an apartment for the chef's use."

The small crowd gasped at the news. Beside Luke, the inn's current chef smiled broadly, the surprise evident on his face. Amanda was delighted. Mr. Lowrey had only told her of the change minutes before the meeting and obviously he hadn't talked to Henri about it.

The chairman asked a few more questions about noise and pollution. Seemingly satisfied, he banged his gavel and adjourned the meeting.

Amanda leapt from her chair, relieved. Heath shook her hand. "Good work, Amanda. That inn might be a gold mine."

"I hope so, Heath."

She was packing her briefcase when Luke approached her.

"So that's it."

Looking up with a smile, she wanted to fling her arms around him in triumph. But his cool demeanor stopped her.

Did I expect hearts and flowers, fireworks, and a parade?

He was never going to forgive her. Would he wear that chip on his shoulder every time they met? If so, she had failed. Together they'd accomplished everything she wanted for Luke, his family, and Mr. Lowrey, and yet she'd been unable to win the one thing important to her.

Luke's heart.

She squared her shoulders for a snappy comeback, something about how lucky for them they'd only have to meet two more times. After the rehearsal dinner and the wedding, their paths would never cross again.

Before she could say anything, however, Mr. Lowrey stopped to shake her hand. "Thank you, Miss Johnson. Good work."

She beamed. At least the inn had been spared. "Thanks, Mr. Lowrey."

He turned and put out his hand to Luke. "I hear you're the man who is creating the sensation about the inn. How did you put it? 'Romance. Magic. Happiness.' My marketing people took a look at your website and social media, and they haven't stopped talking about it."

Luke looked stunned. "It wasn't anything, really."

"Do you keep track of the traffic to your website? You should." Mr. Lowrey handed Luke his card. "Call me tomorrow. I want to talk to you about a job."

He shook hands again, first with Luke, then with Amanda. "Now I must speak to your fathers." He strode off to the other side of the room where Henri and DeWayne were talking to a member of the zoning board.

That left Luke alone with Amanda.

"Romance. Magic. Happiness, huh?" She crossed her arms and cocked an eyebrow as Luke grinned from ear to ear.

"Mr. Lowrey was in our offices yesterday raving about your website. I think the word he used to describe it was 'brilliant.'"

She pulled her laptop from her bag and fired it up. "Not just good, 'brilliant.'"

As they reviewed the pages, Amanda breathed in Luke's clean scent and delighted in the sound of his voice. He stood so close, telling her about the teenagers in the faded pictures. They laughed at the sweet comments from people he knew. As they scrolled through the web pages, they chatted like old friends. Finally he smiled at her with warmth shining in those beautiful blue eyes.

They were still talking about photos Luke had posted when Henri and DeWayne joined them. "Is that our website?" Henri asked, leaning in.

"Yes, *mon père*. Mr. Lowrey asked about my work on the website. Then, he asked me to call him about a job."

Both fathers slapped Luke on the back. "Congratulations." DeWayne beamed a great smile.

"I don't have one yet."

"You will, *mon fils*."

"Please, take a look." Amanda swiveled her laptop so the three men could look at the website.

The room grew quieter as they clicked between pages.

Henri's face lit up as he read. "Look at the comments, Luke."

"Yes, *mon père*. There are hundreds of them."

All kinds of events had happened at the inn over the years. Engagements, first love, last dates, break-ups, make-ups, family reunions. One after another, neighbors and people who visited Deep Creek from all over the country left comments.

The last one was added only earlier that very day. "I met my wife at the Broadview Inn. I had forgotten, but she has just reminded me. I guess you could say I found romance, magic, happiness at the inn."

Luke turned to Amanda. "Did you notice who signed it?"

She leaned in to read the name, which she hadn't seen before. "Ted Lowrey. Luke, this has changed everything." She threw her arms around Luke. "I knew the inn was worth saving. I'm really happy for you, Luke." Realizing what she had done, she backed away. "Sorry. I got excited."

She tried to ignore the heat rushing to her face by smoothing her hair and straightening her jacket.

~ * ~

Amanda's gesture after she hugged him, once a reminder of Luke's terrible last moment with Emily, held no meaning this time. It was merely the movement of a young woman trying to keep up her professional appearance. Nothing more.

He loved Amanda in that moment. His reservations had started fading when they met with Alexandra, then when she told him about the fire, and now as they looked through the comments on the webpage together.

He no longer saw an opponent across a hearing room, or a tough professional putting her career above everything else. It wasn't her fault she worked on this project. After all, she had gone beyond her job description to find a way to save the inn. Amanda, along with the diary, Alexandra's story, his own memories—and now hundreds of others—saved the inn. Amanda was the force that made this moment possible. She'd kept going when others would have given up. Her determination never wavered. *She* saved the inn. *They* saved the inn.

He smiled at her with gratitude before turning to his father. "Were you surprised at the name of the new restaurant?"

"*Bien sûr.*" Henri stared at Amanda with feigned suspicion. "Did you know?"

"Me? Not until just before the hearing. Otherwise, I'd have told you. It was a wonderful surprise, wasn't it?" She paused for a moment. "It is okay, isn't it?"

"It is more than okay. Your Mr. Lowrey not only offered Luke a job, he offered me one. Just now. As executive chef of Henri's."

Luke's eyes lit up. "Papa, are you going to take it?"

Putting his hand on his heart, Henri dipped his head. "I have not yet decided, but I'm honored. I have found happiness in the kitchen, feeding my family and all our guests."

DeWayne rested his arm across Henri's shoulders. "We have found happiness in your dining room."

"Then perhaps I shall tell Mr. Lowrey yes." With a slight bow, Henri turned to Amanda. "*Mademoiselle*, would you like to join us for coffee? Maybe a donut? It's not time yet for lunch but I feel like celebrating."

Luke looked aghast at his father's invitation. "Papa, did I

hear you propose eating somewhere other than the Broadview?"

Henri smiled. "I believe we are going to have to get used to eating in other people's restaurants. At least until Henri's opens."

The way Amanda beamed made it clear how thrilled she was by the turn of events. "I'd love to come along. I'm so happy for the place will still be yours."

"It will never be the same, *mon amie*. Yet I believe Mr. Lowrey and his team will make it a beautiful place. If I accept his offer, we can be assured the food will be worthy of the name."

They laughed together, a happy laugh. The chill dividing her from Luke had been replaced by the warmth of affection.

"Well, Amanda?" Henri asked, scanning her things still spread out on the table.

She raced to collect everything. "Give me five."

"We'll give you ten," he replied.

A few weeks ago, Luke couldn't imagine squeezing into a diner booth with his fathers and the lawyer he was never going to trust again. So much changed since Memorial Day. It started with an old, musty book. Which he would never have found if he wasn't snooping around the wine cellar with Amanda. She latched onto it even before she knew she was part of the case. Then she hung on even after Luke got angry and blamed her for the loss of the inn.

Now here they were like one big happy family, drinking coffee and checking their phones.

"Henri?" DeWayne looked up from his. "Did you know we have a full house this weekend?"

Henri responded with a look of alarm and then grinned. "We only had one room reserved on Monday."

DeWayne looked at Luke. "Funny how a good story changes everything."

Before Luke could comment, their neighbor, Megan Mason, stopped at their table with an expression full of regret.

She offered her hand to Henri. "The past few months have been hard on everyone. I want to apologize for the way we behaved. I hope you will forgive us."

Henri, who hated grudges, stood and kissed her cheek. "*Madame*, there's nothing to forgive. We both wanted the best for our families. What will you and Reese do now that the case is settled?"

"My husband always wanted to live closer to the city. Since he grew up in Baltimore, we decided to buy a condo on the Inner Harbor. Should be quite a change from living here."

"I wish you and Reese well, *ma cherie*."

"Do you have plans, Henri?"

"We are discussing the future now." Henri wore a smile that meant he was keeping a secret as he looked at DeWayne. "We're waiting for our son to decide what he's going to do. Perhaps something closer to Pittsburgh."

Mrs. Mason turned to speak to Luke. "Your website is very nice. My daughter called and told me I had to look. Apparently, you're all over Twitter and Instagram."

He never imagined his work would go viral. It touched him, in fact, that so many people were willing to share their memories of the old days at the inn. It was with some hesitation he added his memories of the Broadview to the site. But he was glad he did. The inn had shaped his family, his past and now, maybe his future.

As Amanda squeezed his hand, his heart welled with joy. How times can change in a matter of weeks. "Thank you, Mrs. Mason. I'm surprised at the response."

"You shouldn't be. Everybody who visits Deep Creek Lake falls in love with it. How could they not? I grew up here, and when I married Reese, he was happy to make his life with me here in the mountains. I suspect it's the same for you."

Henri glanced at DeWayne and nodded. "When DeWayne saw the inn, he told me he found our home."

DeWayne chuckled. "I don't know if I realized we'd stay here twenty years."

"That long?" Mrs. Mason asked.

"Almost. It would have been twenty next year. Luke was eleven when we came here."

She wished them luck in their new adventures and hurried off.

"Twenty years," Amanda whispered. "Such a long time. Perhaps twenty more?"

DeWayne shrugged. "If Henri wants to keep cooking that long."

Returning to his seat, Henri steepled his hands. "I don't

know what I would prefer more. My kitchen, my family, my mountain lake."

"Sounds to me you have decided." DeWayne turned in surprise.

"Perhaps, yes. But we must find something for you to do, *mon amour*."

"Oh no we don't." DeWayne's expression turned to a frown. "Maybe it's time I retired again."

Henri had a ready answer. "It's time for you to take up golf?"

"*Mon pere.*" Luke put up a hand to stop the debate before it went any further. "Pop. We have plenty of time to decide."

"We'll have Christmas in a new home," DeWayne murmured.

"That's true." Henri's eyes lit up like a kid on, well, Christmas.

Luke leaned over to Amanda. "His favorite time of year. The inn never looked more beautiful than during the holidays."

"Plus, we had it all to ourselves," Henri added. "I did it all for my family. Wherever we are this December, I promise we'll have a Christmas just as beautiful. You, *mademoiselle*, will have to come and celebrate with us."

A blush bloomed on her pretty cheeks. Luke took her hand and nodded. "Yes, you will have to come, wherever we are."

"It's a date." She smiled, and the blush deepened. Like Henri, he wasn't holding any grudges. All he wanted was for her to come home. To him.

Amanda held his hand tight as a smile crept across her face. Case closed.

Chapter Twenty-Nine
Romance. Magic. Happiness.

The inn looked no different from when she first she saw it. Still, to Amanda, it wasn't the same.

This time, instead of a rundown building with an ill-kempt garden, she saw DeWayne's attention to historic detail. She understood how he worked so diligently keeping the place running, he didn't have time to worry about the weeds strangling the black-eyed Susans. They bloomed anyway.

Beyond the inn, the blue lake sparkled the same way it did in May. The breeze, though much warmer today, soothed her frazzled nerves.

Luke held open the door to the familiar parlor. It was as quiet as it was Memorial Day weekend. This time, she felt at home. Not awkward as she did as a newly arrived guest. Not angry as she was when she raced away that awful Monday.

Down the narrow hall, the sitting room was filled with her own memories—mostly good. It occurred to her she could fill out her own comment form on the Broadview website. She would love to tell the story of how she and Luke found the diary in the wine cellar, a detail not yet explained. The day she met Alexandra and confirmed the inn's history was one Amanda would never forget. As Alexandra told her stories, Amanda became sure the inn would survive.

She had stories she still wanted to keep to herself. The kiss by the fire. The argument by her car when she believed she would never come here again.

To her surprise, here she was again, wondering what the future would hold. For her. For Luke. For the inn.

Optimism bubbled in her heart. Sometime soon, in eighteen

months or so, it would look as beautiful as it did the day President Cleveland and his new wife Frances came to tea. She knew that story would spark many a young romantic's imagination. "I'm really glad we convinced Mr. Lowrey to keep the inn."

"Thanks to you." Luke invited her to sit by the fireplace.

She took a seat and shook her head. "And thanks to you."

He rested beside her. "You believed and never stopped believing. Even when I was angry at you."

Amanda clasped his hand. "We did it together. We found the diary together and met Alexandra together. You did everything you could to show me how important the inn was. And still is."

"Even so, thank you for believing."

What was it his website said? Magic. Romance. Happiness. She found them all there when their hands touched. All that and an unmistakable spark of hope in the future. For them.

"You're welcome," she whispered, willing him to lean in to kiss her. Which he did.

Amanda savored the moment, refusing to worry about what tomorrow would bring. What mattered most was that she was here again, sitting beside Luke at the Broadview.

Something deep in her soul hoped—no, knew—the roughest of the rough patches was over. There might be others. Of course, there would be others. There may even come a day when she and he decided they had no future at all.

Even so, today, in this moment, at this inn, it felt right. In their kiss, she saw the balance she sought. She understood how her grandfather looked at her grandmother and vowed to make it work through forty-eight years of marriage, two kids, and four grandchildren.

This time, she was the one imagining a future filled with everything she yearned for. Romance. Magic. Happiness. Just as Luke put it on the Broadview's website.

He must have dreamed a future as she saw it now. Maybe that's why he posted the picture of their kiss on the website. Maybe it recalled his own sense of romance. She was angry when she first saw it, but now it warmed her heart.

He rose from his chair, his gaze remaining fixed on her. "I need to show you the diary."

The way he said it alarmed her, and Amanda shuddered.

"Did something happen when I sent it back? I have the receipt. I'll call UPS." She reached for her purse until his smile stopped her as he opened the glass cabinet door.

She breathed in and smelled…nothing. "The smell is gone." Or close to it. Perhaps a faint whiff of four-day-old fish remained. That was fine, a reminder of its long-lost years. "I never thought nothing would smell so good."

He chuckled. "I found a book expert close by, in Cumberland of all places. A book restorer who knew how to clean the book at least enough to get rid of the smell. She couldn't do anything with the mold and mildew stains and did warn me to keep this book away from others. She said the spores could spread and ruin other books. People could even get sick from it. The photographs and the book are in this cabinet by itself so it should be fine. We'll have to keep it locked."

Amanda opened the book to look at the famous entry before turning to the back cover. She wondered if young Rosalind was in love with Alexander when she met the president and new first lady. Certainly, her sweetheart was very much on her mind when she wrote their names on the back inside cover.

"We had the book professionally reproduced too." Luke held up a copy of the book, exactly like the one she held, except for the leather cover. "One is Alexandra's. This one is yours."

Amanda put down the original to take Luke's gift. She was overwhelmed with the sweetness of such a gesture. A treasure of words, of history. A book filled with romance and magic. "You made a copy for me?"

"It was Henri's idea. You did an awful lot for us. He wanted to repay you in some way."

Hot, salty tears slipped from Amanda's eyes. "I feared you all would never forgive me. Just when I found you, I was worried I'd lost you forever."

"There are very few Henris in the world. He has taught me to love, and to forgive."

Seeing the love that lit Luke's eyes Amanda threw her arms around him and held him close enough to feel his heartbeat. "Thank you." Then with some reluctance, she stepped back. "I must talk to your father."

The sounds of clattering pots and the aromas of onion and

garlic let her know Henri was in his kitchen. When she threw open the door, he wheeled around, a wooden spoon in his hand.

His businesslike expression transformed into one of joy. "*Ma cherie.*"

As she hugged him she whispered in his ear. "Thank you, Henri. I love the book."

"Only the book?" Henri didn't mince words.

"No, no, I mean, I love the book and yes, I love you too."

Henri laughed. "*Mon amie*, you honor me. But I meant my son. He loves you, you know."

"Ah, *oui, monsieur*, I think I knew you meant that."

Henri kissed her heated cheek.

~ * ~

The wide square table in the middle of the lobby caught Luke's eye right away. The slice of shining blue represented the lake. Around it was an expanse of rolling green, dotted with trees. Nestled among those hills were low, dark wood buildings that hugged the landscape. Around them were tennis courts and fire pits, a swimming pool, and a spa building.

It was all so modern, with simple lines. Off on a hill by itself, an old Victorian house, graced with turrets and gingerbread recalled a different time on the lake, reminding visitors of what had come before. A new stone walkway would link the two forever.

It wasn't Luke's home anymore, but it would always stay in his heart.

"Do you like it?" Mr. Lowrey leaned over the model beside Luke.

"Yes, sir. It's amazing to see how it will look in three dimensions."

"Can you sell it?"

"I'll do my best, sir." The words were strange to say, but Luke looked forward to the challenge. He was up to the task.

"Come into my office. I want you to meet Sam Wright. He'll be the manager. You'll answer to him." Mr. Lowrey held open the door to his office overlooking the Monongahela River. "That is, if we can come to suitable terms."

For more than an hour, the two men described their vision for the hotel Luke and his family once so strenuously opposed. Luke knew as they shook hands on their agreement, Henri and

DeWayne would be happy with the plan.

Beginning in November, Luke's office would be here, in the offices of the developer he had earlier considered his enemy. He would market a resort that savored the present and appreciated the past. He emerged into the warm sunshine with a new lightness in his walk and a longing for a woman with pretty golden curls. Her office, he remembered, was in the same block.

The minute he got in his Jeep for the drive back to Deep Creek Lake, he made a phone call.

"Amanda. It looks like we're going to be neighbors." That's what he said though he hoped for much, much more. "I took the job with Mr. Lowrey."

"We have to celebrate. Can you stay in town a while longer? It's only three, but I can get away by five. I think."

Her voice was full of excitement, but then the line went silent, as if it were dead. He waited, just in case.

"Never mind what I said, Luke." His heart sank as he braced for the bad news she wasn't available after all. "I just told Quin I was taking the rest of the day off. I'll pay for it tomorrow, but it will be worth it today. Where are you?"

After he told her, he jumped from the car, tossed his tie on the back seat, and patted the always-obstinate door. It was time to get it fixed.

Amanda was rushing toward him, peeling off her trim blue jacket and flashing him the brightest smile. "I can't believe how close your office will be to mine," he said.

"Lucky me." She ran into his arms, and Luke wanted her to stay there forever. He hoped so.

His lips found hers, warm and soft.

They had a lot to discuss. Later. Right now, this was all he wanted: his arms around her, breathing in her floral scent and tasting her sweet kiss.

Chapter Thirty
The Rest of My Life

When Luke took his place as best man beside Frank, the groom threw an arm around him and laughed. "You're next, man."

The first strains of the string quartet's wedding processional kept Luke from responding. While Frank craned his neck to see the bride, Luke was looking for her maid of honor. The woman who owned his heart.

He acknowledged the other bridesmaids with a nod and a smile. Hannah, her dark hair pinned up, and Marisa, her baby bump now more obvious, wore broad smiles as they marched toward the altar in matching rust-colored silk.

When the maid of honor appeared, Luke's heart thudded in his chest. Amanda's dress, long and shimmery, the color of the setting sun, clung to her slim waist and wrapped gracefully around her hips. Her curls had grown and now brushed against her bare shoulders. He focused on her eyes, dark and smoldering, catching her gaze and holding it until she took her place at the altar.

He barely noticed the bride, beautiful and glowing. Instead, he focused his attentions on the maid of honor. He wanted to hand her his handkerchief when she dabbed at a tear glistening in the corner of her eye. They both smiled when Julie's voice squeaked while she proclaimed her vows. He thought how much he loved her when she handed the bride her bouquet with a giggle.

As they listened to all those words of love and promise, Luke caught Amanda's gaze and held it. *Does she feel as I do?*

After the bride and groom began their life as husband and wife, Luke took Amanda's hand to lead her down the aisle.

He couldn't wait to reach the church door to lean over and tell her how beautiful she was.

He wasn't quick enough.

"You look amazing." She squeezed his arm as they emerged into the sunlight.

"I was going to tell you the same thing."

"Do you think so? I had to order my dress online. I missed the fittings."

"You too? I couldn't get to the store when Frank arranged for us to get our suits. Boy, was he angry."

"The wedding turned out beautifully, in spite of us."

The sidewalk outside the Baltimore church grew crowded with bridesmaids and groomsmen, family, and friends. Luke looked around and led Amanda into the garden by the side door.

"Amanda." When he leaned in to kiss her, she dropped her bouquet by her feet and drew him close.

"Luke," she whispered, a smile lighting her face, and love shining in her eyes. *Was it possible she loved him? Despite everything?*

He had to tell her. "I love you, you know."

She smiled as if she already knew a secret. "Henri told me."

"Henri told you?" *What a puzzling thing for her to say.*

"When I went into the kitchen to thank him for the book. That's what he told me."

Luke caressed the pink roses blooming on her cheeks.

Taking his hand, she smiled. "I'm glad because I'm pretty crazy about you too."

There was a time when Luke thought he'd never hear those words from her lips. Now, he leaned in to kiss her again. This kiss tasted even sweeter now that he knew he was holding the woman who loved him. If he once had any misgivings about her, he didn't anymore. He wanted to be with her. He was sure.

The rest of the afternoon flew by. Limousines arrived to whisk them all to the Peabody Library, a classic old library lined from its marble floors to its skylit ceiling with antique books. Luke didn't dare leave Amanda's side as they marched into the hall and into the dazzling atrium where the band was already playing a romantic ballad.

The only people he remembered later from their time in the receiving line were Henri and DeWayne. They hugged and kissed both Luke and Amanda, declaring them the most beautiful couple in the room. Then they hugged and kissed the bride and groom, declaring *them* the most beautiful couple in the room.

As soon as he said it, Henri shot a look back at Luke and laughed. Luke only shook his head.

Amanda squeezed Luke's arm. "You're lucky to have a father who loves you so much."

"I didn't think that when I was an angry teenager, but I certainly know it now."

After Julie and Frank cut their towering wedding cake, the band struck a dreamy waltz.

"Come dance, Luke." Amanda dragged him toward a floor full of couples.

"No, no, I don't dance." Luke was more interested in wrapping his arms around this beautiful woman. Dancing was not his thing. It would be embarrassing.

Still, she persisted. "Everybody dances." She tugged on his hand, and he relented.

Pressing her hand into Luke's strong shoulder, Amanda hummed along with the song she knew so well. It was from an old movie. Did Luke, the film buff, know it too? Gazing into his eyes, she couldn't remember the words. It didn't matter. The tune was enough. Slow and wistful, it sounded so full of hope.

"I love this song." He smiled as he whispered in her ear. "Leonard Bernstein can do no wrong."

Amanda had never noticed they were the same height. She liked it. She could see him eye-to-eye and drink in the happiness on his face. No one ever looked at her that way before. No one. He didn't consider her as competition. Or a threat. Or someone standing in the way of something he wanted. He placed no demands on her, not yet anyway. All he wanted was her presence by his side. That was where she wanted to be. Now and always.

He held her close as they danced more slowly than the rhythm of the ballad. "There's a place for us," he crooned by her ear.

"*West Side Story*." She stepped back to look at his face. "It ended tragically for Tony and Maria."

"Don't think of that." He held her tighter. "Remember the love and the hope in the future they had when they sang this song on the fire escape."

She had to laugh. "You really are a movie fanatic."

"It's all Henri's fault. I told you that. *Star Wars* has always been his favorite. I love everybody from Bette Davis and Gene Kelly to Woody Harrelson and Taraji Henson."

"Do you have any favorites?"

"It's hard to say. I like the old ones...the one with Humphrey Bogart and Ingrid Bergman."

"*Casablanca*."

He smiled in agreement. "Hitchcock except for *Psycho*. Anything with Julia Roberts or Sandra Bullock. Samuel L. Jackson reminds me of DeWayne. Lately, though, I've been watching a lot of Meg Ryan too."

"Really? Why Meg Ryan?"

He ran his finger along a ringlet beside Amanda's luminous face. Such a little gesture but it seemed so intimate. "Because every time she comes on the screen I think of your sweet face."

His comment sent a hot blush to her cheeks, but she had to admit she loved what he said. "That explains it."

"What?"

"You *are* a hopeless romantic." She buried her face in his neck and wondered if they could dance all night like this. Even though the song ended, Luke held her close. "Luke?"

He let her go and laughed. "I got carried away. It's awfully hot in here. Do you mind taking a stroll in the park across the street?"

Lamp light pooled in golden circles on the pathways of the cross-shaped park. At its center, the Washington Monument, Baltimore's round tower topped by a sculpture of the famous first president, gleamed in the growing twilight.

The evening was warm, but a cool breeze hinted at the coming autumn. They passed ornate fountains and blowzy flowers. At a delicate table with two wooden chairs, he asked Amanda to sit. He dragged his chair close to her and lay his hand on her silky bare shoulder.

"I want to say something. I've been practicing it all day, and now I have to say it," he whispered in her ear. "I'm sorry but it's from a movie. It's one of those wonderful lines I always hoped someday I could say."

She pushed away to look at his face, his eyes dark, his lips set in a thin line. "You're not kidding."

He shook his head and kissed her cheek. "When you realize you want to spend the rest of your life with somebody, you want the rest of your life to start as soon as possible."

How did this wonderful man know that quote? "I'll have what she's having" was the classic line everyone knew from this movie. Who remembered this one?

Although she was surprised at first, she understood. Silently, she thanked Meg Ryan and Taraji Henson and all the rest—Henri especially—for making him such a movie fan. She knew without a doubt she loved Luke. He was funny. He was romantic.

She wrapped her arms around him. "Billy Crystal. *When Harry Met Sally*. I love that movie."

"I hoped you did."

Amanda sat back to study his face. She needed to ask a question. It would be so easy to get swept away in the moment, but now it was her turn to be serious. "You're sure you want to spend the rest of your life with me? You're sure?"

"I am."

She smiled again. "I'd like to be as confident as you are."

"Do you mean you aren't?" Disappointment clouded his face.

She contemplated the man in front of her, the streetlamp reflected in his eyes, shining off the planes of his cheeks. It was a face she was willing to study for a lifetime. "Oh, I don't know…"

"Amanda." He stood, took her hand, then drew her closer. "Life just began all over again. I meant it when I said I want to start spending my life with you right away. Promise me, you will believe in us, too."

She smiled and remembered her favorite movie quote as she answered his question.

"As you wish."

His laughter rang across the park as he swept her up for a kiss.

Acknowledgement

Thanks to my children, Sean Truitt, Gina Truitt, and Brigid Truitt, for their advice about life as a millennial. They helped me with everything from work-life balance to what this generation wears to bed.

Thanks to Baltimore attorney Deborah Dopkin for her legal counsel. She helped me with real estate law questions and details about zoning issues, and then I took her sage advice and flew off into a world of my own. If I made any egregious errors about the legal world, they are mine alone.

I am grateful to my critique partners for their honest assessment of my story in its earliest drafts. Talented authors all, they always give me confidence to keep on writing. Thanks, Nellie Jane, Kristie, Kimberly, Alexa, Patty, Amy.

Finally, thanks to Dick Potts at the Garrett County Historical Society for helping me with historic details about President Grover Cleveland and Frances Folsom Cleveland's honeymoon at the Deer Park Hotel in 1886.

About the Author

Mary K. Tilghman, a journalist for forty years, finds inspiration for her books in the sites she visited when she wrote six travel guides for *Frommer's*. These places and their history set the scene for her novels, both historical and contemporary.

Mary is the author of two Maryland-based historical novels, *Divided Loyalties,* set during the Civil War in Sharpsburg, and *Love Letters & Gingerbread,* set in 19th Century Annapolis.

Divided Loyalties was cited in CBSBaltimore's "Five Baltimore Authors To Put On Your Summer Reading List."

The mountains of Western Maryland serve as the backdrop for *Inn By The Lake*. Her upcoming novel, *The Last Gift,* to be published by Champagne Book Group, takes place during an Adriatic cruise.

Mary is a member of the Historical Novel Society, Romance Writers of America, Maryland Romance Writers, and the Maryland Writers Association. A Maryland native, Mary and her husband Ray have three grown children, all of whom still live in Maryland.

Mary loves to hear from her readers. You can find and connect with her at the links below.

Website/Blog: MaryKTilghmanWrites.com
Facebook: https://www.facebook.com/MaryKTilghmanWrites/
Instagram: https://www.instagram.com/mktilghman/
LinkedIn: https://www.linkedin.com/in/mary-k-tilghman-2191133a/
Pinterest: https://www.pinterest.com/mktspins/inn-by-the-lake/
Twitter: https://twitter.com/maryktilghman

~ * ~

Thank you for taking the time to read *Inn by the Lake*. If you enjoyed the story, please tell your friends and leave a review. Reviews support authors and ensure they continue to bring readers books to love and enjoy.

DURING A MAGICAL HOLIDAY SEASON, EMMA AND ANDREW KEEP FINDING THEMSELVES SNOWED IN TOGETHER, AS THEY FACE THEIR PASTS AND FALL IN LOVE.

TURN THE PAGE
FOR A LOOK INSIDE!

Chapter One

Emma Ballard hated snow. Cursing her shoe choice—leather designer boots clearly not made for mid-Atlantic winters—she stomped her feet on the frozen sidewalk under the overhang outside of the Portuguese restaurant in Newark, New Jersey. As she rocked to stay warm, she wrapped her gray wool coat, a Ballard original, a little tighter around her chest, pulled a cap from her oversized bag, and cursed all things winter.

Despite her hatred of the white flakes falling around her, the bitter air cooled her cheeks, still warm from the heat and activity of Russell Westingman's retirement party. Thanksgiving had just passed, and it was early in the season, but the weather people had been predicting a snowy winter, starting with the storm today.

Emma had insisted on keeping the party as scheduled. As CEO of Ballard Industries, she wanted to send Russell out in style, and the five-course luncheon, complete with a band and open bar, seemed to do the trick. If only Mother Nature had agreed with her plans.

She should have left earlier, but after the party cleared out, she and Russell polished off a pitcher of Sangria. With her belly full and her head spinning from the alcohol, Emma had listened to Russell's stories about her father, making a conscious effort not to let her tears fall. Russell missed Daniel "Danny Boy" Ballard, almost as much as she did.

She had known Russell all her life, since her father started Ballard Industries with a flagship store thirty years earlier, and Russell had been his first administrative hire. Later, while her father focused on building the global brand and business, Russell "kept the home fires burning," working out of the Jersey branch and focusing on human resources, office management, and technology. Their competition—Ann Taylor, Dress Barn, the Gap—had tried to lure him away, but he'd been loyal to "Danny Boy" and BI from day one.

When they finally said their goodbyes, Russell thanked Emma for the party, gushed over his generous retirement package, and cried reading the card she'd written for him. His shoes would be hard to fill.

Shoes.

She stomped her feet again, but her toes had officially become numb. They'd received word earlier that the trains to Manhattan were cancelled due to the storm. Emma debated staying in a hotel for the night.

But holding onto one last thread of hope that she could get home to the city, she willed herself to be patient, and waited for the car she'd summoned.

After adjusting her wool cap over her ears, she pulled out her phone and opened her email, figuring she'd give the car another ten minutes before high-tailing it to the nearest Hilton. Snowflakes dropped onto the device as she texted the Assistant CEO, Rhonda Lewis, that she was still in Jersey. She brushed the annoying flakes off her phone as she typed, hating the snow even more.

"Ms. Ballard!" a man's voice called from the street.

"Thank God," Emma murmured, shoving her phone back into her bag. Another minute waiting, and the frostbite would have set in.

A gray, Honda something-or-other idled at the curb, while the man attached to the voice waved from the driver's seat. "Everything okay, ma'am?"

"Fine now." She walked a few careful steps toward the car. The man exited the vehicle and met her on the icy sidewalk, offering an arm to steady her. He was tall, but so was she, and she grabbed his forearm and leaned on him for support. "You can get me back to New York in this mess?"

The man quirked an eyebrow, glancing down at her with green eyes. The snowflakes gathered on his blond, unruly hair—hair that was overdue for a cut. "Oh, um." Looking across the street and then up to the sky, he finally focused on her. "I don't think so."

Her shoulders slumped. Dumb weather. She'd never make it back to the city. "Then why did you answer the call to pick me up?"

"Call?" His broad shoulders, covered in a navy dress coat, shook with his nervous laugh. "Oh, I'm not your driver. I... I work for BI. I was at Russell's party."

Her breath caught, and she groaned, embarrassed. "I'm so sorry." She hadn't noticed him inside and certainly didn't know every one of the company's fifteen-thousand employees, or even the few hundred that worked in the New Jersey branch. Still, she made excuses. "I'm a little out of it. Drank too much and I'm tired. My feet..." She stopped talking. She shouldn't be complaining to an employee, especially a stranger.

"What's wrong with your feet?" He peered down to the ground.

"They're cold." She stomped them with the hope of feeling her toes again. No luck.

Shaking his head, he pointed. "Makes sense. You're not wearing proper footwear for a snowstorm."

Ah, a know-it-all. "Aware, thanks."

"Why didn't you bring your snow boots?" He lifted his foot to show her his perfectly outdoorsy, warm and dry looking footwear. "I did."

Who *was* this guy? "Good for you. But I don't have snow boots. I don't make it a habit to be out in this awful weather."

"Not a fan of winter?"

"Not at all." She scooted back under the overhang of the restaurant before she froze to death or started babbling. Either outcome was possible. "How can I help you, Mr....?"

He held out a gloved hand. "Mooney. Andrew Mooney. IT supervisor, Jersey branch."

She shook it, the warm wool scratching her cold, uncovered palm.

"Nice to officially meet you, Ms. Ballard."

Emma smiled as she racked her brain for prior interactions with Andrew Mooney. "You can call me Emma." In her five years as CEO, she hadn't come across Andrew. That full smile. The angled jawline. Those bright green eyes. Had she met him, she would have certainly remembered.

"Okay, Emma. As much as I'm enjoying holding your hand—"

"Oh!" Her hand was still encased in his. She pulled it away as if it was set on fire.

"—we should probably not be standing in the snow on the streets of Newark. My company policy only allows for a few sick days a year, and I'm already tapped out." He let his jaw drop, feigning shock. "Did I say that out loud?"

Smirking, she wondered how many sick days employees actually received. Her Human Resources Department handled those things, and HR was Russell's end of the business. Now that he was gone, she'd have to learn that side of the company too. "You're fired," Emma barked, pointing at his chest.

The guy gasped. "For realsies?"

She tried to maintain her fake scowl but couldn't stop the grin from forming. "No, for fakesies, I guess."

His cheeks turned a cute shade of pink. "Sorry. I have little girls at home, and that's one of their favorite questions. 'For realsies?'"

Girls at home. A wave of disappointment rushed over Emma upon learning that he had a family. Not for his sake, but for her own. Their short exchange was the most non-business-related conversation she'd had with a man her age in a long time. Maybe she was even flirting? It'd been so long, she wasn't sure anymore.

"Do you mind if I start using that in my meetings? Like, when someone says something inappropriate or completely off the wall, I'll smirk at them like this," she scrunched her face, "and ask, are you for realsies?"

He nodded. "Great technique. Now if you want to add the palm in the air and the hip jut, you'd be exactly like my girls."

She tried again, following his directions. "Like this?"

"Perfect," he said, his gaze dancing. "You're a natural."

"Imagine that." She adjusted her bag on her shoulder. "Well, I hate to do this in the middle of our training here, but I kind of need to find a hotel since it doesn't look like I'll be getting home tonight."

He held his palm to the sky and caught some snowflakes in his glove, studying them like they were magical. "Oh right. That's why I stopped originally, to help you, but then I got distracted by your shoes and stuff."

The way he peered down at her, like a complete gentleman helping a damsel in distress, made her pulse race. But she wasn't a damsel in distress, she was his boss, and she was competent enough to deal with a weather inconvenience. "That's okay, Mr. Mooney. I appreciate the offer of assistance, but I'll be fine."

"Call me Andrew." He tilted his head. "Why don't you at least come wait out the storm at my place?"

She squinted at him.

"That came out weird, didn't it?" he asked, copying her expression. "I mean, you can meet my family, have a meal. I'll show you my company ID if you're worried I'm some wacko kidnapper or something."

"Funny, I didn't think that until you mentioned it." Would she go home with this man? He was a stranger, sure, but he worked for her company and was willing to help. He had a houseful of girls too, apparently. Seemed sincere. She thought for a second. "How about this? I'll ask you a company question, and if you answer it right, I'll believe you work for BI and take you up on your generous offer."

"For realsies?" He rubbed his chin. "Okay, shoot."

"What's the name of the chef from the lunch café in the Jersey branch who ran off with the V.P. of Sales?" Everyone at BI knew this story. The tale was corporate legend.

"Millicent," he answered without hesitation. "Personally, I think she could have done better."

Emma stifled her laugh before it escaped. He wasn't wrong.

"Did I pass?" Andrew asked.

"You did. Still going to text a picture of your license plate to Rhonda, though."

He drew his hands to his chest, feigning pain. "Ouch. But smart. I'll pose next to the car if you want."

"Perfect." She dug her phone out of her bag and waved him toward the Honda.

With a huff, he leaped the two steps and leaned against the snow-covered trunk, crossing his boots at the ankle, and extending his long arms to the side. "My chariot. And my regards to Ms. Lewis."

After she tapped her phone to take the picture, he jumped back to her side, offering his arm. She held on, wobbling her way over the sidewalk, into the street, to the passenger side. He opened the door for her, and she sat in the warm car, texting Rhonda the photo while he scraped the snow that had accumulated off the windshield.

Emma: Know this guy?
Rhonda: Andrew Mooney. NJ office. Something with IT?
Emma: He's giving me a ride. Thoughts?
Rhonda: Neutral. If you go missing, I'll know where to look.
Emma: Great.

By the time he sat in the driver's seat, she'd defrosted and dried off a bit. "Thank you for helping me, Andrew Mooney."

He put the car into drive and glanced at her in the passenger seat. "It's an honor, Boss Lady."

Smiling at the nickname, she had no idea where they were going, but she didn't care. Despite Rhonda's neutrality, Emma's instincts told her she was safe with Andrew. Best of all, in the heat of the little car, she could feel her toes again.

※ ※ ※

Andrew pulled the Accord onto the streets, which thankfully were plowed, and pointed them toward his home, mentally reviewing his factual knowledge of Emma Ballard.

He knew as much about the woman sitting next to him as she seemed to know about him. Very little. Emma Ballard. CEO. Former model. Hired over five years ago when her father died, which would make her his boss's boss. Considered a reluctant CEO, he'd heard she was a good businesswoman, tolerated by the Board of Directors as a legacy to her father but mostly as a placeholder until the Board could usher her out for a more suitable candidate of their choice. Smart. Neutral about employee issues. She didn't bother the staff; they didn't bother her.

He glanced at her in the passenger seat and added to his fact base. Beautiful. Brunette. Long, thick hair. Brown, mysterious eyes with full lashes, perfect for catching snowflakes.

At Russell's retirement party—Russell being his boss's boss—

she'd glided around the room, somehow avoiding attention but at the same time lighting up the place. He vaguely recalled seeing her on the cover of magazines, but had a hard time reconciling the supermodel with the CEO. That afternoon was the first time he'd seen her in person.

That afternoon was also the first time he'd had a woman in his car since Hayley.

When the silence between them became awkward, for him at least, Andrew cleared his throat. "So, Emma. Any big plans for the holidays?"

"Not really. Just working. How about you?" Her friendly tone invited the conversation.

"Hanging with my girls. They already made their lists for Santa."

"Already? But Christmas is still a month away."

He smiled. "They insisted the elves need the lists now to start making toys."

"Smart. How old are they?"

"Six."

She paused then said, "Both of them?"

"Yep. They're twins."

"The Realsie Twins?"

He liked the nickname. "You got it."

"How fun. You and your wife must have a blast with them."

Andrew gulped and glanced at her. "Oh, I'm not married."

"I'm sorry." She groaned. "I'm an idiot. You wear a ring, but I shouldn't have assumed…"

"My wife passed away." He hoped she'd leave it at that. Andrew had loved his wife more than the world but hated talking about her out loud. Even after six years, when he heard the sadness in people's reactions to her death, a vise gripped his heart.

"I'm so sorry," Emma said quietly. "For you and your girls."

She didn't ask any follow-up questions, which he appreciated. "What about you? Any kids?" He knew the answers to these questions from the company gossip hounds, but figured they'd make do for conversational purposes.

"Not married. No kids."

Andrew couldn't imagine a life so free. He had loved his wife, and loved his girls more than anything, but between work and them, he didn't have time for much else. Thankfully, his father lived next door and helped out more than he should so Andrew could do things, like attend the retirement party for Russell. "What do you do besides work?"

Emma shifted in the passenger seat. "Not much. I mean,

sometimes I sew."

"You do?" He hoped the shock in his voice was indecipherable. "What do you make?"

She twisted her hands in her lap. "I love to stitch. I've been making a lot of scarves lately. It's my new obsession."

"Really?" He tapped his fingers on the steering wheel. "Wasn't your mom a clothing designer? I vaguely remember something in our company's history."

"She was." When he peeked at her, her eyes lit up. "She created the first designs my father sold for BI."

"Such an amazing story. I'm proud to work for the company." He smiled and gave a curt nod.

"That's a nice thing to say."

They drove in silence for a few more blocks. Traffic slowed as the sun set and the roads iced up. "Only a few more minutes, and we should be there." He tapped the wheel.

"What about you?" she asked. "What do you do besides work and parenting?"

Andrew pressed his lips together, unsure whether or not to confide in the fancy pants boss lady sitting beside him. He glanced her way. She may look fancy, but she didn't act fancy, and he could probably trust her with personal information. "Promise not to laugh?"

"I'd never," she insisted.

"I like theater."

She gasped. "Me too! Are you an actor?"

"I was, in another life. I still love Broadway. Musical theater is my passion. I've memorized every song in *Heatherby*."

She reached across the console, grasping his upper arm. "Wasn't that a wonderful play? I loved it so much."

He flinched, surprised at the feel of her touch on his body. "I never saw it. I don't have much time to get to the theater with the girls' schedule. It's expensive too."

Placing her hands back in her lap, she nodded. "That's true. Well, I hope someday you get to see it. *Heatherby* is...," she sighed, "...absolutely indescribable."

He smiled. "I bet." He pulled up to the duplex, his tires crunching over the snow in the driveway he already dreaded shoveling. "This side is me. The other side is my dad. He's babysitting tonight so I could attend the party. Want to come in and meet everyone?"

"Sure," she said. "Beats being home alone."

If it weren't for the sadness underlying her tone, he may have taken that as an insult. Instead, it almost made him feel sorry for her. As if he should be feeling sorry for a rich lady, his boss, while he struggled to make ends meet.

Andrew helped Emma over the slick driveway, and then opened the door to his home, the feeling of relief washing over him. He always loved walking through that doorway. Whatever happened on the outside always faded away as his girls ran to give him hugs and tell him about their days.

That evening was no exception. The soft lights and the crackle of the fire had created an orange glow through the house, and a smell of winter and Christmas wafted toward him.

Devon and Bella darted into the room, screaming, "Daddy!" but then stopped short when they saw Emma.

"Devon, Bella," he said, in his best "dad" tone, "this is Daddy's boss, Ms. Ballard."

"Hi, Ms. Ballard," Devon said.

His father hobbled over to join them, extending a hand to Emma. "Jeffrey Mooney, Andrew's father. Nice to meet you, ma'am."

Emma shook his outstretched hand. "Please, call me Emma. I'm sorry to intrude on your evening."

The girls circled Emma as she spoke, inspecting her like she was a great mystery they had to solve.

She addressed them directly, obviously not intimidated by their scrutinizing glares. "Your dad was kind enough to offer me shelter from the storm. I hope that's okay with all of you."

Bella stopped in front of Emma, crossing her arms. "You're my dad's boss?"

Emma nodded.

"She's more like my boss's boss," Andrew added. "And I expect you all to be polite and respectful."

"Yeah, yeah," Bella said, waving an arm around. She turned back to Emma. "Why can't he have more days off?"

"Bella!" he yelled, then looked at Emma. "I'm sorry—"

"It's a fair question." She pressed her lips together and side-eyed him, clearly trying not to laugh. She turned her attention back to Bella. "What would you do if he did?"

Devon joined her sister, striking the same pose. "Go to the zoo. I like elephants."

Emma exaggerated a gasp. "I like them too. I got to see some when I was on a safari in Africa."

"For realsies?" Bella asked.

Andrew's heart clenched at her sweet tone. Even though the girls' schedules were just as busy as his own, he had to find a way to spend more time with them, outside of carting them around to their various activities. He made a mental note to research season passes for the zoo.

Without missing a beat, Emma jutted a hip and lifted her chin, in the pose he had coached her on. "For realsies." She winked at Andrew. "How about this. Since you've all been so nice to me, I'll do my best to get your dad more days off, okay?"

Bella flashed Emma a thumbs up. "And you have to tell us about your safari."

"Deal." Emma offered Bella a hand, and Bella shook it.

Amused, he shot a grin over the girls' heads to his father. Jeffrey raised his brows and nodded toward Emma, clearly impressed.

When Devon waved her down to eye level, Emma squatted before her. "You have a nice nose," Devon said, reaching out to touch it.

"Devon!" Andrew barked. "Leave Ms. Ballard—"

"Emma." Emma smiled and stood up. "Ms. Ballard makes me sound old and official."

Official maybe. Old? Not so much. He vaguely remembered reading that she was thirty-something. He threw his stern dad look at Devon. "Leave *Miss* Emma, alone please. Can you let her take her coat off and get comfortable?"

His father shooed the girls into the living room and directed his attention to their house guest. "How about a cup of coffee, Emma?"

"That sounds perfect," she answered, as she slid her coat off over her arms. "You'll join me?"

Andrew wasn't sure if she was talking to his dad or him, but they both jammed their fists into their front pockets and answered in unison. "Sure."

Something about Emma Ballard had turned the Mooney men to mush.

Chapter Two

Emma woke to the sound of whispers from the other side of the bedroom door. Confused, she glanced around and remembered that she was in Andrew Mooney's house.

"Why is she in your room, Daddy?" the little voice whisper-shouted.

She smiled at the girl's attempt to be quiet. The clock on the nightstand read six-fifteen, and sat next to a picture of a woman, presumably Andrew's wife, on their wedding day. She was beautiful—smiling, beaming, in a long, lace-covered, A-line gown. Emma wondered how she died. How this family had survived without her.

"Because she was tired, and the blizzard would have made it hard to get her home." Clearly, that was Andrew's whisper voice.

"But where does she live?"

"In New York City. I think. Quiet. We don't want to wake her."

"Like Eloise?" the little voice sang.

"Huh?"

"You know, the book? She lives in New York City too."

"I thought Madeline was from New York?" he asked.

"No, Madeline lives in Paris."

"Oh, that's right. Come on. Let's get moving. Go get Devon, and we'll have breakfast."

"But I need my library book. I left it in there."

Emma sat up, focusing as she scanned the room. Books covered the dresser, mostly adult sci-fi, except for the one pink book.

"You'll get it later," Andrew's tone was hushed but stern.

With a long stretch, Emma dragged herself out of bed and grabbed the book with the illustrated elephant on the cover. She looked down at her attire—a long, black, men's T-shirt with a spaceship on it, and a pair of flannel pajama bottoms rolled up at the ankles. She barely remembered changing out of her party clothes the night before, after Andrew convinced her to stay the night.

She shuffled to the door and opened it, as the two stunned faces turned to her. "Good morning. I think this is yours." She held the book out to Bella.

"Thank you," Bella said, as she grabbed the book. Then, in a flash, she stuck her tongue out at her dad and ran down the stairs.

"Hey, you. Watch that attitude." Andrew's loud, deep "dad"

voice couldn't scare a fly, as he called after Bella.

Emma took the opportunity to check him out. He was showered, shaved, his messy hair tamed with gel. He wore the typical IT outfit of khakis and a button down. "These kids," he muttered, turning back to her. "Sorry. It's only a little after six, but that's like noon around here. We didn't mean to wake you."

"Please. It's your house. There's no need to apologize."

"Did you sleep okay?" he asked.

She crossed her arms over the ridiculous shirt, as his eyes did a quick sweep of her. The combination of his warm gaze and the smell of bacon wafting up the stairs woke every wonderful nerve inside her body. "Perfect." She made a show of sniffing the air around them. "That smells fabulous."

"Breakfast is our favorite meal." He pointed down the hallway. "Two doors down is the bathroom. Why don't you get cleaned up and meet us downstairs?" His gaze darted back to hers. "Not that you're dirty."

She raised an eyebrow as he shifted before her.

"But, you know, women do things in the morning in the bathroom I guess. I mean, what they do I'll never know, but you'll figure it out. I think what I'm trying to say is, you look great, but, if you need…"

He huffed as she poked his arm, hoping to put him out of his misery. "Andrew. Stop. It's fine. Yes, I'd love to have a minute in the bathroom."

Clearly embarrassed, he shook his head. His blush was cute. She couldn't remember the last time she'd made a man so uncomfortable, at least outside of the board room.

"Anyhoo," he continued, rocking back on his heels, "we'll eat and then I'll drive you wherever you need to go. The roads are plowed, and the world keeps spinning so… Does that sound good?"

"I'd be grateful, but I don't want to put you out. I can call a car." Emma already dreaded the ride back in this weather. Andrew Mooney's house was so warm and bacon-y, she didn't want to leave.

"It's no problem. You may have to write me a late note for my boss though."

"Who *is* your boss?" she asked, realizing the topic of work hadn't come up at all the night before. Mostly, they'd discussed elephants, nail polish, and television shows. "I'm not exactly clear on where you sit in the company flow chart."

His laugh indicated he'd relaxed a bit. "I have three employees I supervise, so I'm sort of low-middle management. I report to Stuart, who used to report to Russell."

"Stu Borowski? Oh, no problem. I'll text him right now." She knew Stu well and would probably promote him to Russ's now-vacant position.

Andrew held up a hand. "Maybe that's not the best idea. Don't want the rumor mill to get started."

She raised her eyebrows. "Good point. You'd probably be embarrassed that I'm squatting in your house…"

"I don't mean for me, for you. They'll say you're slumming with the IT guy. It would be scandalous." He sputtered out an awkward chuckle.

With a tilt of her head, she grinned. "You've been a perfect gentleman. But whatever you want me to tell Stu, I'll respect that."

"Thanks." He ran a hand over his head, but with the gel it only made his hair stick out at weird angles. "I'm really annoying, huh? How about I go downstairs? You take your time, help yourself to what you need, and meet us down there for breakfast. Deal?"

Anticipating bacon, she nodded curtly. "Deal. And you're not annoying."

"Glad to hear that." He walked toward the staircase.

"Andrew?" she called.

He turned to face her.

"Thank you for letting me have your room last night."

He smiled a warm grin, his eyes crinkling in the corners. "You're welcome, Boss Lady."

* * *

A few hours later, after Andrew dropped her off at home and she had a much-needed shower and outfit change, Emma made her way to BI headquarters. She spent a minute to appreciate her office view overlooking Midtown Manhattan. The snow-lined streets were busy with business people weaving around the holiday influx of tourists who'd taken over the area. She hated snow, but she especially hated snow when it painted her city that dingy-gray color.

The people rushing around in business coats reminded her that she had to send an email to Stu. She opened her inbox and composed a new message, copying Andrew. Seeing his name pop up in the company mailbox made her heart race. He really did work there. She wondered for how long.

She sent a simple message to Stu, explaining that Andrew had "assisted her with business that morning" and thanking him for excusing his lateness. Then, she called Rhonda's office, opposite hers in the executive suite, and asked her to stop by when she had the chance.

Born in Trinidad, Rhonda Lewis had started working for Emma's father at the flagship Ballard store in Brooklyn the month after she arrived in New York, shortly after her sixteenth birthday. She'd worked her way up through the corporation as she pursued her business degree and eventually her MBA. Twenty years from the exact date of her hiring, Daniel Ballard asked Rhonda to be the Assistant CEO, the position she still held. Besides Emma's late father and Russ, nobody knew more about Ballard Industries than Rhonda.

Knowing that Mr. Ballard wanted Emma to learn the business, Rhonda didn't object when Emma was named CEO after his death. Instead, Rhonda had taken Emma under her wing. *Your father gave me a chance when I started out. It's only right he should do the same for his daughter. I respect that man and his wishes more than I care about which office I sit in,* she'd said. As much as Rhonda tried to teach Emma the art of people skills over the past five years, Rhonda was the expert on sensing the tone of the company's staff. The employees often approached her with issues, feeling more comfortable with her than with Emma. Rhonda also knew how to get information on employees, and Emma needed her help.

After a quick knock, Rhonda poked her head into the office. "Hey, Emma. What's up?"

She cleared her throat. Rhonda had known her since she was a child and would be able to sense the curiosity in Emma's voice if she wasn't careful. "Could you find me a personnel file on the down low?" Her cheeks warmed as she shuffled papers on her desk in an effort to appear disinterested.

"Sure. What's the name?"

Emma folded her hands on her desk, sitting up taller and meeting Rhonda's gaze. "Andrew Mooney. The guy from the Jersey branch."

Rhonda lifted her chin, squinting at Emma. "From the party? Did he give you a hard time? If HR needs to get involved—"

"Oh no, not at all," Emma interrupted. "He helped get me home, and I felt terrible that I didn't know who he was, that's all."

"That's all?" Rhonda asked, quirking a brow and studying Emma.

"Yes." *And I want to know more about him,* Emma didn't admit to Rhonda.

"I'll have it to you in an hour." Rhonda smiled and closed the door as she left.

Later, when Rhonda emailed the file on Andrew Mooney, Emma clicked on it but deleted it before reading anything. He'd been nice to her, and she wouldn't abuse her position by stalking him through his company history.

She spun in her chair and then picked up her phone. Thinking of Andrew, she made a few calls, cashed in a few favors, and spent more than a few dollars.

No, she wouldn't stalk him. She'd be direct. She had no idea how it would play out, but one thing was certain—she hadn't felt so alive at Ballard Industries in her five years.

※ ※ ※

A courier delivered the letter after work as Andrew returned home with pizza for dinner. He didn't get a chance to open it until the girls were fed, bathed, and in bed.

His jaw dropped as he read the handwritten note.

Andrew,
I can't thank you enough for helping me last night and for the hospitality your family showed me during the snow storm. I'll never forget your generosity, your bacon, or your beautiful girls' advice on life (secret girl stuff!). I came across these Heatherby *tickets and remembered how much you wanted to see it. It's late notice, I know, but I've set up a car to pick you up and bring you to the city if you are able to go. Please take a guest, maybe your father. I'd love to babysit the girls. They are welcome at my place, or I'd be happy to watch them at your place if you think they'd be more comfortable there.*
I hope you enjoy the play as much as I did. Talk soon.
Emma.

She'd signed the note and scribbled her phone number on the bottom.

The first thing he did, the first thing he always did when life threw him a curveball, was call his father.

Jeffrey hobbled into the kitchen before Andrew had a chance to put down his phone. He grumbled a greeting, then went straight for the leftover pizza, tossing a piece onto a paper plate. "What's this about a letter?"

Andrew shoved the card and the tickets toward his father. As Jeffrey scanned the card, Andrew paced the kitchen. He'd read the thank you note from Emma twice and barely recovered from the shock at the feel of the *Heatherby* tickets between his fingers. "Do you believe this? Is this even real?"

"Nice penmanship." His father held the tickets to the overhead light, as if he were an expert on counterfeiting. "They look real to me."

"Not the tickets, the...the...sentiment."

Jeffrey handed the card and its contents to Andrew and grabbed his slice of pizza. "I think it's appropriate for her to send a thank you to her employee who helped her out. You gave up your room and drove her into that horrid city in the ice and snow. She's a classy lady, with a good upbringing—"

"She's a corporate viper." He tossed the card onto the counter.

"A damn pretty one—"

"Dad! You can't say things like that. It's not the sixties."

Jeffrey scowled and pointed the tip of the pizza slice at his son. "If I think a woman is pretty, I sure as heck can say so."

Andrew rolled his eyes, brewing a cup of coffee as his father bit into the cold slice. After Jeffrey finished, he stood next to Andrew, who focused on the coffee streaming into his "World's Best Dad" mug. He reached for Andrew's shoulder. "I think maybe your...jitters...toward Emma come from a different place than you think."

"A different place?" He felt like the twins snapping at his own father like that. All he needed was to put a hand on his hip and stick out his chin. "So it's not because she doesn't care about her job? It's not because she has no clue how to run a company?"

Jeffrey growled and turned away. "You know that's not true. The woman has an MBA, and the company's doing fine. The stock has held since she took over for her father. Listen, son, it's been six years since Hayley—"

Andrew held up a hand to stop his father's words, words he didn't want to hear because they hurt his heart. "This has nothing to do with Hayley." He picked up the note and tickets and waved them at his father. "It's not like she wants to date me, Dad. She wants me to take you."

Jeffrey huffed. "So then why are you so upset?"

Andrew peeked at the envelope. He didn't know why he was upset. Maybe because he'd never have been able to score *Heatherby* tickets on his own, and all Emma Ballard had to do was bat an eyelash and they fall from the sky. Maybe because she'd assumed he'd leave his girls with her, a practical stranger, while he gallivanted around the city. Or, maybe it was because, like his father had said, she was gorgeous, and had been sweet and nice to him during her stay in his home.

Emma Ballard scared him. Not so much as his boss's, boss's, boss, but because she was likable. He didn't want to like her.

"I should have never stopped to help her yesterday. I should have left her to her own devices."

Jeffrey grunted in disapproval. "That is not how you were raised.

Don't you lose your manners because you're out of your comfort zone, young man."

Young man. His father hadn't called him that since he was a teenager. The whole situation with Emma was completely out of his comfort zone. "I'm sorry."

Jeffrey snatched the note and pulled out the tickets again, studying them. "Friday night. I'll be around to watch the girls."

Andrew furrowed his brow. "I'll call Mrs. Fletcher to watch them. You're coming with me, remember?"

His dad laughed. "Oh heck no. I hate that city, and you know I can't sit through that musical stuff. I fall asleep, and my hip gets sore." Jeffrey hated Broadway, a bone of contention between him and Andrew for years. It didn't help that he'd had hip surgery after his time in the Army, which made it difficult for him to sit for long periods without stiffening up. "I'd rather have a movie marathon with Dev and Bells."

Andrew sighed. "Well, who am I supposed to take?"

His father held up the card, tapping his thumb over Emma's signature.

"Are you insane?" He grabbed the card from his chuckling father's grasp. "She's my boss, Dad. And she doesn't want to go. She said she'd seen it already, and the card says to take you."

"Of course it does. A classy lady like Ms. Ballard wouldn't invite herself out with a man she barely knows, especially one who works for her."

"Exactly."

"But I bet if you asked her, she'd say yes."

"Well, I'm not asking." Andrew huffed again, proving to himself that he was his daughters' father. He sounded just like them. He glanced sideways at his father. "And what makes you think so?"

Jeffrey shrugged. "Just a feeling. The way she looked at you like she needed a friend. The way she poked around the house after breakfast, picking up the picture of you on the mantel, like it was the most fascinating thing ever."

"Oh please," Andrew sang, feeling his cheeks heat. He hadn't noticed any of that. Did Emma really look at the picture of him with his prize-winning tuna catch? "You make her sound like a schoolgirl with a crush. She's an ex-model, a spoiled princess turned CEO of a major corporation. She's a vi—"

"A viper," Jeffrey finished. "Yeah, right. She really seemed viper-ish and spoiled when she let Devon paint her fingernails orange last night."

Andrew ignored his father's sarcasm, taking a minute to think while he cleared the table and crushed the pizza boxes for recycling. Sure, Emma had seemed nice, sweet. But he'd heard stories about her tearing things up in the board room. Stories about how the Board constantly challenged her and tried to force her out, and how she'd never been able to move her agenda. She wasn't strong enough to fight for the company, but that didn't mean she hadn't tried. At least from what he heard through the gossip that filtered from headquarters to the Jersey branch.

Jeffrey stood next to him, leaning his bad hip against the counter. "It's a play. You don't have to marry her. Heck, you don't even have to talk to each other. It would be a common courtesy to ask the person who got the tickets if they wanted to accompany you. Just like you do when Uncle Sal gets you Yankee tickets."

Andrew scowled. Why did his father have to be so smart? He glared at Jeffrey, then sputtered out, "Fine. I'll think about it."

Out Now!

What's next on your reading list?

Champagne Book Group promises to bring to readers fiction at its finest.

Discover your next
fine read!
http://www.champagnebooks.com/

We are delighted to invite you to receive exclusive rewards. Join our Facebook group for VIP savings, bonus content, early access to new ideas we've cooked up, learn about special events for our readers, and sneak peeks at our fabulous titles.

Join now.
https://www.facebook.com/groups/ChampagneBookClub/